# STALKER

## A.M. McCoy

# Contents

For the baddies who think sex should come with a bit of danger, a whole lot of obsession, and a Ghostface mask.
Here's to the thrill of being stalked and turning the game around on him with a spicy light saber or two.

# CHAPTER 1 - PEYTON

## THE LINE WALKERS

"**D**id you survive day one?"

With a sigh, I threw myself back onto the delightfully comfortable bed and switched my phone to speaker, ready for what was undoubtedly going to be a long conversation with my sister, Olivia.

"I think my brain is officially mush from all the information." Despite my weariness, I sighed and smiled silently because there was something else going on within me.

Fulfillment.

"Is the old stiff as anal as you thought he'd be?" Olivia chatted on and I rolled my eyes behind my closed eyelids.

"He's particular." I rebutted, "But he has a right to be. Mrs. Straight said he's worked hard for his fortune, and I think that earns you a bit of grace when it comes to how you like your home run."

I thought back over my entire day, shadowing Mrs. Straight, the current housekeeper, for Mr. Bryce. She was in her fifties and hands down the sweetest woman I'd ever met before. I was temporarily replacing her while she took a three-month vacation to visit her daughter, who lived in England.

Which left me three months to hide from my life and ignore the shitty turns it'd taken recently.

Mr. Bryce was some millionaire tech guru who lived his life in almost complete isolation on his three-hundred-acre estate in the middle of nowhere. Which was the perfect place to hide for three months, so I jumped at the chance when I saw the job posting a few weeks ago.

My family thought I was nuts.

My friends thought I was hiding.

My boyfriend Tyson believed that the time apart was the best thing that had ever happened to us.

Which should have alarmed me more than it did, but to be honest, I just didn't care about the way my future with Tyson was playing out as much as I used to.

"Hello?" Olivia snapped her fingers through the speakers, "Are you ignoring me?"

"I think I fell asleep." I lied, yawning and counting how many hours I had off before I was expected back up at the main house in the morning.

"That's rude." She deadpanned, but it didn't stop her from chatting on and on after that.

I half listened, half imagined what it would be like to be locked away on the estate, essentially completely alone after Mrs. Straight left in two days. Mr. Bryce was away on business that couldn't be completed at his primary residence. According to Mrs. Straight, he hadn't left in almost a year before his current trip.

She also said he only scheduled it because he hated goodbyes, and it was his way of avoiding her departure, even if it was temporary.

He sounded like the cutest little recluse ever.

And I was excited to enjoy the peace his fortune would afford me in return for servicing his home and cooking him meals.

It was more than a fair trade in the end, given the gross amount of money the job paid on top of the solitude.

I would have done it for the vacation alone, but the money would help me figure out what I wanted to do with my life at the end of the three months, nonetheless.

"Don't you think it's weird that you'll be alone with a man you know nothing about past his name and how he likes his underwear folded?" Olivia tried to speak to the small bit of doubt in my brain, but I had a perfectly crafted response since I'd been repeating it to myself nonstop since accepting the position.

"Funny." I mused, "That's exactly how it felt living with Tyson."

"P." She softened her tone, "Are you sure—"

"Don't." Rather than allowing her to start a pity party over my dying relationship, I steered our conversation back to my only focus. "I love it here. I just want to enjoy this break for a while and not stress what waits for me when I get back home."

"Or what doesn't." She sighed.

"Exactly." As I sat up, I attempted to inject some cheerfulness into my voice. "I'm going to go take a bubble bath in the tub deep enough to sink in, and then go to bed. I'll call you tomorrow."

"You said nothing about soaker tubs being part of your benefits package." She scoffed.

"I didn't?" I playfully remarked, "You know what I shouldn't mention? The sauna, pool, and state-of-the-art gym I have full access to during my contract."

"I'm starting to not feel so bad for you anymore." Olivia popped her lips through the phone, "Wait, what the heck does some old tycoon need a state-of-the-art gym for?"

Shrugging, "Old people work out." I stated, even though I doubted the need for the hundreds of different free weight options available when I saw them myself on my tour.

Did old men deadlift?

What if Mr. Bryce was more like seventy-year-old Sylvester Stallone and less like seventy-year-old Mr. Rodgers like I'd imagined when this all started?

Wait, did I actually ever get told how old he was? With the name Lincoln Bryce, I just assumed he was older.

Was this a mistake, after all?

"Hello?" Olivia snapped again, "What the heck is wrong with you P?"

"Mush," I said, rubbing my forehead and forcing myself to focus on my sister for another thirty seconds to get off the phone with her. "My brain is mush. I need sleep"

"Well, don't fall asleep in the tub!" She cried, "You'll drown."

"Well, if it's my time—" I deadpanned.

"Peyton Rosa Everett, that's not even funny!" She scolded me in true older sister fashion.

"I'm kidding!" I walked across the expansive bedroom to the bathroom, "But seriously, I'm going to relax before tomorrow. Mrs. Straight and I have only one more day together. And I have so much more to learn."

"Whatever." She blew out a breath. "At least send me a text when you're safe from the threat of drowning."

"Yes, Mom." I shook my head and clicked the dimming lights on and turned them down low before flipping the lever to shut the drain on the soaking tub. "Love you."

"Love you too." She replied right before I ended the call and set my phone down on the bamboo tray on the edge and turned the water on.

I admired the adorable welcome basket that Mrs. Straight left for me in the guest house and pulled out one bottle of bubble bath, sniffing the intoxicating scent, and then poured it in heavily.

As the tub filled up, I stripped out of my clothes and tossed them in the hamper, avoiding the full-length mirror in the attached closet on my way back to the bathroom. I'd have to cover it with a sheet or something.

Tomorrow, I told myself. I was too focused on the tub to let Tyson's words seep into my brain like usual when I saw my reflection.

Exhaustion had its benefits, I suppose.

I lit a few of the complimentary candles in the basket, laying them around the bathroom, and then sank into the scorching, bubbly water. I forced my mind to go blank as I rested my head back on the pillow rest and took a few calming breaths, desperate to sink into the dreamland where I met the sandman with the dark mask and the burning touches.

Fear that I was going insane tried to move to the forefront of my mind every time I conjured my dark dreams, but I refused to regret them. I was just over everything and needed a break.

I desperately needed the break that Hartington Estate was promising to give to me. And a little hard work in exchange was perfect.

Because my mother always said idle hands made mischief.

Although, maybe dedicating all of my early twenties to a man who didn't deserve my time meant I was due to cause some mischief.

Maybe, just maybe.

# CHAPTER 2 - PEYTON

## THE LINE WALKERS

"Are you sure you don't need any help to get anything to the door?" I asked from the doorway to Mrs. Straight's private apartment inside the main house two days later. She was leaving for her vacation, leaving me all alone on the estate until Mr. Bryce's return, and the idea of solitude suddenly overwhelmed me after seeking it for so long.

"Oh, thank you dear, but I'm all set." She smiled, slipping her arms into her sweater and buttoning it up. "You have my number and my daughter's, as well as both of our emails. And if all else fails, Mr. Thomas is here every day with the landscape and maintenance teams, so go to him if you can't get a hold of me."

"I won't bother you." I tried reassuring us both, "Mr. Bryce and I will be perfectly fine while you enjoy family time."

She beamed at me and rolled the large suitcase behind her as we left her space. "Just remember, if he's crass or stand-offish—"

"Don't take it personally." I finished for her. The sweet woman had repeated that phrase multiple times over the last three days and the more she said it, the more I was questioning how sweet the old man was, after all.

She tsked her tongue goodheartedly, "Good. Well then," She paused at the front door where Mr. Thomas, the head groundskeeper, took her bags down to her waiting car. "Best of luck."

"Enjoy your vacation." I gave her a gentle hug and waved her off as she left for the adventure she'd put off for years in place of keeping Mr. Bryce happy and cared for in her last decade of service to him.

When I closed the front door and typed in the code to the fancy alarm system on the wall, I looked around the grand home with a fresh set of eyes.

"Home," I whispered, running my fingertips over the pristinely polished handrail of the double-twisting staircase. "Temporarily at least."

THE LINE WALKERS

I polished the silverware.

I folded and refolded sheets until the fitted ones stopped looking like a toddler did it.

I dusted woodwork that was flawless to begin with, but I had the time, so why not?

I organized the groceries that were delivered and then redid them for good measure.

And then I explored some rooms Mrs. Straight had glossed over on the first tour of the estate and ones we hadn't gone back in since.

Bedrooms actually.

Mr. Bryce's, to be exact.

The schedule for cleaning his personal bedroom, bathroom, and sitting rooms upstairs in his private wing only called for attention once a week, and they had just been done before my arrival. But I wanted a chance to familiarize myself with them while my new boss wasn't in residence and hovering around any corner at any given time.

Being inside a stranger's bedroom was nerve-wracking enough, without worrying about being caught like you were doing something wrong.

I stopped outside of his bedroom and looked up and down the hall, even though I knew I was completely alone inside the mansion. I shook my head and forced myself to turn the handle, granting myself access to my boss's most personal space.

My tour of his space had been brief as we walked through the hallway a few days ago, but it was my first time inside the room. I expected it to feel old and outdated, but everything inside was masculine and modern, from the black furniture to the dark green walls that made the room feel dark and cave like even though it was daytime. It didn't match the vibe of the rest of the house, and I wondered if his bedroom better resembled his personality or not.

I forced my feet to carry me through the large bedroom, avoiding looking at the massive custom bed that looked fit for an actual king, and walked into the closet.

I told myself it was so I could see if any dirty clothes needed washed or tidying to be done before his return, but in reality, I simply wanted to see what kind of clothes he wore.

Was he a suit-and-tie kind even in his own home?

Did he wear those leisure smoking jackets like Hugh Heffner did?

Did he smoke a pipe?

No, I would have smelled it if he did.

As I walked into his closet, automatic lights turned on and his expansive wardrobe lit up with a warm glow. "Fancy." I mused, walking deeper into the room. The scent of his cologne hit me when I neared the clean clothes hanging meticulously, but it wasn't overpowering like most men. I couldn't even pinpoint what scent it was as I leaned in to take a deeper breath.

It smelled like–the trees?

Nature.

Masculinity.

"Weird," I whispered, running my fingers down the sleeve of a cream-colored sweater before pulling it off the rod to check the size and fit of it.

It was large and cut with a modern style that surprised me.

Maybe Lincoln Bryce tried to seem younger than he was.

But then again, who was he dressing to impress as a recluse?

I hung the sweater back up, barely fighting the urge to rub the soft sweater against my cheek to see if it felt as soft there as I imagined it would.

I ran my fingers over the other semi-casual clothing hanging and then even more surprising loungewear that was folded in drawers on the other side.

Loungewear of the sweatpants variety.

Gray sweatpants, to be specific. One pair laid on top of others in various colors, but that one pair caught my attention and wouldn't let it go.

Social media videos I'd seen on repeat of fit, muscular men wearing nothing, but a pair of low-slung gray sweatpants and a baseball cap backward infiltrated my brain and suddenly my fast heart rate wasn't from the excitement of creeping into my boss's things.

But from something unfamiliar.

Lust.

"My, my, my, Mr. Bryce," I hummed to myself and then closed the drawer. I walked from the closet and then from his room and wing all together before I could do something stupid, like snoop through his nightstand drawers from morbid curiosity.

Technically speaking, I had free access to every room in the house, so I wasn't breaking any rules by being in his bedroom, but I still felt guilty.

Well, every room except one.

Mr. Bryce's office was off-limits to everyone. Including Mrs. Straight.

She told me when I started, that was one of the few rules to follow without fail because if I broke it, I'd be breaking my contract and effectively terminating myself. Which was no problem for me, I was a rule follower to a fault.

There was no way I would break that one.

I moved back through the house and then left through the rear entrance, using my code to grant access in and out without sounding the alarm and alerting god knows who. My hours were seven am to six pm every day of the week, with a two-hour break from one to three in the middle of the day. Since Mr. Bryce was out of town until the following day at some point, I was free to retire to my room for the evening to do whatever I wanted.

To be honest, though, *room* was a generous term for the immaculate guest house I had all to myself a few hundred feet off the back of the main house on the other side of the pool. Apparently, Mr. Bryce's desire for isolation didn't end with his vast property, but inside of his home as well.

All the twelve guest rooms inside the house were empty.

As in bare walls, and pristinely polished light fixtures, but nothing else.

Every single one of them. The only space on the entire property that was available for guests to stay was in the guest house, physically removed from his home altogether.

Well, besides Mrs. Straight's suite, which was still down three different hallways off the kitchen with its own private entrance separate from Mr. Bryce's.

The man enjoyed his privacy; I supposed.

I eyed the large in-ground pool with the attached hot tub longingly as I walked to the guest house, aching to dip into both and enjoy the amenities while I had them.

The apartment I lived in with Tyson back home didn't even have a washer and dryer hookup and the longer I spent on the Hartington Estate grounds, the less it felt like a job and more like a vacation.

After showering the day off, I climbed into bed with the intent of watching a show. After ten minutes had passed, I could no longer resist the allure of sleep, so I surrendered and snuggled in, preparing for a restful nap.

When I felt my body settle and my mind float away, the same dream I'd been having started seeping into my head like a dark and disturbed movie I yearned to see more of.

It happened almost every time I closed my eyes anymore. At first, I hated the dreams; the intensity left me feeling ill and hung over when I woke up with a sickly sweat clinging to my skin and a hazy brain. After a while, though, I stopped treating them like an invasion into my head and started looking at them as a sign.

I even went as far as asking a tarot card reader at a fair what it meant to have the same recurring dream every night.

And her answer had been simple as her aged eyes darkened and her brows rose.

*"Fate, my dear."* She whispered with an eerie gleam to her voice. *"You're seeing your future."*

I didn't have the heart to tell her I was pretty sure my dreams showed my death and not my future. Because in a way, maybe she was right after all, and maybe my future was my death.

Death by the masked man in the woods who hunted me through the darkness for his pleasure.

And mine.

As sleep pulled me under, I felt my body relax physically before falling completely into the subconscious space I ached for so I could see him.

The masked man.

The dark shadow that lurked just out of sight as the forest came into view through dreamland. Just like every other dream, I found myself standing at the edge of a meadow, blinking through the darkness, and waiting for my eyes to adjust as if I had been dropped into the scene from above.

The message in the dream was easy to decipher, even if the dream itself confused me when I woke up.

The meadow was safe. It was light. There was security there that I desperately wanted and longed for. So one would think I'd walk out into it, letting the bright moonlight bask against my skin and offer its protection from the monsters lurking in the darkness behind me.

At least that's what I had grown to resent every time I woke up from the dream in the beginning. Because not once, in the months since the dream started, had I walked out into that meadow and into safety.

Not a single time.

Instead, every single night, I turned and walked deeper into the darkness, feeling my way through the thick underbelly of the forest where light no longer existed until I could feel his stare on me from afar.

His.

My monster.

My biggest fear.

And also, my biggest admirer.

The man that was as obsessed with me as I had become with the dream. To him.

I felt his stare on my skin like a burst of cold air first. And then the hair on my neck rose as my nails dug into the bark of a tree while I contemplated which direction to turn in.

Left.

I always went left.

Two steps to my left, I felt his breath on my cheek and gasped at the sensation. That breath could make me come all by itself; it had multiple times in the dream before that moment. Adrenaline rushed through my blood, and I took off running, swatting branches and bushes from my face as it cut my skin and caused more excitement to burn in my belly.

I felt the ghost of his hands in my wild hair as I tore through the darkness as he reached for me, yet I evaded him. For now. My freedom was always short-lived.

A few more twists, a duck, and a leap through the air before those fingers ensnarled their way into my long red locks, gaining purchase and ripping me backward off my feet completely.

"No!" I screamed as I flailed my arms out, trying to catch myself before my back landed on the ground with a solid thud. Stars danced in front of my eyes as my lungs clenched from the impact and refused to grant access to new oxygen, no matter how hard I tried to breathe.

Shadows of him moved around me as he slowly circled over my prone body, staring down at me. I could see the faint glow of his sinister smile beneath his mask before he moved with lightning speed, flipping me onto my stomach so I couldn't see him at all.

"What a pretty little prize you are." He growled against my ear as he straddled my back and pulled my head back to look up at the sky.

Fuck, he smelled so good; he always smelled so damn good. It was part of the conundrum he created inside of my brain each time he caught me.

"You always look so pretty for me." He ran his face up the side of mine and I could feel the cool leather of his mask before his teeth bit my jaw. His mask left his mouth and jaw free and exposed, not that I would have been able to recognize him from those features alone if I saw him in the real world. But every time I saw glimpses of him in the dream, I knew he was mine.

My monster.

And I was his. I belonged to no one else in this world, and I didn't want to. Even if I fought him each and every time he caught me.

"Tell me, Puppet," He loosened his hold on my hair and wrapped his hand around my throat, "How many times will you come for me tonight?" I clawed at his hand as my body panicked for fresh air around the pressure of his hand. "Three?" He bit my ear and moaned when I rocked underneath him. "You're feisty tonight, I bet you'll come four times before I'm done with you."

"Please let me go," I begged in a hoarse whisper, drawing blood from his fingers where my nails broke the skin. "Please."

"Your mouth does far better things than beg for freedom, Puppet." He lowered his body to lie on mine, and I felt his other hand rake up the back of my thigh, bunching my already torn skirt as he went until he reached that telltale part of my body that always gave me away to him. I gasped when he pushed his fingers under my panties and instantly rubbed my wet, aching core. "Tonight we'll start with this, though." He pushed those thick fingers inside of me and I cried out in ecstasy from the feeling of him filling me. It felt almost as good as his cock would when he would finally push inside of me. "Fight me." He demanded, tightening his hold on my neck again and cutting off my air supply. "Tell me to stop, Puppet. Prove to yourself that you don't want this."

"Stop!" I pushed my palms against the dirt to push up into him, trying to dislodge him from my back, but he was so big. So fucking big. Everywhere. "Don't."

The commands were weak, even to my ears, because we both knew I wanted the exact opposite.

He chuckled in my ear and then ripped my panties until they covered nothing but hung in tatters from my waist. This was the only time my dreams ever changed, after I begged him to stop. Sometimes he would play with me and make me come almost instantly. Sometimes he would edge me until I begged for release. Other times, he would sink into my body and push my face into the soft earth beneath me as I screamed with my ecstasy.

This dream was one I'd had before, though not as often. And I couldn't tell if that was good or bad because the end result was always the same.

Ecstasy.

Though there would be pain before pleasure in this version.

His hand lifted from between my thighs and then laid against my bare ass cheek with a resounding slap as he spanked me powerfully.

"Fuck!" I screamed into the darkness as he released his hold on my throat and buried his fingers into my hair, pulling me up onto my knees so my ass was presented just how he like it. "No!" I shrieked when his hand landed blow after blow to my ass, even as my body arched back into position after each spank, ready and eager for another.

I may have said no, but I wanted more. The voice in my head screamed for it harder each time. I was so fucking psychotic.

I felt the brush of his hand against my ass cheek seconds before his cock pushed deep into my pussy. "That's my good little, Puppet." He groaned, giving away the effect our encounter was having on him as he bottomed out, stretching my pussy out around his massive cock.

So. Fucking. Big.

I arched my hips and spread my knees further to accommodate his punishing thrusts as he fucked me like the madman he really was, and he chuckled darkly. I pushed back into him, chasing the ecstasy he gave me when all of a sudden the dark sky above us broke away like someone punched a hole in it and blinding light shined through the spot.

"What?" I gasped, squinting against the light as he kept fucking me. Another spot exploded in the sky, and more light broke through the cover of darkness. Where the beam of light hit the damp underbelly of the forest, the foliage shriveled up like it was being burned by the light until it evaporated into smoke and dust.

My monster growled from behind me as he fucked harder and deeper, as more light burned up the forest around us.

Another beam shot across the sky and landed on the mossy ground right in front of me and I watched in horror as the green life burned to brown dust. I reached forward to grab for the plants, like I could block the light from destroying them.

Burning pain erupted in my hand when my fingers touched the light, and I reared back from it as panic built in my stomach. "No!" I whispered in panic as my monster chuckled.

"Tell him I said hello, Puppet." My monster said, leaning forward to lie against my back as he bit my ear. "Someday you'll be all mine. Someday soon."

I shook my head, not understanding what was happening. He never spoke that line in any of my other dreams. And the sky had never evaporated around us before, either.

What was happening?

I clawed at his arm as he kissed my cheek like he was saying goodbye, even though he was still buried deep inside my body when he spoke. "You're mine, Peyton." He growled, once again breaking the script from every other dream and using my real name instead of his favorite nickname for me. "Be ready for me when you wake up. Because you've always been mine, and I'm done sharing you."

"No." I gasped, no longer fighting against him, instead fighting for him. "Wait."

The sky exploded around us, and I closed my eyes against the painful light and high-pitched noise as the entire dream evaporated around me.

I blinked my eyes rapidly, lurching forward as reality took hold again, dropping me back in the bedroom of the guest house at Hartington Estate. My skin was wet with perspiration, and I gasped for breath as I looked around, trying to figure out what happened.

Never before had my dream been interrupted. Never before had my monster abandoned me like that, causing me to cry out in agony as I felt trapped between two worlds, unfulfilled in both. "No." I whispered, clawing at the bed sheets as the noise began again and I realized my phone was ringing a shrill, annoying sound.

That was what had disturbed my dream and torn me from my monster's clutches before either of us found pleasure, like usual.

I ripped my phone off the nightstand and loudly groaned when I saw Tyson's name flash across the screen, angry and worked up. And then my monster's words fluttered back through my ears like he was right there with me again.

*Tell him I said hello.*

My monster was talking about Tyson like he knew what was breaking up our time together.

"Fuck." I moaned, laying back flat on the bed in exasperation. I stared up at the ceiling panting, as I tried to reason with myself that I wasn't a psychopath having a sexual affair with a shadow monster in my dreams while my douche canoe boyfriend called my phone for a third time.

Before I could come up with a better reason to ignore him besides the fact that I was aching for sexual release, I answered the phone and tried to slide out of the headspace where I was a slut for my stranger's cock, and back to the dutiful girlfriend I'd been for the last four years to a man who never grew up to become the man I'd hoped he would.

"Hello?" I answered, rubbing my hand over my forehead.

"Why didn't you answer the first two times I called?" Tyson snapped, and I rolled my eyes, sitting up in bed to hang my legs off the side, further forcing myself to leave my dream man in the darkness and return to the world of the living.

"I fell asleep."

"It's not even ten pm." He scoffed, "Do you ever do anything but sleep these days?"

I gritted my teeth and got out of bed so I could pace around the guest house as I forced my way through the conversation. "I was tired. It's been a long few days."

"Hmm." He hummed and then moved on, in true Tyson fashion. "You want to video chat?"

Knowing that the only time he ever wanted to video was when he wanted to jack off while I sat there topless for him to stare at, I couldn't help but cringe.

"I can't right now." Opening my fridge, I grabbed a water. "The service here isn't great. I don't think the Wi-Fi signal reaches out to the guest house."

"The billionaire doesn't have adequate Wi-Fi?" He replied like a child, "Well, then send me a picture at least."

"Tyson." I sighed, feeling sick to my stomach at the idea of taking yet another picture for him to jack off to. The man had an entire phone's worth from our four years together, yet he always demanded more. And every time I did it lately, I got the ick from it like I was cheapening myself even though he was my boyfriend. A man I was supposed to love and do anything for.

Yet every chance I got; I imagined my dark monster instead of the man I was dating. Never mind the fact that every time I'd had sex with Tyson since my dreams started, it was that dark monster and his touch I imagined while I lay there and waited for Tyson to get done. I even managed to have more orgasms in the last few months because of the mental stimulation during sex than I had during all of our other encounters over the past four years.

"What?" He whined. "You go off for some soul searching and I'm left with nothing but my hand and you won't even send me new nudes? Do you hear how selfish that sounds?"

"We're on a break." I reminded him. When I brought up the fact that I was taking the three-month-long job a few hours away, he demanded we take a much-needed break. He claimed he wasn't going to be "stuck waiting around for me." All of my friends were getting married and having kids, and I was back to semi-single with a suitcase full of baggage tagging along in the shape of a grown man-child who didn't know how to survive without me but wouldn't actually commit to me.

Why the fuck did I even answer the call like I owed him anything?

I took a sip of my water and fought down the nausea the entire conversation was causing me and tried to remind myself that deep down I loved Tyson, and it was only because of my midlife crisis in dreamland that I was left lacking the connection we'd built for years. "Look, Ty,"

"Peyton, this is bullshit." Tyson interrupted me and I sighed, letting him talk over me like usual. "You wanted to take this job and in a way, I agree we needed some space so we could desire each other again," He said and my brows rose to my hairline in surprise. He didn't desire me anymore? Then why was he always demanding sex and nudes? "But if you're going to blow me off like this, I'm going to have to go to someone else to satisfy my needs." *Excuse me?* "I'm a man for Christ's sake, Peyton. I need to come."

I gritted my teeth and fought so hard to keep my words down like usual when he said insensitive things like that to me. "Ty, I'm not going to send you nudes," I stated firmly. "And if you feel you need to go elsewhere for your sexual needs, then that's your decision to make."

Long before the job listing ever crossed my computer screen a few weeks ago, I knew I needed to break up with him for real. I just had no clue how to start over again as an adult with mutual friends and mutual financials and all of that headache. I was pretty sure that was the only reason I hung on as long as I did.

"Whatever." He snapped. "Just remember you pushed me into someone else's bed when you're the one crying about me moving on."

"I—" My voice rose in response, ready to tell him where to shove his stupid ego and miniature penis when the call clicked in my ear, signaling that he hung up.

I screeched in frustration and slammed my phone down on the counter. "Piece of shit." I hissed, shaking my head and then rolling my shoulders so the frustration of being denied sexual satisfaction in my dream and life beating me down for too long wouldn't choke me out completely.

For a while, I gazed out the window, and as I did, my vision blurred and I stared unseeingly. I was stuck between happiness and emptiness, and some days it felt like I only ever felt alive when I was asleep living a fantasy.

I needed to figure out how to make my real life and my fantasy similar. But short of lurking in the woods waiting for a stranger to chase me down and fuck me, I was low on options.

*Unless.*

I glanced at my laptop, resting on the coffee table in the living room, contemplating another dive into the captivating lifestyle website I stumbled upon by chance. The one with different tabs for different kinks. I randomly made an account a week before I placed my application for the housekeeping job, and I could almost directly correlate a change in my emotions and actions to that same night. It was like I was finally taking control of my life, first with the site and then with the job.

Sure, I knew joining a kink sex site where people hooked up, chatted, and shared personal bits of their lives wasn't exactly something a person in a relationship should do, but I also knew deep down that Ty and I weren't meant to be. I just hadn't come to terms with it enough to make that last cut. So instead, I lurked on the website, seeing if there was something meaningful about my new interests.

My profile was essentially blank, giving only brief answers to the standard questions and an avatar for the photo.

That first night I searched the site, I found the kink I thought described my weird obsession with being chased. For some reason, I hadn't been brave enough to click it yet. What if I was right and officially had a label for the perverse desires in my brain that made me feel more like a weirdo than I already was? Never mind the fact that I was pretty sure once I labeled my obsession, I'd never be able to go back.

Back to normal. Back to boring.

Yet part of me already knew I could never go back because deep down I had a need and I would continue to go crazy until I fulfilled it.

Before I could stop myself, I opened my laptop, starting an incognito tab because I didn't need my new boss's internet provider knowing how fucked in the head I actually was, and then went to the kinky site.

Sitting cross-legged on the couch, I held my fingertips over the keypad, hovering over the title of the kink I was most interested in.

*Primal.*

The word beckoned to me, and also terrified me, but what did I have to lose by exploring it?

My sanity? Gone.

My relationship? Over.

My dignity? Overrated.

My finger clicked the icon, and the page changed, blooming into another expansive amount of options with pictures and lists to further explore the interest.

My heartbeat picked up and my body throbbed needily as I read each listing until I found the one I wanted.

*The Chase.*

The new screen exploded with videos, pictures, stories, and articles all related to the kink of being and giving chase for sexual pleasure.

And for the first time in so long, I felt like I was home.

# CHAPTER 3 - LINCOLN

THE LINE WALKERS

I watched the screen closely, zooming in as far as possible on the camera, but I was unable to see the images on her computer.

She was sitting just far enough that my ultramodern camera system failed to show me her computer screen.

But it was no hardship for my hacking abilities; those knew no bounds.

With a few clicks on my keys, a firewall or two dismantled, and a link sent through the Wi-Fi signal she lied to her boyfriend about being too weak to video over, and I was in.

There wasn't a single piece of her life she could hide from me digitally. Not when my entire life had been dedicated to dismantling barriers and walls meant to keep me out. And she didn't even have a good cyber security system in place to make it fun for me, either.

Peyton.

My new housekeeper while Mrs. Straight, abandoned me for her own flesh and blood. Selfishly, I might add.

I rolled my eyes at my stupid inner monologue, knowing that the woman deserved the three-month break from me and my obsessive nature; to visit her daughter. I just hated the idea of the void she'd leave in her absence for the time.

Or at least I had until I read through the stack of applications she left on the breakfast bar for me one morning.

And Peyton's was on top.

Pick number one circled with red in Mrs. Straight's pristine handwriting.

*This one looks perfect.*

Her picture alone had been reason enough for me to dismiss the notion of hiring the young woman. Not because there was anything wrong with her, but because my cock had hardened to stone within seconds of gazing at her smiling photo attached to the application. And that was problematic.

It was unsafe to allow myself to be aroused by anyone who would be in my general vicinity, let alone someone locked away in solitude with me in my own personal jail cell.

Nothing like locking the sweet treat in the cell with the captive man, desperate for a taste.

No, I should have dismissed Peyton's application right then and there.

Should have.

What I did instead was lock myself away in my office and investigate every single thing there was to know about the beautiful redhead.

And I mean everything.

Including her closet obsession with being chased through the woods by a masked man before he used her for sexual pleasure.

That had been unexpected, sure.

It had also been the straw that broke the camel's back and forced me to accept her application, offering her the job electronically with a benefits package far too enticing to turn down.

I needed her to accept and wouldn't leave anything to chance to get what I wanted.

Which she did, immediately.

And I'd been obsessively stalking her ever since.

Then she appeared, and sat in my guest house, on my couch, searching a porn site for her dirty drug of choice. So I watched.

I was always watching.

The monitors laid out on the wall behind my desk showed me every single thing I ached for. One showed the camera in the living room of her guest house, zoomed in on her so I could see the pulse point on her neck throbbing harder the longer she explored the site. Another one was screen shared with her laptop, so I could see everything she was looking at, even where her cursor was on the screen.

The others were on the normal things I monitored in my in-home office. Security footage, internet hacking, and other coding stuff.

But I'd never been more interested in what was being displayed before me than I was at that moment. Before Peyton took up residence in my home, I lurked through her computer only. Since her arrival, though, I had her within reach.

Yet, just far enough away to keep her safe. Because I was the worst kind of monster, and she was too perfect to break.

She scrolled through more articles on her newest fascination, primal kinks, and then clicked on an amateur video of a woman being chased through a haunted house.

The video was shaky, and you could hardly make out the woman past her screams of terror and delight as the man got closer to her at every turn until he caught her. I watched in fascination as Peyton's lips parted and her little pink tongue ran over the fullness of her bottom lip while she watched the woman thrash around as the man set his camera down on a chair before pushing her up against the wall.

Peyton swallowed almost audibly when the woman bucked while the man lifted her short little schoolgirl skirt and pushed himself inside of her without warning. The woman moaned and Peyton sighed, running her fingers over her collarbone absently as she stared, engrossed in the film.

My cock was so fucking hard it pulsed in my jeans. I fucking hated jeans, but I hadn't taken the time to get changed after getting home. I all but ran right to my office to stalk my new housekeeper the second I walked in the front door. She had no idea I was back at Hartington, and I wanted to see her unreserved self.

I palmed my erection as I stalked her, watching the kinky porn balancing on the precipice of consent. She was so entranced by it she leaned back into the couch and ran her fingertips down the front of her chest, gently dragging them over one of her hard nipples through the thin fabric of her sleep shirt.

I only had one camera in her house, the one in the living room because even though I was a dirty fucking bastard, I couldn't bring myself to spy on her where she would be naked and vulnerable. She always wore clothes as I watched over the last three days because the large windows overlooking the pool had no blinds on them, ensuring she never stepped foot out of her bedroom or bathroom naked.

If I ever saw her naked, she'd know I was watching her.

I wouldn't take that from her in secret. She'd know I was looking, and she'd give it to me willingly.

But fuck if I didn't ache to know what her breasts looked like bare. What they tasted like. What she sounded like when I took a bite.

Obsessed didn't even begin to describe it.

I knew if I kept watching, I'd see something I didn't deserve, but I wasn't willing to stop completely. So instead, I redirected her attention.

I typed out the code to interrupt her porn video just as the woman on the screen begged for more and then watched in fascination as Peyton leaned closer to the computer screen to see what I did.

I sent the pop-up message through the site to the center of her screen, pausing her video remotely, giving her no choice but to allow me to interrupt her.

**What is it about the chase that excites you?**

She leaned back against the couch like she was trying to create space between the computer screen and herself and then glanced outside at the darkness. Did she think someone was watching her? Did she feel my eyes?

Her fingers hovered over the keyboard as if she wanted to reply, but didn't quite make contact with the keys. So I prompted her again.

**Is it the thrill? Or the fear?**

Her chest rose and fell and then her fingers danced on the keys. My heartbeat sped up in my chest when I realized she was replying to me.

*Aren't they the same thing?*

I smirked at her reply and watched her on the camera as she chewed on her bottom lip while waiting for me to answer. As she waited, she clicked on my profile, like she was looking to see who I was or what I looked like, but my profile was fake. It was a ghost, it only existed for her and it was blank other than my location, which was two towns over from where we were currently. I wanted her to know I wasn't some ghost on the internet, but a man who was close enough to follow through with what I said. I replied, drawing her attention back to the message window.

> **I suppose.**

> **What's your favorite part of being chased?**

She swallowed and looked back outside through the unobscured glass and then back to her screen.

> *Who are you?*

I grinned and typed out my reply, knowing eventually her good sense would kick in through the haze of arousal.

> **A shadow. A nobody.**

Her reply came instantly.

> *How are you messaging me? This looks different from other messages that come through.*

I ignored her first question and asked what I was more interested in.

> **Do you get messages through this site often?**

> *A few times.*

> **From men wanting to chase you through a haunted house and fuck you into the wall?**

I shouldn't have noted specific things about her, but I enjoyed the way the fear of being watched bloomed over her skin like a shy blush. Was she shy? Or did she redden from the excitement of it all?

*They all offer pretty lines and good times in varying forms.*

She chewed on her fingernail, glancing around her again like she felt my eyes on her. Fuck, I was rock hard and only had twenty lines of communication in so far. But it was the first time she'd spoken to me, even if it was through chat, and I hungered for more.

**You don't want pretty lines, do you?**

*No. I don't want anything pretty.*

**So tell me then, what draws you to being chased?**

*Are you some freak emptying my bank accounts while distracting me?*

**Answer me.**

She was trying to avoid the question with humor and distraction, but she didn't realize how tenacious I could be.

Especially for her.

*I dream of it. Every time I close my eyes, I dream of being hunted. So I guess I'm trying to figure out why.*

I didn't reply as I watched her while her words danced around inside of my brain. She dreamed of being hunted, but why would the girl with the perfect life randomly uproot herself to the middle of nowhere and long for something so dark? And what did it say about me that I wanted to give that to her?

> **So, are you on this site looking for your hunter?**

> *I don't know.*

She thought avoiding the real answers would give her something. Perhaps protection from the truth, or even maybe a bit of her sanity, I wasn't sure. But until she had the answers and was willing to give them, I couldn't make a move.

> **Well then. Until you find the answers or the bravery to give them, goodbye P.**

She sank back into the cushions again as I remotely closed our blank conversation window and resumed her dirty movie, but she paid it no mind. She knew nothing about me, yet I'd be on her mind for a while, nonetheless.

Which was exactly what I wanted.

# CHAPTER 4 - PEYTON

THE LINE WALKERS

I stared at the blinking cursor in the blank message bubble before suddenly the entire thing disappeared. Poof. One minute, the most complex and terrifying thing was right in front of me, and then it was gone like it never happened.

Did it happen?

Did I imagine the entire bizarre interaction?

After exiting the porn video I had been engrossed in, I completely left the dirty site and then opened the anti-virus software that my sister had installed on my computer when I bought it. I ran a scan to check for any security problems.

But I had a feeling even before it was done, there'd be nothing new to find. Something about the blank chat window and the creepy messages already told me there would be no trace of its sender.

And something about that intrigued me, as well as terrified me. Someone knew what I was doing at that exact moment, down to the scene playing on the video in front of me. Yet I was alone.

I was always alone.

I closed my laptop, running the messages back through my head while I tried to decipher something from them that would give me a clue as to the sender. And the entire time I was doing that, I heard my monster's voice in my head with his last warning from earlier tonight during my nap.

*Be ready for me when you wake up. Because you've always been mine, and I'm done sharing you.*

My monster. His warning had been make-believe, something dreamed up in slumber from some deranged part of my psyche. Despite my longing for him in real life, I was educated enough to know that it wasn't possible.

And then there was the messenger. Though he didn't just give me a message, he dove deep into the hidden parts of me I thought only I knew. Maybe he knew more about me than I could fathom.

Maybe he was a stalker.

Two different men playing with my life.

Both were dangerous, real or not.

Both were also the only things that made me feel alive for as long as I could remember.

I swallowed down the heat that rose in my stomach where fear should have been. I should have been terrified that someone hacked into my computer to watch me search for porn. Instead, I was fucking horny.

"Get a fucking grip, P." I groaned, standing up and pushing my laptop under the couch. I didn't need to leave it open so my stalker could watch me through the webcam.

I paused as that thought crossed my brain and heated my blood even more.

Nope, we're not doing a free cam show. I shook my head and forced my feet to take me away from the offensive piece of technology before I did something stupid. The internet was for forever, after all.

I knew I was too wired up to sleep, thanks to the impromptu nap earlier, even though I had my first real day of work for Mr. Lincoln in the morning. Suddenly, a better idea came to mind, one that would prevent me from becoming a perversion for anyone's personal gratification. In a hurry, I switched into my bikini in my bathroom and grabbed an extra bath towel.

As I passed by the couch, I looked over at the blue blinking light of my laptop from underneath it, beckoning me back to it while I wondered if my stalker would reappear if I did. But I refrained from giving into temptation and went out the front door of the guest house instead.

The night was hot and muggy still as I walked up the brick path to the peaceful water of the large, in-ground pool. I leaned over the side and dipped my toes into it, sighing when the cool water lapped at them. "I can indulge. It's allowed." I reminded myself as I glanced up at the main house above the pool for any sign of Mr. Lincoln.

I didn't know when he was due to return, but I doubted he would wander out to the pool in the middle of the night if he did. Didn't old people go to bed early?

My dad always fell asleep in his recliner with the ten pm news.

Before I could back out, I laid my towel down on the lounge chair near the stairs and slowly wadded into the water. God, it felt so good. I was always down for a steaming hot bubble bath at the end of the day, but there was something about a cool dip in the pool to recenter yourself, too. Especially after spending the last few hours worked up sexually, with still no release from it all.

I swam out to the center of the large pool and lay on my back, staring up at the sky as the water moved around me. The stars were so bright beyond the soft blue glow of the lights beneath the water below me, and I was in awe of the beauty surrounding me.

When was the last time I admired the night sky? Months? Years?

I couldn't remember the last time I was far enough away from the city lights to enjoy the show, to begin with, let alone indulge.

What if I got to admire nature's beauty that way every day for my entire three-month contract? Would it feel any less spectacular?

I waded around for a while and then noticed the enticing hum of the jacuzzi on the edge of the pool and decided to overindulge myself by letting the jets relax me even further and climbed in.

The thing was massive, with more than enough room for probably ten or more people, but I could quickly find a molded seat in the stone to relax into. "A girl could get used to this kind of life," I whispered to myself as my arms floated around me on the current from the powerful jets. On one pass by the seat beneath me, I felt the buzz of a jet on a raised ledge between seats and I held my hand over it questioningly.

What a peculiar place for a jet, someone could unintentionally give themselves an enema if they weren't careful with how strong it was.

I paused mid-idiotic banter with myself and looked down in the bubbly water at the space next to me. The ledge was rounded and raised up almost six inches above each seat on either side like its purpose was to keep you seated and separate from your jacuzzi mate who may be relaxing next to you.

But my horny brain instead imagined the rounded edge with the powerful jet poised perfectly in the middle would make one hell of a sex toy for a lonely girl like me.

And before I realized what I was doing. I slid over onto the ledge, letting my legs part over it to kneel on each seat. I rocked back and forth, trying to get the angle right, but it just wasn't possible with my feet jammed into the backs of the seats, so I shimmied my way around to face the wall and as my grandmama called out every Wednesday night at the Firehall back home, *B-I-N-G-O.*

Was her name, Ho.

I gripped the stone ledge in front of me and widened my stance until that beauty of a jet worked my clit through the fabric of my bikini like a well-trained man.

Not that I had any experience with one of those, I imagined it was similar.

"God, yes." I moaned, tipping my head back to the stars but kept my eyes closed as my pleasure bloomed in my belly at lighting speed thanks to the continuous edging I'd endured earlier until I was panting and riding the jet like it was my job.

And the fact that I was technically getting paid while I rode it made it even better.

I held on with one hand and let my other wander, thankful for the dark and empty residence in front of me as I untied my bikini top, freeing both of my breasts before pulling my bottoms aside as well, giving the jet and my fingers free access to play with my most sensitive areas.

I rocked back and forth over the jet, letting it tease my clit and then move away, building pleasure towards ecstasy slowly so I could enjoy it longer while I tweaked my nipples and pulled on them.

My mind wandered with my eyes closed, and I instantly fell into my go-to fantasy of me and my monster alone together. I needed little build up to my fantasy thanks to the toy between my legs and my dream earlier, so I jumped right to the part of my fantasy where he pushed his thick cock into me from behind. It was right where we left off before Ty's phone call rudely woke me up.

My monster slammed into me, while my nails dug into the dirt beneath me, searching for something to brace against as I pushed back onto his thick cock. He fucked me so hard his balls slapped against my clit with each thrust and I timed it with my motions above the jet so I could pretend it was all real.

*That's my good little puppet.*

I could hear his voice in my head as I imagined him fucking me and I wrapped my free hand around my throat, tightening it down until a hazy euphoria consumed me and I exploded.

I screamed a hoarse cry of ecstasy through the constriction on my throat and fell forward, gripping the sides of the jacuzzi for support as I jolted and jerked from the intense pleasures I found in fantasy land.

I laid my forehead against the rough stone and panted, coming down from the high with a satisfied smile on my lips.

"Holy fuck." I moaned, already pushing back to find the delicious jet again, intent on chasing another orgasm with its help.

"I'd say." A deep gravel voice startled me from above and I screamed, opening my eyes and locking onto a pair of black bottomless ones twenty feet away on the pool deck.

"Oh, my god!" In horror, I screamed and quickly sank below the stone edge to conceal my tits from the stranger. Unfortunately, that put the jet aimed powerfully against my clit with only an inch of space between. "Who are you?"

"I could ask you the same thing." The man said, and I feverishly scanned him for recognition, but found nothing familiar about him.

He was mid to late thirties, tall and massively wide in the shoulders, with dark hair and light stubble on his jaw. The darkness of the pool deck obscured most of him, but I could make out that he was wearing a long black button-up and dark jeans.

Admittedly, he didn't look the part of a serial killer, but I was hesitant to relax completely given the fact that I was still naked, riding the jet and adrenaline careening towards another massive orgasm.

"Peyton." I gasped, clawing at the edge, hoping he'd leave or turn around so I could dismount my pleasure spout and cover myself up. "My name is Peyton. I'm Mr. Bryce's new housekeeper."

"Peyton." He repeated my name like it was foreign to him and he was trying it out for the first time.

"Can you—?" I nodded behind him, "For a second?"

"Can I what?" He raised one dark brow at me and put his hands in his pants pockets.

"Turn around."

"Why would I need to do that?" He replied instantly, taking another step toward me.

"Don't!" I screeched, ducking further into the water and pressing my clit directly against the jet. I bit my bottom lip so hard to keep from moaning as the percussion of the water pressure nearly pushed me over the edge of bliss again. "I'm not dressed!"

He straightened up and stopped walking toward me, but he didn't turn around. "Why would the new housekeeper be naked in the hot tub?"

"I—" I moaned lightly, but I knew he heard me as I considered just sinking beneath the water completely and drowning myself in embarrassment. "Look, just turn around and I'll get out."

"Tell me why you're naked in my hot tub first, then I will."

"Please, just—" I froze and took an alarmed breath in, "*Your* hot tub?"

No fucking way was my old wrinkly new boss the massive fit thirty something year old standing over me.

He nodded to me and adjusted his stance, crossing his arms over his wide chest. "I'm Lincoln Bryce." He said firmly, making my head swarm with confusion and horrific embarrassment. "I'd offer to shake your hand, but I'm afraid of where it's been in the last few minutes."

Well, I had a good run, but I was going to meet my maker through the drain of the hot tub because there was no way I was getting out and showing my face around my new boss ever again.

"I—" I stammered, opening and closing my mouth, trying to come up with some excuse for the predicament I found myself in.

"Will get out and make sure this never happens again." He finished for me. "And you'll make sure my groundskeeper drains that damn thing in the morning and puts enough chlorine in to remove your orgasm from the walls." He turned and finally gave me the decency and privacy I desperately ached for, but the damage had been done. "I expect my breakfast in the kitchen by six!" He called before disappearing through the darkness up the steps to the main house.

I never saw him enter it, but I had been in my precarious position for too long. The moment he was out of my sight, I reached the peak of another orgasm. I bit my knuckles to stifle the moan as I propelled myself off the seat and plunged into the center of the hot tub, going under and screaming in horror.

Not only did I just get caught by my new boss using his hot tub for my sexual enjoyment, but I then orgasmed again from how fucking hot I got as he chided me.

If I didn't already question my sanity for having a sex affair with a monster in dreamland, I was officially off my rocker for getting off while being disciplined by my sexy as fuck new boss.

I was fucked.

But at least I got two world-class orgasms out of it, before I quit, I suppose.

# CHAPTER 5 - LINCOLN

## THE LINE WALKERS

It was six on the dot and I rounded the corner into the kitchen, anxious to see what was waiting for me. I resisted the urge to watch my desirable little housekeeper on the cameras all night and then again this morning as she prepared for day one.

I ached to see her move around my home but refrained so I could judge her actions accordingly in real-time.

Last night I'd been watching her after our online chat and when she left the guest house in her skimpy little black bikini, I moved through the house to the darkness of the back patio so I could finally watch her in person.

I'd spent my entire life watching people through cameras, and normally I preferred it that way because I couldn't actually stand *literally* anyone. But with Peyton, I wanted to share air with her like no one else before.

So I lurked in the shadows as she floated around in the pool, stargazing and relaxing. I fixated on her, which should have been alarming, but I couldn't look away. She consumed nearly every thought since her application crossed my desk. And knowing she was in a skimpy bathing suit in my pool left too much temptation to resist.

I had planned to simply watch her, which was my specialty. However, when she got into the hot tub, she was too far away from the patio to watch, so I stalked her around the edge of the pool, keeping myself hidden in the dark until I was less than thirty feet away.

And then she straddled my stone jacuzzi and rode it like a pony until she came with a scream of ecstasy. And I couldn't help myself.

I revealed myself.

I. Never. Revealed. Myself.

Ever. That was rule number one and a fucking mistake I couldn't afford to make, even with my staff.

Yet I walked into the light and spoke, drawing her drunk eyes up to mine as her big tits swung free and bare to my starving eyes. Fuck, what I would have given to take a bite of them right then and there.

Instead, I played with her, like a peculiar new pet I wanted to fuck with. I tormented her and made her squirm, both physically and figuratively, as she tormented herself with that same jet she used to come the first time, desperate to hide her nudity from me.

Her boss.

Her mean, crass, and judgmental boss.

At least that was what I wanted her to think of me. It was the only way to keep her safe from me.

Until I was ready to play with my new toy.

When I returned to the shadows of the house, I turned back and watched her shatter on yet another orgasm, eating it up like my new favorite drug.

Oh, the ways I'd make her sweet voice scream for me when I finally touched her.

But if my original plan was going to work, I had to see it all through.

So there I was, walking in for breakfast like any other day before Mrs. Straight abandoned me and anxiously awaited if Ms. Peyton Everett had the potential to be a good girl or not.

And what a good fucking girl she was.

As I neared the breakfast bar in the kitchen, she laid a steaming plate down at my preferred spot, wiping her hands on an apron that wrapped around her waist. Images of her bent over the kitchen counter in just that apron while I fucked her from behind filtered through my brain as I took my seat.

"Good Morning, Mr. Bryce." She greeted me hesitantly as I unrolled my silverware and laid my napkin down on my lap, ignoring her.

I picked up the cup of hot coffee and took a sip, only then gracing her with my attention as I swallowed down the molten lava. "Did you give your instructions to my groundskeeper?" I asked, in place of a greeting.

"Um—" She hesitated and blushed at the quick mention of last night's events. "He's not here until seven. I'll make sure to take care of it immediately after he arrives."

"Very well," I hummed, as if that answer was unacceptable.

"Is there anything else—" She started, nodding to the meal laid out on the bar as I started dressing my omelet with salt and pepper.

"No." I cut her off, "That's all."

"Yes, Sir." She mumbled, dipping her head in a slight bow and backing out of the kitchen as if I'd strike if she turned her back to me.

What a silly little act, feigning innocence and a demure nature when we both knew she was anything but. She just didn't know how much I knew about her. Yet.

But she would.

# CHAPTER 6 - PEYTON

## THE LINE WALKERS

I managed to avoid the terrifying man most of the day, interacting briefly as I laid his lunch on the table outside of his office door and knocked but didn't enter, as instructed. Nonetheless, I was on edge, like he was going to walk around the corner at any minute.

I couldn't quite describe the feeling I got in his home, but it was like he was always near, but just out of sight. And it made me jumpy.

So jumpy that when Mr. Thomas the groundskeeper for the estate came in through the back patio door to tell me that the hot tub had been drained and cleaned as requested, I screamed and flung the tray full of silverware I had just polished for the second time in two days all over the butler's pantry.

The whole day was all a fricken wreck, to be honest. I even cried in the bathroom.

Twice.

Mr. Bryce was so cold and abrasive that it made it hard to find any common ground in his presence. And sure, masturbating in his hot tub probably didn't help my case, but it felt over the top. And did he have to be so deliciously good-looking at the same time? Last night in the dark, I hadn't been able to see him clearly through the shadows and steam. At breakfast, however, his good looks were on display for me, and I had to resist not to stare. He was so tall, even more so than I imagined, looking up at him from the jacuzzi on my knees the night before. He wore black-framed glasses at breakfast, and it darkened the entire look he gave off as he stared at me powerfully like some dark and dangerous Clark Kent. I still didn't know his exact age, but he shaved his jaw before breakfast, and the overall effect, along with his black-framed glasses, exuded dirty college professor vibes, leaving me to wonder more than a few times if he had ever spanked a bad girl.

Further proving I was psychotic, lusting after and imagining him in any sexual nature at all was the opposite of helpful, and I needed to figure out how to stop.

Perhaps it was from nerves and hormones. New jobs sucked on a good day. And I hadn't had one of those in months.

But dinnertime was breathing down my neck, meaning Mr. Bryce would make an appearance any minute. Even if I was so not ready to face him again.

"Ms. Everett." His deep voice surprised me from behind and I jumped, whipping around to face him as he came into the kitchen from the servant's stairwell, because even in the year 2021, of course, his mansion had separate stairwells.

"Mr. Bryce." I wrung my hands together in front of me and questioned my outfit for the hundredth time since putting it on before coming back to the main house after my break. My dress was serviceable and black, but the black silk stockings and semi-modest heels made it feel fancier than a normal outfit. Dinner service felt like the time to impress.

Especially because he hated me.

Maybe he wouldn't hate me if I was at least physically appealing to him.

*Fuck, my plan was so stupid.*

If the man found me repulsive while I was naked and orgasming in his hot tub, some expensive stockings weren't going to make him suddenly approachable.

"Is my meal ready?"

"It is," I ducked my head stupidly, "I'll bring it right out."

"Good." He walked past me to the dining room where he ate his meals, and I couldn't help but follow him with my eyes as he left. Same as this morning when he came down for breakfast, he wore a pair of black sweatpants and a casual long-sleeve cotton shirt. He looked better suited for the gym or lazy Sunday movie marathon; not the expansive mansion he was roaming around.

I took a deep breath and picked up the bottle of wine Mrs. Straight noted as a favorite of his and followed him.

He sat down at the head of the fancy table that fit sixteen chairs, watching me as he flicked his napkin out over his lap when I approached. His dark eyes felt eerily haunting as he tracked my every move and a shiver broke out over my skin, raising every hair as I got near him.

I swallowed my fear down and offered him a small smile, "Would you like some wine?" I held the bottle out to him, and he glanced at it before looking back at me.

A long pause filled the space between us before he broke the stare and pushed his glass toward me. "Did you pick that bottle out yourself?"

I uncorked it and tried not to drop it or mess it up as he watched me closely. "Mrs. Straight left a list of your preferred picks," I replied, pouring the recommended amount into the glass and sliding it back to him.

"Put it here." He tapped the space on the other side of his plate across the table, catching me off guard.

I knew where a wine glass was supposed to be placed for dinner service but didn't refuse his demand. Instead, I gently leaned forward and placed the glass where he indicated, trying not to notice how close I had to get into his personal space to do so.

"I'll be right back with your meal." Upon my return to the kitchen, I removed the cover from his resting braised pork dinner. I garnished the plate, added the side dishes, and returned to him. "Here you are." Gently leaning over his arm and catching the woodsy scent in his hair as I stood back up. It was the same scent I caught in his closet when I snooped before he returned.

"Did you cook this?" He asked, eyeing the meal before looking over at me. He was so damn tall that even with my heels on and him sitting, we were still almost level.

"Yes," I whispered, overwhelmed by the closeness to his perfection and power, aching to get as far away from it as possible while simultaneously wanting to see if it would burn against my skin how I imagined.

"Where did you learn how to cook?" He asked, cutting through the meat.

"Nowhere, really," I replied and took another step backward to create more space between us, even though he hadn't released me yet. "Family and self-taught."

"You didn't study somewhere abroad?" He took a bite of the pork and chewed slowly before looking up at me.

"No, Sir." I answered, and then for some stupid reason I asked, "Do you like it?"

He finished chewing and swallowed, transfixing me as I watched the muscles in his neck move. I expected him to ridicule me for seeking his praise, or perhaps even insult the meal completely, even though I knew it was delicious. Instead, he held my stare with his dark bottomless one and licked his lips before saying, "It's divine."

I froze in place as he continued staring at me. He placed another bite in his mouth and chewed it. Why did he have to be so damn sexually appetizing and a massive jerk wrapped into one?

One or the other would have been enough torture.

"That's all. You can leave now." He interrupted my thoughts where I stood at the side of the table.

Backing away, I mentally kicked myself for thinking anything fond about the vapid man as I replied automatically. "Yes, Sir."

As I left his house through the back door and crossed the patio to the guest house, the clicking of my heels annoyed me so much that I tore them off. I then walked across the stone in my expensive stockings, shredding them with every step.

In an attempt to ignore the embarrassment still burning in my gut, I purposely avoided looking at the hot tub altogether.

Questioning every decision that led me to Mr. Bryce's front door, I slammed the door shut to my guest house and leaned against it.

My cell phone pinged in my pocket, and I opened it, hoping maybe it was a funny meme from my sister or something to distract me, but found an icon lit up I didn't recognize.

I walked through my space on autopilot as I clicked on it and paused when the message thread from last night with the mysterious person popped up with a new message.

*Are you feeling braver tonight?*

I eyed it momentarily and then laid it down on the bathroom counter as I stripped out of my dress and put on the bathrobe I bought myself for my birthday last year. When I saw it in the store, I thought about snapping a photo of it and sending it to Tyson as a gift idea but realized before I even got my phone out that day, that he wouldn't get it for me even if I put it in his cart digitally and told him just to click buy.

He'd find some reason not to.

So I grabbed the sexy pink thing and bought it for myself.

And as I walked around the guest house of the bajillionaire I worked for, with a fresh glass of wine in my hand and a message from a man on a sex site I didn't know on my phone, I felt powerful.

Fuck Tyson, and his little boy issues. And fuck the big man in the main house who continuously made me feel small all day.

I picked my phone back up and leaned back in the large reading chair in the corner of my living room and opened the message back up.

> Depends. What do I get for giving you anything?

> **Feisty. I like a little fight with my chase. What do you want?**

> Information. Your profile is blank and I'm not about to talk to John Doe just to find out he's some creep in his mama's basement with a limp dick and a boredom kink.

I smiled down at my phone triumphantly for finally feeling big and bad, even if it was to a faceless John on the internet. I needed to feel in charge of something in my life.

> **Ask your questions.**

Before I could even start typing out the hundreds of them that came to mind, another reply popped up.

> **But for every question you ask, you give me something in exchange.**

> What, exactly?

> **I'll name the price after I give you my answer. Ready to play?**

> Fuck it, sure. Why did you message me? My profile is blank, just like yours.

> **Yours isn't blank, it's just evasive. I saw enough to interest me. So I messaged you. Now I want a picture.**

I instantly prepared for the annoyance or disgust to bloom at his request that came every time Tyson demanded nudes from me. But it didn't come.

> Of what?

> **Your decision. But it has to be taken right now.**

He was letting me choose the direction I went, instead of demanding to see my body or something revealing. Something about that made me want to send him something scandalous. I contemplated sending him a photo of the fake plant in the corner or something equally as disappointing, but found some middle ground between nudes and herbology porn.

I crossed my legs, letting the pink silk of my robe part just enough to reveal my knees and lower legs down to my French tipped toes, and snapped the photo.

The lighting was low, adding to the sensuality of it and perhaps it was the wine I was quickly consuming or the intrigue of talking to a stranger, but arousal bloomed in my belly.

I wondered what my monster would think about me playing with fire with my stalker from the internet like I was. Would he punish me if he was real?

> **Those toes could make you a lot of money selling feet pictures.**

I took another sip of wine as his next message came in.

> **Those legs would look good on my shoulders.**

I ignored his comments, because I couldn't quite come to terms with why they excited me so much.

> *Your turn.*

> **For what?**

> *A picture. Or an answer to a question.*

The cursor on the message thread blinked mockingly as more time passed with no reply from him, and I wondered if he spooked that easily. But then, an image popped up on my screen and I sat up straight and set my glass down so I could focus on the deliciousness sent to me.

It was a photo of him leaned back in a massive office chair with an exuberant number of black computer screens behind him like an enormous wall of televisions. Each screen had back lighting, creating a kaleidoscope of different neon colors in the dark room. His phone must have been resting on something across from him because I could see his entire body down to his bare feet, yet the vibrant lighting behind him obscured his face and distinguishing features in shadow.

But what I could see—damn.

He was shirtless, wearing only a pair of black pants. And black ink everywhere but on his feet and hands from what I could see, and his body was magnificent.

And I was hooked.

Yet I wanted to see his face. I wanted to know what color my stalker's eyes were. I wanted to know if he had a beard or was clean shaven.

He replied after that.

> **Where's my compliment? I complimented your toes.**

> You don't actually like my toes?

I teased instead of telling him just how sexy I thought he was. Something told me a man like him had an ego big enough for both of us. And besides, I wanted to play a little hard to get.

> **I'd suck your soul straight out of your toes before I moved up to the heaven between your thighs.**

Fuck. Me.

The man was dangerous and had a mouth on him. Though it didn't give me an ick like it would if most men spoke like him.

> **Now that I have you warmed up, answer my question from last night. Are you here looking for your hunter?**

> *One more answer from you, then I'll answer that. Why do you chase? What do you get out of it?*

> **The darkness is the only place I feel sane. When I'm hunting for the fun of it, I feel in control of myself.**

I hadn't expected that answer, and I wasn't sure it made me feel any more comfortable with him once I had it. Did it mean he was insane anytime he wasn't chasing women? Was I really imagining him chasing me, with the end goal being to let him fuck me?

Yes. There was no denying that anymore. I wanted to try it. I needed to give the primal kink inside of me free rein to know if I was obsessed with it as I thought I was.

> *I'm here to find my hunter.*

> **I think we both know you already have.**

> *What happens now?*

> **Now, you tell me how much control you want or don't want in the chase. Now, you tell me how far you want to go. Now, you tell me how far to push you.**

> *All the way. I want to lose myself to it. I want to let loose for once. I want everything.*

> **Then clear your schedule on Friday night.**

> **Friday night you're mine.**

Friday was two days away. My heart raced as my thumbs hovered over the keys, trying to figure out what to do.

> *What do I do? Then and now?*

> **Now, you just imagine how good it's going to feel to be helpless to your monster in the dark. Now, you fantasize about how it's going to feel when I push my way through your hesitations and reservations deep into your body. Now, you trust your monster will make you feel so good.**

> **And then, on Friday, you run.**

> **You fight.**

> **You let every emotion you've ever repressed free, and you let it all go.**

I panted, reading his messages as they kept popping up until I knew without a doubt that I wanted what he offered.

> *Yes, Sir.*

> **Call me, Dane. Sirs are weak, they give commands expecting them to be fulfilled. I'll make you do what I want you to.**

Yes, Dane.

*Good girl. I'll be in touch.*

# CHAPTER 7 - LINCOLN

THE LINE WALKERS

I n the shower, I stood with one hand on the stone and the other wrapped around my cock. I didn't stroke furiously like I normally would when I needed to release.

In a relaxed manner, I ran my hand up and down, gradually increasing the pressure around the tip of my cock before easing it back through my firm grip.

Peyton was going to be mine. Tomorrow.

Tomorrow night, I'd have her.

Not as Lincoln, but as Dane. She'd cower and hide from me if she knew the truth, but not in the way I crave. I needed her to give in to her deepest desires and instincts the first time I had her.

I needed her to be free and open.

Mine.

The plan was set; the pieces leading up to the actual main event were already started, and I longed to be able to fast forward to tomorrow night when I'd feel her fear and excitement in my own hands.

The buildup would have to do until then, though. Which was why I pulled my fist off my cock and took two long deep breaths, feeling my body give way to my mind and allow me to do what I wanted.

My whole life I'd been called unpredictable.

Dangerous.

Unhinged.

The problem with that was, no one even knew the depth of those words besides me.

I was a fucking monster inside my head. And I rarely kept myself in check and controlled my urges to do whatever the fuck I wanted to do. That was why I lived in absolute solitude, away from anyone who could get hurt if I let go of control and snapped.

I wasn't normal, and I stopped longing to be years ago.

Normal was boring, and there was a part of even the most poised and perfect person who longed to taste the crazy occasionally.

Hence my particular sexual tastes being more *primal* than most. Who cared if I was a fucking animal in the dark, if that was what my partner craved.

Granted, usually, my partners didn't understand the level of darkness they would get from me until it was too late. But for Peyton, I'd stay in control.

For her, I'd be the perfect fucking depraved gentleman, giving her as little or as much of my dirty tastes as she wanted.

She said she wanted everything, but I'd break her in slowly. Offering her glimpses into what she could have with me, before giving it to her.

Or taking it rather.

"Mr. Bryce?" My sweet Peyton's voice called from my bedroom, and I grinned, shutting off the water and wrapping a towel around my waist.

"What, Ms. Everett?"

"I was just checking to see if you were still in here." She cleared her throat uncomfortably. It's Thursday, and I thought you'd already be in your office, considering I have to clean your rooms.

"I'll be out in a few minutes." I called, silently stroking my still rock-hard cock through my towel. She couldn't see me, but hearing her voice while I stroked myself was almost enough to push me past the restraint I'd mastered years ago until I was coming on the floor.

"Yes, Sir." She called and then I heard the soft click of my bedroom door closing again.

That fucking title again.

Someday she'd stop calling me Sir, but until she knew the truth about who I was, I would have to deal with it.

I dressed in a pair of gray sweatpants and then a long sleeve shirt to cover my ink and walked out of my bedroom. She was standing against the railing overlooking the grand foyer below with her head down as I stepped out.

When she heard me, she looked up, and I watched as her eyes traveled up from my bare feet over my legs and stopped at my groin. Because I was the worst kind of monster, I left my rock-hard cock free behind the thin fabric of my sweats and forwent underwear so she'd see how big I was.

Did she know I was hard because of her? No.

Did I care as long as she knew what kind of man I was beneath the belt? Also no.

"All yours." I said, and she quickly looked into my eyes, her cheeks turning red as she realized she had been caught staring at my erection.

"Thank you." She whispered, and I closed my eyes as I passed her, fighting back a growl at how good those words sounded on her lips. Someday she'd say them on repeat after each and every orgasm I gave her.

Friday, to be exact.

"You're welcome, Ms. Everett." I replied, walking down the hall to my office and scanning my finger over the biometric screen and entering as she stared after me.

She had no idea how close she was to being bent over the railing, staring down at the marble floor twenty feet below as I fucked her tight pussy until she came all over my cock while she hung precariously between thrill and fear.

That was where she would bloom like a fresh spring flower. She needed the bit of fright to lace with her pleasure and that was why she ached for a primal fucking. And I was going to fucking give it to her.

THE LINE WALKERS

I watched Peyton through the security cameras in my home as she moved through the spaces, cleaning and tending to the tasks of her position. And I'd be lying if I wasn't really fucking keen on her being in my bedroom.

Of course, it wasn't her first time in there. The other night she had gone in and snooped before she masturbated in my hot tub. But she didn't know I knew that, and I wasn't going to tell her I knew. Yet.

But watching her move around the space, changing the sheets on my bed and pausing to run her fingers over the softness of my mattress briefly before shaking herself out of whatever thought she was hung up on, made me ache for her even more.

And not just in the usual way. Not just in an exchange of power and pleasure, but in my home. In my space.

In my life.

Which wasn't something that could ever happen, because I'd destroy every bit of her if she dared to stay near me for too long. But I could still imagine it briefly when I watched her.

The joy of having access to her visually all day long was even better when I brought up the messaging thread again from the site and sent her a message from Dane.

Watching her read my messages and her reaction to them was a fucking drug for me.

> I've sent you something. It's at the post office in town under your name.

She was standing in my closet, hanging up my clothes that she had just washed, when the message pinged on her phone. She stared at the screen for a long time like she was trying to process the new information before her thumbs started typing.

> I've never told you my name. Or what town I'm in specifically.

> Your point? Do you want your gift or not?

She chewed on her bottom lip and then leaned forward to rest her elbows on the large center island in my closet. She didn't know it, of course, but it gave me a perfect view of her plump tits through her cell phone camera I was also watching her through. I hadn't planned to see them before she let me, but the other night in the hot tub I couldn't help but stare at her big, full, perfect tits as they swung freely above the water while she orgasmed.

They would look incredible with my cock between them.

I could almost feel the heavy weight of them in my hands. Peyton was curvy everywhere, technically plus sized by society standards, but I was obsessed with every fucking inch. I craved the thickness of her body against mine.

> I want it.

> Good girl. You're not allowed to open it until tonight when you're solely focused on me.

> This seems like a stupid question, considering the bad guys never admit they're bad, but are you dangerous Dane?

> Do you want me to be dangerous? Would that make it hotter for you?

I ran my fingers over my jaw as I watched her take a deep breath, still leaning over on the island. Her eyes were so full of wonder and uncertainty as she stared at my words on her screen and a part of me ached to see her green irises blurry with tears.

I just couldn't tell what kind of tears I wanted to make her cry.

> I want you to be dangerous. I want you to be bad. I want to be vulnerable. That's so fucked up, isn't it?

> I'm a monster, the very worst kind. I don't make promises to anyone, but I'll promise you two things because I'm feeling generous. Promise number one, I'll ruin you in the worst way possible. Promise number

> **two, you'll thank me for it when I'm done, because it's exactly what you crave.**

*Okay.*

> **Now do something for me.**

*What?*

> **Take your panties off and send me a picture of them. Show me the fabric that's been against your pussy all day.**

She swallowed audibly and licked her lips as she looked around the closet as if I was going to materialize behind her while she contemplated obeying me. I didn't think she was going to do it, when suddenly she set her phone down and lifted her skirt.

I forced myself to look away from the screen on my phone as I walked, sticking to my promise to myself that she would know when I was seeing her nudity.

A moment later, a message popped up on the app, and I clicked it. Lace.

Of fucking course, she wore lace even at work; she was perfect.

Her white lace panties laid on the island in my closet and she followed directions perfectly. The small triangle of fabric that rubbed itself against her pussy all day laid on top so I could see exactly what I craved.

It was damp.

She was wet for me.

And obeyed me so prettily.

Unfortunately, now she needed to be punished for it by Lincoln.

# CHAPTER 8 - PEYTON

THE LINE WALKERS

"**W**hat are you doing?"

I jumped a mile, pulling my panties off the counter in front of me and crumpled them up in my hand as I turned around to face Mr. Bryce where he stood in the doorway.

"Mr. Bryce." I gasped, trying to figure out exactly what I was going to say to get out of my latest fuck up. "I'm folding clothes." Thank god I'd pulled my skirt back down before I sent the picture to Dane. Fuck, that would have been even worse.

"What's that?" He crossed his arms over his enormous chest and nodded to my hand pinned behind me against the counter like it wasn't making it obvious I was hiding something.

"Nothing." I whispered, shaking my head as I looked around me. The hamper I used to bring the clothes up from the laundry room was to my right. If I could grab it without dropping my panties, I could use the handle to conceal them and get the fuck out. "I'm all set in here. I have to go start lunch."

"Ms. Everett." He snapped, and my heart nearly beat out of my chest. "What is behind your back?"

"Nothing," I repeated, taking a step to the right.

"I won't have a thief in my home. Show me." He stepped to the right, and then took one toward me, blocking me completely.

"I didn't steal." I shook my head quickly. "It's just a girl thing." I tried grasping at straws to come up with a reason not to have to show him my panties.

"Give it here!" He held his hand out and my eyes widened in horror. "Now. Or you're fired."

"Sir," I pleaded, begging God and any other divine entity to get me out of the mess, but he was unwavering.

"Fine, you give me no choice," He shook his head disappointedly.

"No!" I cried and shoved my hand forward and into his, dropping my crumpled panties into his palm and then covering my mouth as I shook like a leaf.

His eyes fell to his palm, and I expected him to act as though the fabric burned him once he realized what they were, given how disgusted he acted that night on the pool deck. What I didn't expect, though, was for him to hook his fingers into the band and uncrumpled them so he could see exactly what he was holding.

"Mr. Bryce," I tried again, silently begging the floor to open up and swallow me whole. "It's not what it looks like."

His dark eyes snapped up to mine, finally leaving my panties, though he continued to hold on to them. "It looks like you were caught masturbating. *Again*."

"No!" I cried, shaking my head, "That's not it."

"Then what is it?" He cocked his head to the side, fisting my panties in his hand and staring at me unwaveringly.

"I—" I panicked and said the first thing that came to my mind. "They were uncomfortable. So I was trying to adjust them and then you walked in and—"

"Adjust them?" He glared at me and I tried not to cry. Fuck, I really did not want to cry in front of him.

"Yeah," I brushed a lock of hair back behind my ear. "I promise I wasn't—" Do not say the word. You cannot say that word to your boss. "I was just adjusting them."

He clenched his jaw and then held his hand out between us, dropping my panties into my hand and watching me closely. "Strike two, Ms. Everett. You're on thin ice."

"Yes, Sir." I dropped my head and grabbed the basket from the floor, eager to leave now that it seemed he was dismissing me. "I'm sorry Sir. It won't happen again." And then I ran. I ran so fucking fast my bare ass could have been flapping in the wind behind me, yet I didn't care. All I cared about was getting the fuck out of Lincoln Bryce's presence. Maybe I didn't have what it took to be his housekeeper after all.

But I was so not ready to go back home with my tail tucked between my legs so I had to get my act together and impress my boss.

THE LINE WALKERS

I drove through the quaint town, searching for the post office to collect the package that was sent to me. I should be figuring out how to come face to face with Mr. Bryce again after my absolute horrific experience earlier in his closet.

Instead, I was getting sex mail from a stalker.

Great life choices, P. You're really proving to everyone that you're an adult.

I parked and jumped out of my car, eager to get back to the mansion before my break was over, I did not need something else to pile on top of my list of offenses.

The post office was small, as expected, and a lady who looked older than the building stood up from her desk behind the counter when I walked in. "Hello, dear." She smiled brightly. "Let me guess, Peyton Everett."

I paused, looking around the space, "I am." I finished walking to the counter. "How did you know?"

She chuckled and grabbed a wrapped box from a shelf and set it on the counter. "There isn't a single name in this town I don't know." She patted the top of the matte red gift box, "Nor do I get packages hand delivered for newcomers either. Secret admirer?"

I ignored her question and asked my own. "Do you know who dropped it off?"

"I've never seen him before in my life." She cocked one eyebrow at me, "Two new people in one day." The woman smiled, "Enjoy yourself young lady, because he sure could do damage to a woman's sensibilities."

"Was he—" I paused, unsure how much information I wanted to berate from the old woman, but she picked up on my direction and chuckled, slowly walking back over to her desk and sitting down gingerly.

"If I was twenty years younger, I would have ridden that man right there on the counter for the whole church choir to see on their way in for practice across the street."

I snorted and waited for her to make a joke out of her over the top statement, but she just stared back at me.

"You're serious?"

She deadpanned, "The man belongs in People Magazine's Sexiest Man Alive contest."

"Interesting." I picked up the box, surprised by the weight of it, and stepped back toward the door, pausing briefly before I opened it. "Hey, if I go missing in the future, tell the police to start with him, would ya?"

She grinned, "Got it. Enjoy the ride." She winked and went back to reading some trashy tabloid magazine, dismissing me.

The entire way back through the winding hills and twisting roads to Hartington Estate, I eyed the red box on my passenger seat.

Dane told me not to open it until I was free after work, but every bit of me wanted to break his rule, then I remembered what he said.

*Call me Dane. Sirs are weak, they give commands expecting them to be fulfilled. I'll make you do what I want.*

I was pretty sure I didn't want to find out what happened if I disobeyed. So I made myself wait and be a good little girl for him.

My phone rang, distracting me, and my sister's name popped up on the screen, so I approved it.

"Why are you avoiding me?" She asked in place of hello and I smiled to myself at her antics.

"We talked yesterday." I reminded her.

"But I've sent you three texts, four reels, and I even resorted to sending you a message on TikTok." She shuddered like it all was exasperating.

"You're so dramatic."

"Where were you?" She kept on.

"Working, Olivia!" I cried, "You know this job that I took so I could—"

"Find yourself," She cut me off, "Yeah, yeah, yeah, we all know you're on a soul-searching journey through manual labor for some rich old man. But that doesn't make you a slave. Can't you answer a text once every few hours?"

Flashbacks of the message I dared to answer and the shit show that erupted in consequence assaulted me. "No. There are no phones allowed while I'm working." I lied.

"Rude." She sighed, "It's 2021, everyone has a phone."

"I know." I replied, suddenly tired. "What's up?"

"Can't I just call you to chat?" She stammered.

I rolled my eyes so far I saw my brain. "You just chased me down like a madwoman for a chat? Olivia!"

There was a long pause and then a sigh. "I miss you, P."

"Livy," I sighed, slowing life down around me to take my sister's words to heart. "I miss you too. Life has been weird lately even before I moved, I know. I'm sorry."

"Don't be sorry," She replied, "I'm a million percent in support of you taking time for you after the last two decades of serving everyone else. But that doesn't mean a part of me isn't selfish in wanting to at least be a small part of your new independent life."

"I know." I replied, "You've been kind of MIA lately too, you know. You're kind of like this mysterious cool sister who has a whole other life that I know nothing about."

She snorted and I smiled to myself, "Sometimes another life doesn't mean it's any more exciting though."

"But is it?" I questioned. Olivia had always been a kind of rebellious soul over the years and even though she had a steady job at the bank and her own apartment, there was always a bit of mystique in her life, like I knew there was more she didn't share.

"Meh, it can be. But it's not as cool as you think it is I'm sure."

"Well, then maybe we should add some excitement to our lives," I offered, glancing over at the present again and remembering the way my stalker's words excited me. "We deserve to divert off the path we thought we'd follow and choose what makes us happy, don't we?"

"We do." She agreed, and I could hear the smile in her voice finally. "Let's just agree if the other one calls looking for bail money, we don't tell mom or dad. Fair?"

I chuckled and shook my head. "Yeah, I'd rot in jail before I disappointed them that way."

"Same." She said, but there was something veiled in her voice I didn't recognize. Something new that hadn't been there before as I thought back over our conversations in the last few months.

Something I'd dig deeper into someday.

# CHAPTER 9 - LINCOLN

*B*e nice.

　*Be nice.*

*Be fucking nice.*

I repeated the mantra in my head the entire time I sat at the table waiting for her to bring my dinner to me. Earlier, I set her up with the panties in my closet, and all afternoon I could see the weight of it on her shoulders as I watched her through the cameras from my office.

Although I wanted to push her away, I had to take my time breaking her down. I couldn't do it too fast, or she'd quit and leave forever. I needed to give her just enough hope that it would work as my house-keeper, so she'd stay close. If she left, I'd never get her completely free during the chase.

She had to hate me to let *Dane* have a chance to give her what she desperately needed. But I didn't need to destroy every piece of her self-esteem in two days, so I forced myself to rein in it.

I heard the click of her heels before she entered into the dining room. Last night, she'd worn a tight black dress that hugged every inch of her lush curves. Forty-seven times at least while I ate my meal I imagined sliding my hand up her silky thigh and lifting the fabric of her skirt until it was bunched around her waist and then lay her back on the table and feast on her pussy instead of the delicious meal she made me. Tonight, though, she wore black slacks and a long sleeve navy blue top.

I hated it. And I knew she wore it as a barrier against my crass ass.

So for the meal, I'd soften just a bit. Give her hope and maybe ease some of the weight on her shoulders for an hour until she could retire to my guest house and talk to her stalker.

I could tell by the way she continuously checked her phone through the day that she wanted him to reach out to her. Yet I didn't, even though I longed to dive into her brain all day instead of all my other work.

"Wine?" She asked, holding up a bottle of red and I leaned back in my chair, holding my glass out to her so she didn't have to reach.

"Please." Fuck if I could remember the last time I said please to anyone but Mrs. Straight. And that was usually in sass after she admonished me about something in the way a mother would.

At least a mother who loved her child.

"Dinner will be out in a moment." Peyton announced and turned away, but I reached out and grabbed her arm as she turned, surprising her.

"What did you make me tonight?" I gentled my hold on her arm and then let go completely as she stared at me like I had four heads.

"Tortellini." She whispered softly and then cleared her throat and added with more conviction, "Chicken and tortellini in a sundried tomato cream sauce."

"If it tastes as good as it smells, I'm sure it will be delicious." I brought my wineglass to my lips and swallowed it as she continued to stare. "I'm nearly salivating for it."

"I'll be right back." She scurried from the room, her face flushed with embarrassment, and I couldn't help but grin at her discomfort. I pledged to soften myself a bit in her presence, but not that I wouldn't make her squirm. It was half the fun.

When she returned, there was a bit of a pep to her step as she carried a large steaming plate out and gently set it down on the table in front of me.

"Enjoy." She smiled politely and took a step back.

"Aren't you going to wait to see if I like it or not?" I unwrapped my silverware and eyed her as she froze with her hands behind her back as I moved the food around with my fork. "Or don't you care what I think?"

"I care." She replied instantly, "I just didn't want to hover."

"Have you eaten?" I forked a piece of chicken and brought it to my mouth, chewing it slowly as a warm spice erupted across my taste buds. She could fucking cook. I thought maybe the pork had been a one off, but she was hitting each meal out of the park.

"I ate earlier." She hesitated. "Do you like it?"

I wiped my mouth with my napkin and looked at her squarely, "It's the best thing I've tasted in a long time, Ms. Everett." I held her wide green eyes until she blinked and broke the connection, blushing and dropping her head.

"Good." She smiled shyly like she wasn't used to praise. "Is there anything else I can get for you, Sir?"

*To stop calling me that.*

I shook my head and gave her a nod, "I'm all set, have a great night."

"You too." She left, leaving me with nothing but the soft scent of her perfume and the distant click of her heels as she left my home.

Leaving me in silence and solitude, just like every other night.

Someday it wouldn't be like that though, I thought to myself as I opened the app on my phone to our messages and simultaneously pulled up the camera in the guest house.

She was just walking in and toeing off her high heels as I watched.

The red box I sent her sat unopened on her kitchen counter and she stared at it as she walked by to her bedroom.

*Come on, sweet girl. Open it. Open your stalker's gift.*

When I first contacted her on the app, I figured she would zero in on the fact that I was obviously not some normal man on the site. I knew things about her she couldn't explain, yet she only balked at them briefly, and then let me into her head deeper than I managed on my own.

I wanted in all of the way though. I wanted to know every single piece of her personality and her feelings and her moods. I wanted to know her good and bad. I wanted it all.

And I would get it.

As soon as she realized what she wanted was within reach and finally allowed herself to shed her past like an old skin. Shed her boyfriend, and her friends who didn't care. Shed her life and her reservations about what she really wanted for herself.

Only then would she come to me willingly.

And until then, I'd take what she gave me under the guise of sexual satisfaction and exploration.

I ate my meal in silence, watching her camera until she came back out of her bedroom in that same pink bathrobe she wore in the picture she sent me. Someday, I'd drape her body in silk and satin and any other materialistic thing she craved. She'd have it all.

I watched her eye the box once again, on her way to the wine fridge and then after she poured herself a glass she picked up her phone and I tapped into her cell camera, getting an up close view of her perfection as she typed something on the screen. With just my phone, I couldn't monitor all of my screens to see her and what she was doing on her phone, so I settled for watching her until a message popped through the app to me.

I grinned to myself as I took my plate to the sink and rinsed it off before putting it into the dishwasher and starting it.

As I walked back upstairs to my office I opened the message and felt an adrenaline rush through my veins as she came to me willingly.

> *I'm in for the night. May I open my present now?*

I made it into my office and pulled up the other views of her that I desperately wanted, the one of her phone screen, her webcam and the one in her home. I had her on all angles and I was ready to play with my toy.

> *Are you excited to see what I got you?*

> *Very. You know nothing about me, other than I want to be chased like a piece of prey. So I'm anxious to see what you could have gotten me.*

> *Pretty little, Peyton. I know more about you than anyone else does. But I won't bore you with those details right now. Open your gift.*

I watched her hesitate briefly before laying her phone down on the counter and slowly pull the red ribbon bow free, releasing the top of the box and then tentatively lifting it. Her ruby red wine stained lips parted as she stared down into the box and froze with her fingers perched on the edge of it.

Satin and lace awaited her. In the same shade as the box. She gently lifted the dress out of the box and held it up, letting her eyes roam over it like she couldn't believe what she was seeing. It would hug every inch of her body from her shoulder to the tops of her thighs, leaving her arms bare and dipping low in front. I desperately wanted to see her in the dress, wearing what I bought for her, and my cock hardened, knowing how fun it would be to rip the thing to shreds when I caught her during our game.

She set the dress on the counter and took out the pair of designer stilettos and gaped at them as she laid them on top. I put my hand on my hard-on as she pulled out the lingerie next. It was black and completely see through, making my mouth water as I imagined her supple flesh spilling out around the fabric. I growled when she ran her fingers gently over the see through fabric of one bra cup, imagining how her hard nipple would poke through the material when I pinched them.

I was so busy fantasizing about our night together; I didn't see her pick up her phone until her message came through.

> *Dane.*

> *Yes?*

> *I don't know what to say. No one has ever gifted me something so thoroughly thought out before.*

> *You mean Tyson doesn't shower you with gifts?*

I knew it was bold, to mention the fuck wad by name. But I ached for the power I had over her to be recognized. She looked around her living space again and then replied.

> *I need to know how you know so much about me. I want to not care, but I can't. Alarms are ringing in my head and I want to silence them for this, but I need something to help me.*

> **Send me a picture first. Then I will give you an answer.**

She took a deep breath and hesitated, so I sent her another message. I could almost read her thoughts as she fought with herself. She wanted this, but was afraid to dive in. It made sense, given I was a stranger stalking her life and offering her deepest desire on a silver platter.

> **Don't you dare think about him when you're talking to me. He doesn't deserve your time.**

> *I know that.*

> **Give me what I want, Sweet Girl. And I'll give you what you need. I'll always take care of your needs.**

She hesitated again, but then grabbed the shoes off the counter and walked into her bedroom. My heartbeat erupted in my chest as I fought the urge to stalk her through her phone's camera. Instead, I screen recorded what it was seeing and exited out, staring at the empty living room of her house for two minutes.

Then three.

Then four.

When five rolled around, I was losing all resolve to lock myself out as a message came through.

> I hope you know how fucking insane I feel.

I growled deep in my chest and squeezed my cock tight as her image took up an entire screen directly in front of me.

Fucking sinful perfection.

My sweet girl had pulled the chair in her bedroom over right in front of the floor-length mirror on the wall. The image was her reflection in the mirror and her phone was in front of her face, but so much more of her skin was on display for me. She sat in the chair, wearing nothing but the sexy stilettos on her feet. Her legs were wide open, with her toes sensually pointed.

One hand sat flat on the chair between her thick thighs, blocking my view of her naked pussy and her arm covered one breast while the other holding the camera blocked her other breast.

Essentially nothing was displayed, yet somehow, everything was.

She was a fucking goddess, just how I knew she would be. And she gave me the gift of seeing it.

> Pretty Girl.

> My perfect, beautiful, sensual, pretty girl.

> Do you like it?

I could hear her voice in my head repeating the phrase she asked me each time she fed me.

> I've never wanted anything more than I want you. Ever.

> Why me? Tell me how and why you found me.

> Do you believe in fate? Or a driving force, pushing something into existence for no other reason than it was meant to be?

I never used to.

> I came across a picture of you by chance. And something called to me in it. So I did what I do best. I studied. I stalked. I immersed myself in you and your life until there wasn't a single secret left unknown to me. I know about your boyfriend. I know you're only with him because it's what is expected of you by your parents. I know you play with yourself when he's not around because he can't make you come. I know he doesn't treat you like the goddess you are. I know he can't give you what you need. What you crave. But I can. My dark matches yours, pretty girl. My monster matches your call for danger.

I dared to unfreeze the feed to her cellphone camera again and watched her eyes flick back and forth across the screen as she read my message. She was still naked, still in the chair but nothing was on display for me.

> Put your robe back on. Because I'm watching you, and I refuse to see anything you don't specifically show me. Not until you give me permission to see it. But you're tempting a monster who's trying to be a gentleman in that aspect at least.

Her breath hitched, and she looked over her shoulder and then back at her phone before pulling her robe back onto her body.

Where?

Do you really want the answer to that? Because the places I can't see you are far less than the ones I can.

I want to see you.

What part of me do you want to see? I showed you all but two parts last night.

You didn't show me your face. Or your cock.

And I don't plan to show you my face. Not until you're ready to accept that this is more than some sexual adventure for me.

I know I should ask what that means, but all I really want to know right now is if you'll show me your cock since you won't show me your face.

You want a dick pic, pretty girl?

I want to know what to expect tomorrow night. Something tells me you aren't lacking in that department.

I didn't even fucking hesitate, as I pulled my pants down my thighs and bared my rock-hard cock, wrapping my hand around it and stroking it in front of the camera for her. She wanted a picture, but I'd do her one better and send her a video.

I didn't talk, but I backed up enough that she could see the one monitor in front of me, which was showing her through her cell phone camera as she chewed on her nail, staring at her phone. And I stroked myself for her while she waited. And when she licked her lip seductively, I groaned, stroking faster for her.

Before I came, I ended the video and sent it to her. And then I sat there in silence and watched her through her phone camera as she played my video. I knew the second she looked away from my fat cock and caught herself on the screen in front of me. Her lips parted, and she stared directly into the camera on her phone in surprise.

And that was when I fucking came. With her eyes on mine, and the picture, she sent me on another screen.

My pretty fucking puppet.

Mine to play with.

Mine to keep.

# CHAPTER 10 - PEYTON

## THE LINE WALKERS

There was something seriously fucking wrong in my head. I didn't even think twice about sending Dane a nude photo. I even went so far as to play with myself briefly before I posed, so my skin was flushed and the arousal was fresh in my eyes.

Not that I wasn't already fucking hot after opening his gift. The man knew how to buy a girl a present. Never mind that everything was the perfect size.

And I knew he was a man, there was no doubt in my mind after seeing the anaconda of a cock he was blessed with in the video he sent.

I almost reached down between my wet thighs and started playing with myself as I watched it until something in the background caught my attention. Don't ask me how I tore my eyes away from the sight of him jacking off, because to be honest, I'd never seen anything sexier in my life. But when I recognized the pink in the image on his computer screen, I realized it was me and it was a live video through my cellphone camera as I waited for him to send me the picture.

I'd heard rumors about hackers gaining access to webcams, it was one of the reasons I'd hid my laptop under my couch after he messaged me originally, when I knew he hacked me. But I didn't even think about him having access to my cell phone.

And even as I continued to hold it in my hand and stare at the message thread, wondering what to say, I knew he was watching me.

And it didn't bother me like it probably should have.

> **Goodnight, puppet. Dream of me tonight and I'll see you tomorrow night.**

Jesus fuck. I dropped my phone on the floor and walked away from it in confusion.

He called me puppet and told me to dream of him. Just like the monster in my head always said. What the fuck was wrong with me!? And why did I like it?

THE LINE WALKERS

I laid down hours later, no longer able to fight the fatigue trying to pull me into slumber.

I didn't want to dream; I didn't want to close my eyes and accept defeat. For the first time in forever, I didn't want to see my monster.

What if my monster was Dane? What if he revealed himself to me for the first time and it was the man from the internet?

Would it ruin everything, or perhaps I'd feel fulfilled that there was at least a smidge of hope in having my fantasy come to life if the main character in that fantasy was actually alive.

I couldn't hold off anymore and as I slipped into dreamland, Dane's words fluttered through my brain once again.

*Goodnight, puppet. Dream of me tonight and I'll see you tomorrow night.*

I expected to see the trees, feel the humidity on my skin, or smell the moss on the forest floor like usual when I fell into that familiar dream. But I didn't. There was nothing around me but darkness.

It felt like sleep. It felt like rest.

Something I hadn't had freely in months. I felt disappointed for a moment, saddened that my monster hadn't taken me to our dreamland as usual.

"Puppet."

The voice was ethereal, floating around me as I tried to find the source. There was none though, there wasn't even light. I felt nothing, I wasn't standing, I wasn't sitting, I wasn't lying down. It wasn't my monster's voice. His was always strained like a fictional demon's would be in a movie. This one was a man.

Dane's?

"Are you afraid, Puppet?" The voice floated around me again.

"Should I be?" I asked, surprised by the sensual lightness in my voice. "Do you want my fear?"

"If you want to give it to me. I'm here for you."

"Who are you?"

He tsked his teeth, and I felt the air heat around me. "Puppet, you wound me."

"How?"

"Thinking it could be anyone else but me. Thinking anyone else could give you the world."

"You haven't given me anything yet." I tried to sound strong and sturdy, but I was anything but.

"What do you call the dress you're wearing, then?" He asked, and I looked down, and suddenly I could see my body, wrapped in the red lace from the gift box. "And the shoes?" His voice was nearer now as I kicked one foot out and saw the sexy heels on my feet that I wore in the photo. "And this?" I felt his breath on my neck as his fingers traced over the strap of the lingerie showing on my shoulder. "You don't think I've given you anything?"

"Dane." I moaned, leaning back into his feverish body as his hands slid over my stomach. I hated anyone ever hugging me from behind because it made me self-conscious about my stomach. Not with him, though. He was so fucking tall and strong that he made me feel small and I didn't worry about outweighing or overwhelming him.

"Puppet." His lips brushed the side of my neck as he gripped my hair into a ponytail and held it out of his way. "My perfect little puppet."

"This isn't real." I closed my eyes and sagged into his arms further when his fingers toyed with my hard nipples through the dress. "It's a dream."

"Wrong." He kissed up my neck to my ear, and then ran his tongue over the shell as he drifted his fingers lower to my aching center, brushing against it briefly before sliding his fingers under the hem of my skirt and pulling it higher so he could rub my clit directly through the black panties he bought me. "This is a premonition. This is a glimpse into our future together."

"No." I shook my head.

"You've dreamed of me every night for months, P."

"No." I arched my back and spread my legs further for him even as I tried to get my brain to tell him the truth. "I dreamed of my monster."

"I am your monster, sweet girl. Your dreams knew you'd find your way to me, eventually."

I turned in his arms, but he wore a hood pulled down low over his face, and darkness cloaked it.

"Why can't I see your face, then?" I argued, fighting the part of me that wanted to just go along with what he said. "If I truly belong with you, why can't I see your face finally?"

"I told you that already." He sighed and took a step back, creating space between us and backing up further into the darkness. "I won't show you my face until you believe that this is meant to be."

"I—" I snapped, feeling the weight of living in limbo for so long thinking I was nuts and then worrying over the fact that I had a real life stalker trying to burrow his way into my life without giving me anything in return.

"Until tomorrow, Puppet." He cut me off. "I can't wait to hear your screams."

And then he was gone.

# CHAPTER 11 —LINCOLN

THE LINE WALKERS

I watched her all day long on my computer, even taking all of my meals in my office, so I didn't fuck something up and give up my secrets to her before our chase.

She was a nervous wreck, too. She messaged Dane twice, asking for the details, but I didn't respond. I needed her to be as on edge as I was, because it would make the hunt that much more intense.

So at six, I sent her a message from Dane and watched her on the cameras as she left my kitchen for her guest house at the end of her day.

> **Get dressed in the clothes I bought you. Wear your hair long and free. And wait for your next instruction.**

> *Yes, Sir.*

Cheeky little trouble maker. I cracked my neck and then my knuckles before responding.

> **Just for that, I'm going to spank you before I fuck you.**

She didn't respond to the text, but she smirked to herself as she read it. And then she left her phone in the kitchen as she disappeared into her bedroom. Locking me out.

I smiled to myself as I changed into my black outfit and left the house silently, making sure she did not know I was gone.

I parked outside of the first stop of the night and sent her another message.

> **Eight Ball Bar on Halstead Ave. Park directly out front. Go inside and sit at the bar. Order one strawberry margarita and pay with cash. Then wait for your next instruction.**

> Yes, Dane.

I could almost hear the purr in her raspy voice in my head and fought the urge to skip the first part of the plan altogether so I could get my hands on her. But playing with my toy was my favorite part of the entire thing, so I kept my plans in place and then walked into the biker bar.

The place was rough, the bikers inside were already on their way to sloppy drunk and rowdy. And I was letting my pretty girl walk in looking like an expensive decedent sweet treat, ripe and ready for the taking.

Because I wanted her to *feel* how fucking desirable she was. I wanted her to know just how far each and every man in the place would go to feel her body under his. And I wanted her to be afraid that one of them just might get that gift.

I wanted her fear pumping through her veins before she even ran from me.

As I stepped inside, the smoke from cigarettes clouded the air and the stench of stale liquor hit my nose. Heads turned in my direction, easily spotting an outsider amongst the dirty trailer trash bikers, but no one said anything.

They all knew I'd be there. They all knew what their jobs were when Peyton walked in, too.

To look.

To call out and leer at.

To teeter her safety and sanity on the edge of their sharp knives as they riled her up.

"D." The president of the MC nodded to me as I walked past the bar. I took the offered beer from him and nodded in greeting.

"Blade." Of course, he had the most corny rider name out there.

"We're all squared up here. The boys know what to do."

"Good." I walked away and took my place in the very back of the crowded bar at a booth on the wall. I didn't need to hash out the details with him anymore, because we both knew if he or one of his men fucked it up, I'd wipe out his entire club and their entire bloodlines.

Men like him called me *The Ghost*. No one ever saw me coming until it was too late, and then they were dead. My reputation spread far and wide, but I seldom combined my business and pleasure. I knew I could keep the small-town MC in line though, so I dared to blur the lines just the one time.

It didn't take long for Peyton to arrive at the bar as instructed. I watched through her cell phone camera and the tracking device in the shoe's sole I bought her. The moment she walked in the door, I felt the air in the room change as every man took notice of her instantly.

I watched from the shadows, like a voyeur, viewing my dirtiest fantasy in real life. She was breathtakingly beautiful with her sexy red dress on. Every set of eyes in the room locked onto her as she effortlessly moved through the crowd as it parted for her.

She kept her eyes locked on the bar straight ahead, as if she didn't even notice the men drooling over her sinful body. But I knew she was acting tough through her fear as she followed my instructions.

She was terrified. I could almost smell her fear from my seat in the corner.

My cock hardened as I watched her lush body settle on the empty barstool waiting for her. The female bartender instantly walked up to her, taking her order.

"Damn, call girl in the bar tonight." One biker hollered from the other end of the room and his friends laughed, calling out their own jeers at Peyton.

She stiffened her spine as she waited for her drink, even though the entire room could see the way her hands trembled as she reached for the strawberry margarita she ordered.

"Come on, baby. Stand up and let Hammer slide in deep. He'll fuck you so fast you won't even know what happened." Another call rang out.

"Just bend over the bar. Those heels will leave that plump ass angled perfectly!"

"I call dibs on her mouth!"

"I'm fucking that ass first. I bet she's never had a man there."

She drank a large sip of her margarita, ignoring the men as their calls got louder and more crude. Whether she noticed or not, the men were getting closer, too.

I could see her eyes in the mirror over the back of the bar as one of the dirty bikers leaned right over her shoulder and sniffed her hair. He didn't specifically touch her, but he was close.

Too close.

She flinched, and he laughed at her, licking his lips and fisting his cock as he leaned against the bar top next to her. He kept rubbing himself through his jeans as he stared at her.

She took another large sip of her drink, eager to finish it as quickly as possible. When she was done with the drink, she could leave.

The man sat on the stool next to her as Blade, the president, took the one on her other side, both boxing her in with their bodies.

Blade leaned in close but his voice carried as the room quieted, watching their president work the sexy woman over. "I bet your pussy is wet right now, isn't it?"

She pursed her lips tight and then lifted her glass to her lips, finishing it and then turning to face him head on. "Dripping." She replied boldly, and my cock throbbed at her stupidity. Blade licked his lips, and his nostrils flared as he fought to stay on the script. If he fucked it up, I'd blow his brains out before he even stood up. He knew that. But Peyton didn't, and she turned on her stool to face him after laying a twenty down on the bar, "But not for you."

She stood up on her mile long legs and flicked her eyes around the room, briefly looking my way as she took in the entire room. I knew she couldn't see me, but it heightened the fun of it for me.

"Better run then, baby girl." Blade stood up, towering over her in her personal space. "Because men like us don't care who got the pussy wet as long as our big cocks get to enjoy it."

I sent the next message to her phone and watched as she ignored him completely to open it.

> **Leave through the back door by the restrooms. Turn left and walk away from the parking lot.**

She tucked her phone back into her purse and took a step back away from the menacing man in front of her, bumping into a brick wall of a man behind her and jumping away from the contact.

"Run, pretty girl." Blade grinned salaciously down at her. "We love a good fight."

She walked away, turning on her heels and all but scurrying down the dark hallway to the bathrooms. She looked over her shoulder a dozen times in the brief space and burst through the back door to the dark parking lot.

Blade's eyes found mine in the crowd as I stood up to follow her and he nodded, with the amused grin on his gnarled face. "Bring her back someday for some fun."

I ignored him, already heading to the front door and leaving them all in my wake. They served their purpose and effectively riled her up enough that she was nearly running through the darkness to get away from the bar.

Good girl.

I lifted my hood and followed her with my own heart racing through my chest as she hit the thick forest that backed up to my property. I took my phone out and sent my last instruction before turning it on silent and zipping it away.

The hunt was on.

# CHAPTER 12 - PEYTON

**M**y heels sank in the soft earth with each step, but I didn't take them off. If Dane had wanted me to be barefoot, he wouldn't have sent the over the top gifts slowing me down. Which was also the point of their existence I was sure.

My heart was beating a mile a minute in my throat as I reached the end of the parking lot and kept going through the grass. When the trees started blocking out any moonlight from above I glanced over my shoulder to make sure no one from the bar was following me.

At least none of the bikers.

They were scary as fuck, and my skin still crawled from the things they said to me in my short five minute stay. I knew that was Dane's plan the whole time, and I could also tell that the men weren't actually going to touch me, though I didn't know what the fuck made me stupid enough to test that theory.

When the one had cornered me at the bar and asked me about my wetness, I felt so fucking powerful, tempting him and testing the invisible barrier between us. I was high on adrenalin as I left the bar and I could feel it amplifying in my veins with every step taking me further into the woods.

My phone vibrated in my purse and I ripped it out to read the message and nearly cried out in ecstasy from just the words on the screen.

> *Run, Puppet. Run from your hunter and try to escape. Because if I catch you, all three of your holes are going to know my touch by the time I'm done with you.*

And I fucking ran.

I tucked my phone back into my purse and shot off through the dark woods, using my hands as barriers from the brush and twigs, slapping me as I ran. I had no idea if he was even actually with me in the woods, or maybe he was pranking me from some remote location and fucking with my head for his own enjoyments, but I still ran.

The adrenalin and fear made me feel the most alive I'd ever felt before. I felt high, and even the mild experimenting I'd done with drugs in my life couldn't come close to recreating the high I was on as I ran from my hunter.

And then I heard a noise behind me and I whipped around to see what made it and lost my footing, losing one shoe as I caught movement behind me in the shadows.

"Fuck." I hissed, kicking the other expensive shoe off and mentally cried out at the loss of the pretty material item as I left it behind. I couldn't afford to let them slow me down anymore, because I was actually being chased.

I twisted around a large tree and cut to my right, running further into the dark woods, but with every panic induced gasp I took, I heard another noise from behind me.

"Puppet!" A deep baritone voice echoed through the woods and I screamed in fear, ducking beneath some lower brush to hide, crawling across the damp ground on my hands and knees.

He was so fucking close and I no longer cared about my fancy dress, silk stockings, or the manicured nails I'd perfected for him.

I fucking fled with regard for nothing else.

"Come here Puppet," His voice echoed off the low branches around me and I froze, as the noise encircled me, making it sound like he was in front of me. "When you asked me to hunt you down, I thought you'd actually make it hard on me, but you're just giving up. You're making it too easy."

I got up on my feet and turned in another direction, gasping when I slipped in mud and slid down a steep hill that came out of nowhere on my knees. In an open clearing, I landed in a heap; the impact reverberating through my body. Slowly, I climbed back to my feet, wincing at the soreness. Surveying my new surroundings, a feeling of isolation washed over me. The dark forest enveloped me, its dense foliage blocking any sign of escape.

I had no idea where I was anymore. I couldn't tell where I'd been or where I was going.

Movement caught my eye, and I shrieked in horror as a large dark shadow jumped down the hill beside me.

It was him.

Dane.

He landed on his feet with a muffled thud in the mud and fear bloomed anew in my heart, seeing his gloomy silhouette for the first time. I jumped to my feet and cut across the opening into darkness once again, but I heard the thudding of his boots on the ground behind me.

And his sinister laugh.

Fuck, it was so hot.

"That's my girl, P. Run. Run from me like it will make you like it any less when I catch you." He called out from behind me, and it sounded like he was right on my tail.

He was so much bigger than I was; it took no time at all for his long legs to catch up to me. His hand grabbed a fist full of my hair first, and I screamed in agony when he pulled me to a stop by it. He slammed into my back and had one arm around my torso with the other still holding me by my hair.

"No!" I screamed, clawing and thrashing in his hold as he forced me to the ground under his bulking form. "No!"

His weight was overwhelming on my back that stars danced in front of my eyes as he pinned my wrists behind my back and tied something tight to them, completely immobilizing me.

"My pretty little prize." He growled in my ear as I panted in fear and anticipation for what came next. He sat up on his knees and straddled my ass, keeping one hand in my hair at the back of my head to keep my cheek flat to the earth. "You got my gifts all muddy."

"That's what you wanted." I panted, fighting anew, kicking my feet and trying to hit his back or break through the hard plastic cutting into my wrists. "You wanted me dirty."

He chuckled and leaned down over my back again until his breath hit the shell of my ear again and I moaned breathlessly at the sensation of him against me. "You were dirty long before you met me, Puppet." He bit my ear and licked my cheek, "You just didn't allow yourself to embrace this side of you."

He flicked his wrist out to the side of my face and I stilled in absolute panic when a knife shot out of a steel handle menacingly.

Oh, I fucked up.

He was going to fuck me and kill me for being so stupid and gullible.

FUCK!

I fought anew, thrashing under his giant body, causing the ties on my wrist to cut into the skin. My flesh scraped across the dirty beneath me and I screamed in horror when he laughed evilly above me.

"There she is, my pretty little plaything, finally actually fighting me like you mean it." Growling, he pressed one knee between my thighs, wedging it deeper and spreading my thighs wide around his thick, trunk-like leg.

"Please!" I begged pathetically, and froze again when I felt the tip of his knife against the back of my leg directly above my knee. "Please don't hurt me." I whispered, and tears fell from my eyes, dripping down into the dirt. "Please, Dane."

That deep growl emanated from above me again and my body tingled with the vibrations. "Say it again, Puppet."

"What?" I gasped nearly incoherently with fear.

"Beg me. Use your pretty words for me."

"Please, Dane." I cried. Somehow, knowing who the monster was that was attacking me, didn't lessen the fear at all. And it wasn't like I actually knew Dane, either. A name doesn't prove familiarity.

"Mmh," He moaned as the knife trailed higher up the back of my leg. I felt it snag on the edge of the lace dress he bought me and with one quick flick of his wrist, the knife split the fabric. "You're going to scream my name in ecstasy tonight, Peyton." He stabbed the knife into the soft earth next to my head mockingly. I was so close to it, if I could just get my hands free, I could grab it and arm myself. But he knew I was stuck. His warm hands groped my ass as he shook it erotically. I bit my lip to keep myself from moaning through the quick gasps of fear.

"Please don't hurt me." I cried again. "I didn't want to be hurt."

He tore the fabric of my dress, separating it completely up the back so my entire body was on display for him. The black mesh thong and bra did nothing to hide anything.

Every inch of cellulite, every roll, and every blemish on my back was visible. And for once, I didn't cringe at that. Not like I did with other partners. Maybe I was too wrapped up in being harmed by some lunatic in the woods to care if he thought I was fat or not in person.

"Someday you'll realize, Puppet," Dane ran his hands down my body again like he was mapping out the dips and curves. "I'm the only man in this entire world that will never hurt you." Before his words even registered, though, his hand came down in a resounding slap against my bare ass cheek. The noise echoed off the trees and my scream followed suit. I couldn't make sense of his words and actions, and I was thrown into a whirlwind of sensation and emotion.

I was afraid.

I was anxious.

Worst of all, I was fucking aching with need.

But Dane wasn't ready to put me out of my misery yet, "Your deadbeat boyfriend hurts you every time he sleeps with someone else on his business trips." His hand fell to my ass again, and I yelped and groaned when his other hand tightened in my hair. "You may not know every time, but you know he isn't faithful, yet you stay."

"Stop." I gritted through my teeth, "He doesn't matter."

"Yes, he does." Dane spanked me again, and a moan escaped my lips against my control. "He matters because you won't walk away from him, yet you're willing to spread your thighs for a stranger from the internet in return. You'd never act so stupidly if it wasn't for him. For driving you to insanity and desperation. You wanted to feel alive, that's why you came to me."

"*You* hacked me." I yelled and screamed with the next spank. "*You* stalked me. I didn't come to you!"

He growled and spanked me three times in a row and then lifted my hips up into the air so I rested with my knees and face in the dirt. "You dream of me, Puppet." He spanked me again, and then pushed my thighs wider and my body instantly opened for him, arching my back and spreading my knees out wide. Fuck, I was so desperate for him. "You came looking for me. You need me."

"Then fuck me!" I screamed in frustration. "I wanted a man to fuck me like I need to be fucked! Not dissect my life, my like some limp dick therapist asking me how my boyfriend's infidelity makes me feel!" I pushed back against him with my ass and felt the rough fabric of his pants against my barely covered pussy. "I need to be fucked so I can fucking breathe again!"

The next slap of his hand landed directly against my exposed pussy and I cried out in ecstasy as he tore the black thong off my body and brutally pushed two fingers into my wet hole.

"Yes!" I moaned, pushing back onto his fingers as he thrust them in hard. I mewled and moaned for him incoherently. "I need it, please!"

Gasping in agony when he pulled his fingers from my body and then I screamed when his thick cock thrust deep into my body. Fuck, the thing was so perfect. It burned and stretched me effortlessly. "Is this what you needed, Puppet?" He hissed and fucked me hard, using my tied hands as a leverage point to pull me back onto his cock after each brutal thrust.

"YES!" I cried out, slamming back into him desperately. "Yes, yes, yes!"

He grabbed my hips and pushed my torso into the dirt harder and then leaned over my back, slamming deep with each thrust so I had nowhere to move away from them and I couldn't chase him for more when he pulled out. I was his toy. His to use and to fuck like I didn't matter.

But I wasn't stupid enough to think I didn't fucking matter to Dane.

I was stupid to get myself into the situation I was in to begin with, but I knew he wanted me in ways no one else ever had before. He saw me. He looked for me. He stalked me.

He was obsessed.

And it was that very thought that shot me off into space with the biggest orgasm of my life. "More. Yes, Dane. God, you fuck me so good."

"Mmh," He moaned his agreement and spit on my ass, pushing a finger into me. It took me by surprise but it shouldn't have, he told me I'd know his touch in all three of my holes when he was done with me. I tried looking over my shoulder to see him. I wanted to see if he looked as animalistic as I imagined him to look while fucking me raw and possessively. But no matter how hard I fought against his hold on me, I couldn't see him.

He actively avoided me every time I tried. All I could see was the black pants and shoes he wore and his fist gripped in the fabric of my torn dress or hair as he adjusted his hold on me.

He was a ghost, effectively hiding from me while pleasuring me in ways no man ever had before him.

"I'm going to fuck this ass, Peyton." He spanked my ass cheek, and I moaned wildly even as fear bloomed in my chest again. "Someday. Not today."

"Tonight is the only time." I gasped, "This is a onetime thing."

He chuckled, and cut my arms free releasing his hold on my hair, only to replace his hand around my throat and pull me until I was sitting on his thighs as he kept fucking me. The change in angle pushed his fat cock directly against my G-spot with each thrust, and I clawed at his arms in agonizing ecstasy.

"This is just the beginning, P." He pressed his lips against my ear and tightened his grip on my throat. "You can either accept that and come to me willingly, or I'll come to you." He thrust harder, "Late at night, to the rich fuck's massive property." Harder again, "I'll sneak in under the cover of darkness and make you my personal little fuck toy right there on his guest bed." I mewled and cried out when his free hand landed on my clit, slapping it and then drawing pleasurable circles around it. "What do you think your boss would have to say when he finds out you squirted all over his pristine guest house for me like a perfect little toy?"

"Fuck!" I screamed, orgasming yet again as the dirty thought of Mr. Bryce catching me in an indecent predicament again excited me. He was just so tight laced and serious, the idea of him yelling at me again made my pussy throb. How fucked in the head was I that I was thinking about my asshole of a boss with his massive sexy body and his boorish personality, while the literal man of my dreams pounded my pussy with his perfect cock? Super fucked in the head.

"Did you know he jacked off after finding you with no panties on in his closet?"

"What?" I moaned, leaning into Dane harder. "How do you know that?"

"He hid himself away and stroked his cock, fantasizing about bending you over that counter in his closet and fucking you. Just like this."

"No." I tried to shake my head, overwhelmed with the fantasies and ecstasy he was forcing down on me. "He's not into me."

Dane chuckled in my ear and pinched my clit harder before bringing his fingers up to my mouth and pushing them in. "Taste your pussy straight from my fingers, P. And tell me how any man in the world wouldn't salivate for it after smelling your arousal in his own home?"

I locked my lips around his thick fingers, tasting my arousal. I had never been so brazen before, but it didn't matter. Dane didn't care, he took what he wanted, anyway. And in return, he gave me everything I could ever dream of. I licked his fingers, sucking them deep into my mouth and moaning around them as I neared yet another orgasm.

I'd never come more than once at a time during sex, and even then, I wasn't likely to get off at all from intercourse before I met Dane. And that was exactly why I needed tonight more than anything else. I left my inhibitions in my car on the street outside of the biker bar and survived off instinct and need for the last hour.

I mean, for fuck's sake; I was on my knees in the middle of the woods, taking a stranger's cock as I sucked my wetness from his fingers like a fucking aphrodisiac, coming repeatedly like a madwoman.

I was free.

"That's it, Puppet." He growled in my ear, "I watch you, Puppet. I study you. I perfect myself for your wants and needs."

"Dane." I moaned, laying my head on his shoulder as his words of depraved devotion hit me far harder than they should have. He wasn't normal, he wasn't sane. But for once, I didn't care.

"No one will ever make you feel like this, but me." He pulled the ripped remains of my dress off until I wore only his black see through bra, on the dirt ground between his thighs, taking his cock, and silently begging for more of him. The second his big hand palmed my breast and started toying with my nipple, I shot off again.

"Dane!" I screamed for him. I screamed because of him. I screamed at him.

"That's it, P." He growled, circling my clit again and prolonging my orgasm until I couldn't stop coming even if I wanted to. I never wanted to. He controlled me perfectly, and I gave into it. "My turn to taste ecstasy." He pulled out of my body abruptly and stood up, releasing my body completely, and I fell forward on my hands. "Open that pretty mouth, Puppet." Dane stood in front of me and grabbed and handful of my hair, pulling my head back to look up at him for the first time before pushing his thick cock into my mouth. "Taste us together, baby. Familiarize yourself with it, because you're going to taste it often."

I fucking sucked his cock like my life depended on it. I stared up at him in the darkness, but the moon shining above him cast a shadow over his face under the cover of his hood. How the man kept a hood while he fucked me like a rabid animal was beyond me. But I didn't care. I wanted to see his face, but it wasn't necessary anymore. Not after I felt him from the inside out.

I swallowed his cock as he pushed it forward to the back of my throat, moaning from how my pussy tasted on his skin and then dug my nails into his jean covered thighs as I twisted my tongue around him on the way off.

"You're so perfect on your knees with my cock in your mouth, Puppet." He loosened his hold on my hair and gentled his hand as he trailed it over my cheek as I sucked on the head only of his cock. I was sure I looked like a fucking disaster as I tried to be seductive, thanks to the mud, dirt, tears, and anything else smeared on my skin.

But it didn't matter, his praise was the only thing I needed.

"I want your come." Gasping, licking my way up his cock as I stared up into the darkness of his face. "I need it, Dane."

"I already told you, P, I'm the only one who will ever give you everything you need." He held the base of his cock tight as I deep throated it over and over again and then pulled back. I couldn't see his face but I could feel the power in his body as he towered over me, losing control in pleasure. Pleasure I gave him.

How could I feel so powerful when he repeatedly told me I was his toy to be used?

Because it was Dane, I guessed as he tipped his head back and roared into the dark sky as the first shot of come coated my tongue. With his head tipped back, I could make out the edge of his chiseled jaw, covered with dark whiskers as he pumped my mouth full of come.

And I'd never been more attracted to another human being than I was to Dane at that moment. I swallowed him deeper, letting his come shoot down the back of my throat and stroked the part of his cock I couldn't take, milking him dry like a good girl. I wanted to be such a good fucking girl for him.

He dropped his chin to his chest as it rose and fell in pants, staring down at me. He brushed his fingers through my hair almost tenderly as I licked his cock gently, cleaning him. I didn't want it to end, but I knew since we were both satisfied, it was done. So I was just trying to prolong it for a few more seconds.

"Peyton." He whispered through the darkness, hooking his thumb against my bottom lip as he backed up, pulling himself free.

"Don't say anything." I sank back onto my feet there in the dirt as reality started creeping back in around us.

"Why?" He cocked his head to the side as I gingerly got my feet under me and slowly rose onto my feet.

I had nothing on except for the see-through bra, and I, feeling self-conscious, began to mind that he was still fully clothed and staring at me. He turned away and reached around the back of one tree, retrieving a bag that he must have hidden there before everything.

"How did you know where we'd be?" I questioned, as he pulled out a hooded sweatshirt and pajama pants.

"I know everything." He kneeled at my feet and gently lifted one of my feet up and into the leg of the pants, repeating the same gentle motion with the other before covering my body with the softest fabric I'd ever felt before. He didn't look up at me though, even though I silently begged him to. "I always will."

I dutifully lifted my arms as he slid the large hoodie over my head and covered the rest of my nudity. I stared at the fabric of his shirt and then took a step back from him. No words felt right to ruin the night with so I silently backed up another step.

"Go this way." He stepped to the side and nodded behind him. "There's a trail that will lead you right back."

"Okay." I turned and walked the way he said, and just as I broke through the trees onto the path he told me I'd find, I turned back for one last look. Because regardless of what he said, I knew it would be a onetime thing. Even if my entire body ached for more of the free feeling he gave me, I couldn't indulge.

I had obligations and expectations back home to fulfill.

I made promises I had no choice but to keep. Even if it'd feel like I was cutting off a physical part of myself to fit into the role they wanted.

# CHAPTER 13- LINCOLN

THE LINE WALKERS

I paced back and forth in my office, watching the monitors obsessively as Peyton slept peacefully in her bed. I broke my rule and stalked her in her own bedroom.

Technically, I also entered her apartment after she passed out, returned all of her scattered items from the woods, and intentionally positioned her phone on her bedside table so I could see her clearly as she slept.

But the invasion in her bedroom was the only part I felt bad about. It didn't stop me, though. I was a runaway train, unable to stop or control myself after having just a taste of her perfection. I was a man of order, control, and routine. Yet within a week of meeting Peyton Everett, I threw it all out the window and ignored my own limits.

My phone rang, pulling my attention from the screen, showing a sleeping Peyton still passed out in her bed. She would get up soon to come in for work, but I didn't want to lose a single moment of watching her, so I ignored the call.

True to form, the phone rang once more, and with a sigh, I reluctantly picked it up.

"What do you want?" I barked into the speaker, throwing myself down in my chair to stare at Peyton.

As my brother chuckled unimpressed on the other end of the phone, I clenched my teeth, bracing myself for his annoying mood.

"Well, good morning to you too, sunshine. How have you been?"

"Tamen." I growled in warning, cracking my knuckles.

"You're grumpy for whatever ungodly hour it is there right now. Did someone piss in your morning cereal? Surely Mrs. Straight wouldn't treat you so poorly."

"Tamen!"

My brother ignored my warning though and kept right on in his over-the-top theatrical way. "Oh, that's right, Mrs. Straight isn't there is she?" He asked, and I paused, knowing full well I didn't tell him about my housekeeper's departure. "Of course she isn't, because I just saw her walking around the shops in England."

"Leave it alone—" An icy chill broke out over my neck as I realized my brother knew something he shouldn't.

"She had the most fascinating tale to tell about a bright and bubbly young woman taking her place for three months there, locked away with my crass older brother." He jeered and my blood boiled. "What on earth would you be thinking to let someone like that near you?"

"Fuck off, Tamen." I snapped. He wasn't wrong, he was one of the few people in the world to know the real me. The fucked-up parts of me.

And that was only because he was just as fucked in the head as I was.

"I'm coming to visit, Linc."

"No." I growled, envisioning him anywhere near Peyton, turned my vision red with fury. "Stay the fuck away from here."

"See you soon, big bro." He chuckled, ignoring me in typical little brother fashion, "Can't wait to meet your new toy."

"Tamen—" I yelled, but he hung the phone up before I could even finish my threat. "Fuck!"

Thanks to our awful upbringing, we were both equally fucked in the head. But where I was sly and sneaky, using technology to get what I wanted without even having to go near my target, Tamen was more hands with his damage. He had a blood thirst that knew no limits, and his skills to get that blood were unmatched.

And the idea of him stepping foot on Hartington Estate was enough to throw me into a tailspin. We'd never used our skills against each other, basically because we were each other's only allies in the world. But he was just psycho enough to rile me up by threatening Peyton for a thrill.

And I would be damned if anything or anyone ever got near her. As if on cue, her sleeping form moved on the screen and she stretched her arms up over her head, waking up as the sunshine started peaking in through her curtains. Her blankets slid down her body, revealing her sexy form.

I pushed aside my anger with Tamen, ready to watch my most fascinating show as Peyton's eyes fluttered open.

She was wearing a thin sleep tank and her full breasts barely remained covered as she moved around. It was as if it took her a few minutes to remember everything that had happened last night though, because she paused after a while and froze, staring up at the ceiling.

I could almost hear her thoughts racing through her mind. She looked over at the clock on her bedside table and noticed her phone propped up on the charging stand, and cocked her head to the side.

She had dropped it in the woods last night with her purse, but I retrieved it and returned it after she went to sleep. The trail I led her towards after fucking her led right to the back of the guest house, meaning she never even bothered to get her belongings. Instead, she'd walked right back into her apartment in a daze.

Peyton leaned up on one elbow and stared at the phone and then looked around her room, clocking the freshly cleaned high heels she ditched in her run, as well as her purse laid out on the chair by the mirror.

I leaned forward on my desk, completely entranced by her realizing I'd been there while she slept. I didn't know if she'd throw the phone and freak out, or just accept that I was always around now.

"Dane?" She spoke with a sleep heavy voice, breaking the silence around her as she stared at her phone. "Are you watching me?"

I should have remained silent, letting her wonder. But I couldn't stay away when she so openly beckoned me into her life.

With a few strokes of my keyboard, her phone screen opened her camera so she could see herself leaned up in her bed, mirroring my view, and I sent a message to pop up directly on the screen.

*Always, Puppet.*

She licked her lips and read the text before it disappeared so she could see herself clearly again. I watched her, unable to even breathe as she stared back silently. Did she have any idea what she fucking did to me, by simply existing?

Peyton took a deep breath, "Then I hope you enjoy the show. Because it's your fault."

I scowled at the screen, not understanding what she was talking about as she reached over the phone to the drawer in the table and pulled something out.

And then I couldn't fucking breathe again.

In her dainty little hand was a teal blue dildo vibrator with little prods aimed out of the base. She kicked her blankets off and shimmied out of her panties as she stared directly at herself on the phone. I had a perfect view of her entire body from where I propped the phone up and my cock hardened to a brick as she pulled her sleep tank down, letting her big fucking tits pop free as she spread her legs and turned the toy on.

"Fuck." I groaned.

Her soft voice filtered through my speakers as she ran the vibrating tip over one nipple and then the other. "I don't think I've ever been so horny before." They both hardened to peaks on top of the mountains on her chest, rippling with each movement and I regretted not fucking her on her back last night, so I could have seen them shake with my thrusts. "And it's your fault."

I was so entranced with the show she was putting on that I almost didn't reply, but I wanted to keep her talking as she tormented me, so I obliged.

> Did I not satisfy you last night?

She glanced at the screen and read my message as she spit on her fingers and rubbed them over her clit. *Fucking hell, P.*

"Quite the opposite, actually." She breathed and then laid the tip of the vibrator on her clit and moaned, melting into the pillows. "I woke up dreading going to work. And then I remembered what you said about Mr. Bryce." She rubbed the toy over her clit and then pressed it against her hole. I didn't have a clear view, but I knew what she was doing as she moaned again, pushing the toy in deep. "And then I imagined him fucking me on that counter in his closet and my pussy throbbed before my eyes were even open."

My girl knew how to dirty talk.

> **Turn and lay back so I can watch you fuck that pussy with your toy, Puppet. And then we can talk about how you're fantasizing about taking another cock as you masturbate for me.**

She smiled seductively and then pulled the toy free, turning on her bed so her legs hung over the side as she sat up. Those fucking tits were so big they took up the entire screen and I hit the screen record button to save what I was about to see. I wanted to watch it again and again until she was mine completely.

She propped pillows up behind her and leaned back, bringing her heels up to the mattress and spreading her legs wide. God, I was fucking sucked right in as her pretty pink pussy opened up for me like a perfect prize.

I pulled my aching cock out of my pants and stroked myself as she put the toy against her clit again and pinched her nipple. "Like this?" She purred.

> **Perfection. You're fucking perfection.**

She moaned, reading my words, and I grinned, feeding on my girl's praise kink.

> **Tell me what you're thinking about as you fuck yourself.**

"You." She gasped, toying with her nipple and fucking herself deep. "And him." She gave me a naughty smirk. "Does that make you mad?"

My hand tightened around my cock, knowing she was thinking of nothing else but me, even if she thought we were different people. My plan was working perfectly.

I snapped a picture of my hand wrapped around my cock and sent it off to her, watching as she saw it. She paused the motion of the toy and leaned forward slightly, parting her lips and then licking them.

> **It makes me hard.**

She picked up speed with her toy and then paused with it deep inside of her. The probes laid right against her clit, dancing across it with powerful vibrations and she put both hands on her knees, letting it just toy with her body while I watched.

"You confuse me." She palmed both breasts and pinched her hard nipples. "You tell me not to think about Tyson, and then on the same day, you tell me about my boss fantasizing about me. Causing this new fascination to bloom in my head. I thought you'd be angry at me for getting wet at the thought of fucking him."

> **Lincoln Bryce is no threat to me, Puppet. If you want to spread those sexy thick thighs to him, go ahead. Take his cock. Take his come. Take whatever you want from him. You'll still always belong to me.**

She took hold of the toy again and started fucking herself with it. I watched with rapture, memorizing every single thing she did and what made her moan and how she rocked her hips as she took it. I had no idea my girl was so dirty.

It was a fucking blessing I didn't deserve. But I was going to keep it forever.

Peyton was mine. Last night and this morning proved that. I wanted to prove it to her, too. So I screen grabbed footage from my security cameras last night that watched us fucking in the woods and then sent it to her screen.

The video blocked her view of herself, but I could still see her through the camera as the video started playing.

She froze as her voice played through her phone speakers. *"He's not into me."* She was on her knees on the forest floor, taking my cock as I pushed my fingers into her mouth, making her suck her taste off them.

"You recorded us?" She gasped, pausing her motions as she watched. I refrained from replying so as not to interrupt the video she was watching. I wanted to see her absolutely lose herself to me last night, even as we talked about her boss. It was necessary for her to witness the evidence firsthand.

She would always be mine.

"Oh god," She moaned, tipping her head back as I told her in the video how I studied her and perfected myself for her. She wasn't even fucking the toy into her pussy anymore, but she shattered, coming loudly as she watched the video. "Dane."

Her voice nearly mirrored the recording of her begging me last night as I stood over her and pushed my cock down her throat. *"Taste us together, baby. Familiarize yourself with it, because you're going to taste it often."*

God, she sucked me so good last night.

"Fuck!" Peyton screamed and grabbed the toy, thrusting it a few times as she watched herself deep throat my cock like such a perfect pet. "Fuck! Fuck! Fuck!" She screamed, tipping her head back and pulling the toy out as she started squirting. "Dane!"

I covered my bare stomach with come as she squirted all over the floor for me in unison. Cutting the video off, I opened the microphone on her phone to speak to her. I deepened my voice to disguise it like I had last night as I praised her.

"You're so perfect, Puppet. You came so hard for me." She sat upright and stared at her phone in shock as I spoke to her. "Look at that pretty little mess you made for me."

"Dane." She whispered as she looked down at the floor next to her bed.

"You squirted for me just like I told you last night." I growled, and her eyes widened. "Maybe I should send this video to Mr. Bryce, so he has some new material to jack off to."

"Oh god." She sank back onto the bed and ran her hands through her hair in exhaustion. "You're turning me into a whore."

I chuckled into the microphone and then groaned again, "Baby, you've always been this dirty little slut deep inside. You've just repressed your urges. Until now. Until you met me."

"Mmh," She picked her head back up and then closed her legs and dropped them to the floor, cutting off my view of my new favorite place on earth. "I have to go shower."

"Have a great day at work, Puppet." I teased, and she groaned, knocking her phone off the stand until it was face down onto the table.

As if that would stop me from watching her.

She had a rear camera, after all.

# CHAPTER 14 - PEYTON

"**M**s. Everett."

Mr. Bryce's warm voice called from across the great room as I dusted the wooden shutters on the windows and I forced myself to take a calming deep breath before I turned to face him.

"Mr. Bryce." I replied, and then nearly swallowed my tongue as he strolled toward me in a three-piece suit cut for Adonis himself. The man was so infuriatingly sexy, and he didn't even deserve it.

You should have to be a good person to be that drool worthy.

"I have a meeting in the city this afternoon. I have a couple of errands I need you to run for me while I'm there. So grab your coat."

"My coat?" I stammered, not following what he was saying.

"We're leaving in ten minutes." He looked at his watch, "It's supposed to rain later, so go change into something more appropriate for fine dining. And grab your coat." He looked back up at me and raised one of his perfect eyebrows. "Unless you're looking to join a wet t-shirt contest while we're out."

My pussy spasmed as his eyes flicked down to my white blouse and I nearly choked at his statement. "No, Sir." I grabbed my supplies. "I'll be right back."

"Good girl." He said fleetingly, pulling his cellphone out and walking back through the house.

*Good girl?*

Fuck it, I had a full-on waterfall between my thighs and it was all Dane's fault.

I ran through the house, closeting my supplies and then racing to the guest house. All day long, Dane's dirty words about fucking Lincoln Bryce played on repeat in my head. I was a horny mess, and it was hardly one in the afternoon.

I was supposed to be on break, but instead I was flinging clothes out of my closet trying to find something appropriate for *fine dining*.

Who the hell was going to be dining? Him? Was I going to be serving him?

"Jesus fuck." I groaned, hating my wardrobe more with each discarded option. My hand landed on one hanger and I paused, looking at the outfit hanging on it as a rant of thoughts flashed through my head.

*Don't do it.*

*It's not appropriate.*

*You're just a horny teenager that wants to make your boss hard.*

*It's not worth it.*

My phone pinged in the back pocket of my slacks and I would have ignored it because of the time crunch, if I didn't recognize the sound as Dane's hackery notification ping.

The man somehow set his own ringtone to my phone to alert me to his presence.

**So, what are you wearing on your date?**

I rolled my eyes and decided not to reply. But I did set my phone up on the chair along the wall by the mirror so he could see my room, but not me.

A few seconds later, his voice came through the speaker. "Oh, come on, Puppet. Don't I get a show?"

"Your stalking knows no bounds, does it?" I snapped, as I started stripping out of my work clothes, staring at the outfit on the hanger.

"Not where you're concerned." He deadpanned like it wasn't problematic. "So, what are you going to wear?"

"Why do you care?" I flicked my bra off and threw it toward the camera, snickering to myself when he groaned.

"Naughty Puppet." He sounded playful, and I smiled, quite enjoying it. "You're teasing me."

"You'll survive." I changed into a seamless thong and then slid silk stockings up my legs, adding a garter and clipping the thigh highs in. "You can always just rewatch the creepy videos you took of us last night if you're lonely."

"They're not creepy. They're sexy as fuck. I've come three times already from watching them. Not including the time with you this morning."

I paused and looked over at my phone, knowing he couldn't see me. "You came this morning?" I pulled the rose gold lace body suit on over my body, doing the awkward dance of trying to hook the crotch part together. And men wondered why we wanted privacy sometimes. There was nothing seductive about snapping a body suit together like a hunched over gorilla.

He hummed deeply, and I could almost feel the vibrations of his deep voice against my skin. "The same time you squirted for me. I came all over my stomach at the same time."

"Why is that so hot?" I questioned more for myself than him and then shook it off. I had zero time to daydream about Dane stroking his fat cock in mutual masturbation when I was trying to rush back to my demanding boss. Especially if I didn't want to soak my fresh panties before I even got in the car.

Fuck, were we riding together? Alone? In a car?

Fuck, fuck, fuck.

I pulled the garter up to my waist and then checked that my thigh highs were secure before sliding the long calf length pencil skirt up over my hips, shimmying into it and then zipping it up. I grabbed the black cape blazer that essentially sat on my shoulders with my arms draped in it and looked in the mirror.

Fuck, it screamed dirty sex kitten.

But I was out of time to change anything about it, if I had a hope or a dream of fixing my face.

I rushed to the bathroom and pulled the claw clip from my hair, dousing it in dry shampoo for some more volume and then reapplied my mascara and grabbed my trusty red lip stain. It was probably over the top for one in the afternoon, but it would last all day and into the evening.

"Do I get a little preview at least?" Dane's voice filtered through the phone again and I grinned to myself, knowing I was going to give him more than just a preview. The man drove me wild with sexual excitement, and I wanted to tease him like he had been doing to me.

I picked up the sexy shoes he bought me, and returned silently overnight, and then walked over in front of the phone. My image was up on the screen and I leaned over, pretending to check my red lipstick. I adjusted my tits in the cups of the v cut top until they were nearly spilling over and then winked and stood up, so he got the full image. I gracefully stepped into his shoes and then turned, checking out the way they made my ass look lifted and plumper. Which was saying something, because as a big girl in a very giving pencil skirt, I was already looking snatched.

"Puppet." He growled deeply and then sighed. "You're an evil, naughty little vixen."

I smirked and turned so my ass was to him and shimmied as I looked over my shoulder. "Maybe you should spank me for it." I giggled at my attempt to be the vixen he thought I was and picked my phone up. "I have to go. And you're not allowed to interrupt me for the rest of the day."

"Hmm," He hummed, "Challenge accepted."

Oh shit.

THE LINE WALKERS

M r. Bryce ignored me when I returned to the main house, simply staring at his phone and walking ahead of me to the garage. Did I expect him to at least admire my fancy outfit? Maybe. Was it better if he didn't? Absolutely.

Dane's dirty words fucked with my head, and I forced myself to ignore all of them as we got to the garage. I had seen none of Mr. Bryce's cars before, but the obscene number of flashy, super modified sports cars lining the large space took me back.

Mr. Bryce was into going fast. Noted.

My heels clicked mockingly across the shiny epoxy floor as I admired them. I saw one across the space that caught my eye with its rainbow iridescent paint job and shook my head at the obscene price it must have cost.

"Pick one." His voice interrupted me and I was so caught up on the warmth of it for the millionth time that I missed what he said at first.

And then it clicked. "Pic—pick one?"

He nodded and fanned one arm out across the dozens of cars, "Which one should we take today?"

"I don't know the first thing about cars." My head shook after I stammered. "I drive a Corolla."

He smirked, and I stared at the slight movement on his face, realizing it was the first time I'd seen him smile in any way. "I didn't ask for your professional opinion on the fresh air intake on them." He put his hand in his pants pocket and the relaxed motion made my body go warm with appraisal. "I asked which one you wanted to ride in."

While I chewed on my bottom lip, attempting to redirect blood flow from my kitty to my brain, I concentrated on his question. I glanced over the array of options and found the one in the corner that had caught my eye first. "That one." I nodded with my chin, "The color changing one."

He eyed the fancy car and then turned back to me, "The Ferrari SF90." He mused and then held his hand out for me to walk in front of him toward it. "The second most expensive car in this garage."

I tripped, skidding to a stop and turning so fast that he nearly ran into me, stopping only an inch away.

Fuck, he was massive and smelled so good up close.

"I change my mind." I swallowed. "I'll drive my car and follow you."

"Why?" He raised one eyebrow at me but didn't back up, so I stepped back to create space between us. I was far too deep in my newfound slut journey to be trusted so close to him. For fuck's sake, the man had already watched me orgasm in his hot tub, and then found me holding my wet panties in his closet.

And apparently jacked off after that.

Did I believe Dane's tale? No. However, a big part of my slutty brain liked the idea that someone like me would attract the stone-cold billionaire. And I was already getting too many fictional fantasies to come true to trust myself from doing something naughty in front of my boss.

Like sinking to my knees at his feet and begging him to let me suck his cock.

*Down girl.*

"I'll ruin it somehow." Shaking my head with wide eyes like it was obvious. "I'll spill something or scuff something."

He didn't reply but stepped forward, putting his hand on my elbow and herded me back towards the car. "Keep your panties on and I think you'll be okay." He said, and my heart sank to my stomach in shock.

No, he did not just talk about my panties. Bastard.

He reached around me and opened the low door for me, crowding me in against the opening. "Get in the car, Ms. Everett. I'm a busy man."

"Yes, Sir." I whispered, sinking down into the low car, trying desperately to keep my skirt from splitting as I took my seat. Thank god I chose the long skirt instead of a short one.

He closed the door and walked around the rear of the car as I buckled my seatbelt, completely shook that I was sitting in such a flashy car on a seat that felt like butter against my skin.

A ping on my phone sounded, and I frantically pulled it from my purse to silence it as Mr. Bryce took his seat gracefully. For such a tall man, he fit into the seat with ease.

I shielded my phone from his view as I skimmed the message from Dane.

> **Is your pussy dripping for your boss like it does for me?**

"Everything okay?" Mr. Bryce asked, and I nearly choked on my tongue as I held down the power button on my phone, turning it off completely before shoving it deep into the bottom of my small purse.

"Mmh-hmm." I hummed, nodding my head rapidly.

"Good." He hit a button on the dash and the overhead door to the garage opened silently as he hit another button and the car turned on. It was almost soundless, aside from a slight vibration from the engine. "Because I'd hate for someone to be distracting you when you're mine."

I looked over at him and found his dark stare zeroed in on me and a blush crawled up my chest. There was something about the way he said *'mine'* that made my skin buzz with familiarity. "I'm all yours." In a nearly hushed tone, I replied, fully cognizant of the dual significance of the words. "I'm focused."

"Good." He looked away, shifting the car into gear with his big hand on the gearshift between us, and the car peeled out, roaring through the opening and out onto the blacktop.

I squealed like a ninny and grabbed onto the door for leverage as he raced down the winding driveway and then straight out onto the road without even braking to look for oncoming traffic. "Oh god." I gasped and then bit my lip when he looked over from the corner of his eye.

"I didn't take you for a scaredy-cat." He shifted gears and raced down the road at breakneck speeds.

"What gave you any impression at all?" I asked and then regretted it when I realized what impressions he got from me to start with.

He snorted lightly and shrugged. "Hot tub masturbator and closet stripper were some big tells."

I groaned, wishing I'd fought harder to drive my car to the city. It was an hour away and I could not stomach sitting next to him that long if he insisted on bringing it up. "Can we just move on past that? I assure you, both incidents were very isolated cases of misunderstanding that won't happen again."

He glanced at me briefly, shifting gears again as he merged onto the highway. "Shame."

What the fuck?

I opened my mouth to say exactly that, when his phone rang through the speakers and he accepted it.

"You're on speakerphone and I'm not alone." He said in place of greeting and I gritted my teeth at the very inconvenient interruption to what was probably going to be the bravest conversation of my entire adult life.

The contact name just had the letter Q on the screen and the voice that came through was a man's. I could tell he was hesitant to speak at all, after Mr. Bryce's greeting but they found a rhythm of conversation where they gave me almost zero clues to what they were actually talking about, but managed to discuss quite a lot in the time it took to reach the city limits.

When he ended the call, he glanced back at me, yet I continued to look out the window as if I wasn't trapped in a small space with someone who disregarded my presence entirely.

"Do you know your way around a stick?" He asked, and I forgot my plan of ignoring him and whipped around to look at him in shock. "Standard car and all." He gripped the gearshift, changing from fourth to third as we slowed down.

"Why?" I shook my head in confusion and embarrassment.

"I need you to run errands while I'm at this meeting. I already told you that. So I need to know if you can drive this car, or if I need to arrange for one to pick you up."

"Why didn't you say that before we left?" I scowled, "I'm not driving this car. I'll get an Uber or something."

"So you're an average American that can't drive a stick shift." He surmised, "Got it."

"I didn't say I can't drive a standard car. I said there's no way I'm driving a car worth a hundred thousand dollars."

"Five." He added nonchalantly.

"What?" I snapped, irritated and frustrated with myself.

"The car is worth five hundred thousand dollars, base price. With all the modifications and upgrades, this one was nearly seven hundred thousand dollars." He said, as if he was talking about the cost of a loaf of bread. "So if you can drive it, prove it."

He lifted his hand off the gearshift and sped up on the open street. I could tell by the whine of the car that it desperately wanted the next gear and that he was toasting the transmission to prove a point.

"What is wrong with you?" I shook my head, grabbing the gear shift and slamming it into fourth as he hit the clutch.

"Again." He said plainly, accelerating even more. We were nowhere near the traffic of the city yet, thank god, but we were going far over the speed limit. The whine of the car rattled my nerves like nails on a chalkboard and I shifted into fifth.

Or at least I tried, but it was harder than one would think to shift a car from the passenger seat, even given my extensive experience driving standard cars, and I missed.

Grind 'em till you find 'em. At least that's what my mom always said when she was driving my dad's truck growing up.

"Jesus Christ." He groaned and wrapped his hand around mine, maneuvering it into fifth with ease. "Maybe an Uber is better after all."

"It's because I'm over here." I grimaced as the light turned red ahead of us and he started slowing down. He didn't remove his hand as he shifted down, one gear at a time when I knew he could have doubled us down to a stop.

His hand dwarfed mine on the shifter and I caught myself looking down at it, perplexed by the entire thing.

"So you can handle it?" He asked, as the light turned green, so he sped up. He removed his hand from mine, and I instantly missed the feel of it, but I effortlessly shifted through the gears, with zero grinding. I smiled triumphantly, and he rolled his eyes, making him look almost... normal.

"I can shift your car, but that doesn't mean I want to drive it." Now that I had proven my point, I removed my hand.

He scoffed and took over, "Well, you don't have a choice, because here we are." Bringing us into the parking lot of a swanky office building, he stopped in the valet spot. He tapped a few buttons on the screen and a list of items and places popped up. "These are what I need from you. Can you handle it?"

I skimmed the list. Lawyer's offices, a few shops, and a hardware store.

"Easily."

"Good." He undid his seat belt. "Be back by six thirty."

"Yes, Sir." I said and jumped slightly when my door opened, revealing a valet attendant.

"Wait there." Mr. Bryce snapped and got out of the car, walking around the hood and straight to my door. The attendant backed up, stammering something as a tense stare down happened from the hulking entrepreneur I called Sir. When Mr. Bryce blocked off the door to the car and held his hand out to help me up, I took a deep breath, preparing myself to touch him. It wasn't like I could shimmy into the driver's seat with my obnoxiously tight skirt on. "Peyton." He said, and I slid my hand into his, reveling in the tightness of his grip, and as gingerly as I could, stood up from the low car.

When I was safely on my feet, I adjusted my skirt and expected him to back up, but his eyes held mine powerfully from far above, forcing me to tip my head back to look up at him. I still couldn't get over how fucking tall he was.

Just like Dane.

Damn, would he be mad if he knew I was lusting over my boss? Again.

No, because it was his fault I was even thinking the indecent things.

"Don't break any speed limits." He said, taking my elbow and leading me around the hood. "And don't be late getting back, or I'll take my reservation at Menton without you." He named the highest rated restaurant in Boston as I got to the driver's side door and I swallowed quickly, but he wasn't done with me yet. "I hear the food is orgasmic." I stared up at him, expecting to see the relaxed mirth he'd shown in the car on the way into the city, but there wasn't anything light in his dark eyes.

There was only darkness I didn't recognize. "Six-thirty." I whispered, "Got it."

# CHAPTER 15 - LINCOLN

"**W**ine, Sir?" The server leaned over slightly, presenting the wine menu to me. I glanced at it briefly and saw exactly the wine I wanted for Peyton, and then dismissed him.

I didn't want anyone around her. Period.

Aside from Dane.

I smirked to myself as I stared down at the menu, already knowing how I was planning to play with her during the meal. And after.

God, the after was going to be so good.

"Do you have any recommendations?" Peyton asked, drawing my eyes up to her bright green ones. The way I could lose myself in those green eyes should alarm me. I shouldn't want to be that close to anyone at all. "The menu is a little extensive and I can't decide."

"Do you like duck?" I glanced back down at the menu again. Although I had never been to the restaurant before, French cuisine was something I quite enjoyed.

"I don't know." She chewed on her bottom lip, "I've never had it. I've had nothing on this menu before." She laid the menu down and stared at me. "I'm out of my depth here, Mr. Bryce. I believe I will excuse myself and allow you to enjoy your meal undisturbed. I'm not a fancy restaurant kind of girl."

She put her napkin on the table and I quickly put my hand on top of hers on the table, stilling her. "Wait." I could feel how on edge she was and could see the doubt burning brightly in her eyes. "Take a deep breath, Peyton." Her nostrils flared slightly at her name, something I hardly used in place of the appropriate Ms. Everett. "This isn't meant to be stressful."

She took a deep breath like I told her to. "I just don't want to order something wrong and then waste it."

"Then I'll order for us both, and you can try a couple of different things. Explore your options a little." I knew what I meant by that, but she didn't.

"It's a lot of money to chance." She held my stare.

I grinned, unable to keep my usual stoic face. "I'll worry about my fortune, and you worry about what kind of dessert you're going to try first."

She smirked, pressing her lips together to hide it, and flipped her menu to the dessert page. I knew my girl had a sweet tooth, but I was going to enjoy getting to see her experience it first had.

"Ma'am." The Maître de leaned over to her side politely. "There's a package for you at the front desk."

"Me?" She stammered, "I think there's a mistake—"

"Peyton Everett?" He clarified and her lips parted in surprise before she nodded, chancing a glance over at me. "The front desk, Ma'am." The man stood up and held his arm out toward the front entrance, waiting for her to follow his directions.

"I—" She paused, looking back to me and blushing.

She knew exactly who had something delivered to her. Dane.

"Go ahead." I leaned back and took a sip of my water, challenging her to leave me for her stalker. "I'm not going anywhere."

She scurried from her chair, following the man to the front desk, and I smiled to myself. Hook, line and sinker.

Time to play with my pretty little Puppet.

# CHAPTER 16 - PEYTON

## THE LINE WALKERS

A s soon as I stopped at the front desk of the fancy restaurant, I already knew exactly who had something delivered for me.

Dane.

He challenged me when I informed him he could not interrupt me during my workday with Mr. Bryce, displaying once again his disregard for boundaries.

The Maître de retrieved a small red box from behind the desk and handed it to me with a polite smile.

I leaned forward and asked quietly, "Do you know who delivered this?"

The man's eyebrows rose, but he simply shook his head, before turning to someone checking in for their reservation, dismissing me.

I walked away from the desk in a daze, catching the dim hallway to the bathroom in my peripheral. I guess a dark hallway was a better place than the table to find out what kind of unhinged gift he sent this time.

Because I knew it would be unhinged. He had no other speed.

I glanced around to make sure no one was in close proximity and pulled the small envelope off the top, flicking it open to reveal the card inside. I paused as I ran my thumb over the handwritten card, as if the manly script made it feel more personal somehow. And then I read the message.

*Put this on immediately and do not take it off until I tell you. If you disobey, I'll make you regret it.*

*-Your Stalker*

My heart was racing as I lifted the top of the box, revealing its contents, and instantly slammed the lid down on it.

"No." I whispered in horror. My face was the shade of a tomato as I looked around again and then ran into the restroom, locking myself in a stall before I dared to open it again.

To hell with dinner and Mr. Bryce's sudden niceness. I was going home. There was no way I could do what Dane demanded of me.

No way in fucking hell.

I lowered the lid on the toilet and sat down, cradling the box on my lap, and peeked under the lid again. And as expected, the high-end sex toy I'd had in my cart online for months now sat atop a satin cushion like a prized jewel. "Fucking hell." I whispered.

It was a wearable vibrator shaped like an elegant butterfly. I had seen it talked about in a spicy group on Facebook and intrigue colored me tickled pink as I looked it up that same night. The problem was, it was three hundred dollars. Who the hell was buying sex toys that expensive?

Dane, apparently.

My phone dinged in my purse and I gritted my teeth, knowing full fucking well I turned it off hours ago. Grabbing it, I wasn't surprised at all to see Dane's cryptic and creepy message bubble on my screen.

**I want to watch you put it on.**

I rolled my eyes, knowing the bastard was stalking me through my camera because he was that crazy. But to be honest, his obsessive interest in me made me so bubbly and excited. There was no actual anger towards him, but I was stressed to no end that my boss was waiting for me at the table and I was holding a sex toy in my lap in the restroom, gifted to me by some hacking stalker that fucked me in the woods the night before.

> **Do it Puppet. Or I'll send the video of you squirting in your bed to Mr. Bryce's phone immediately.**

Trying to ignore the way my nipples tingled, I cringed at the idea.

To check if anyone else was in the restroom, I looked under the stalls as best as I could, but it was empty. I turned back to my phone and glared at the camera, whispering "I so don't have the time for you right now."

> **Then do what I said and go back to your date.**

"It is not a date!" I snapped and rose to my feet. Thankfully, the fancy restaurant had large stalls because before he even threatened me, I knew I'd do exactly what he wanted me to. I hung my purse on the hook on the door and propped my phone on top so it was staring at me.

As I shimmied my skirt up to my waist, revealing my garter and thigh highs, I stared directly at it and then took the toy out of the box. My eyes lingered on it, my hesitation lasting just a second longer than it should have. But then, I decided to throw caution to the wind.

I wanted to fucking feel alive, and Dane did that for me.

So I pulled my underwear and bodysuit to the side and put the toy right against my clit, sliding it back and forth to wedge it exactly how it was supposed to be and then covered it back up with my clothing. Before I pulled my skirt down, a new message popped up.

**Turn around. I want to see your juicy ass.**

I rolled my eyes but turned my back to the phone and spread my legs, popping my ass out and shook it for him. Fuck my hesitations and reservations. I was horny and more excited about life than I had been in months.

Maybe even years.

**Good girl, Puppet. Now go back to your date.**

"Yes, Sir." I hummed, pulling my skirt down and blowing the phone a kiss mockingly, knowing calling him Sir would annoy him. The last time I did it, he spanked my ass red before he fucked me. I wondered what he would do this time as I pushed my phone into my purse, along with the note, and leaving the stall. I threw the box away, washed my hands, and stared at myself in the mirror before heading back to Mr. Bryce.

With bright eyes and flushed skin, I exuded a captivating and sexy vibe.

Dane did that.

His attention and affection, even as weird as it was, made me feel sexy.

"I'm so fucked in the head." I whispered, walking back across the restaurant to the table.

As I got closer to Mr. Bryce, I couldn't help but be mesmerized by his undeniable sexiness, even though I despised him. Our table was in the corner, tucked near the fireplace, and I didn't realize how downright romantic the entire thing looked and felt until I got to my chair.

He rose from his seat and pulled my chair out, putting his hand on the small of my back to help me down, and I shivered from the contact.

"Everything okay?" He asked, standing next to me, so I had to lean way back to look up at him. On my eye's way up, they stopped at his belt which was nearly eye level and I swallowed down the groan that wanted to escape my lips.

"Perfectly."

"Good." He took his seat and motioned to the wine that had arrived in my absence. "I ordered for us while you were gone."

"Thank you." I lifted the glass to my lips and the second the wine touched my tongue, I hummed in appreciation as a flavor I'd never found in a wine burst across my taste buds. "What is that?" I asked questioningly. I was no wine connoisseur, but I drank enough to know it wasn't normal.

"Chocolate." He watched me carefully as he took a sip of his own.

"Interesting." I took another sip and nearly choked on it when the butterfly buzzed to life against my clit.

In theory, I knew Dane would turn it on, eventually. That was the point. He was playing with me like a toy. His toy. His Puppet.

But the sensation was light and teasing in an incredibly pleasant way.

Whether he was warming me up or teasing me, I didn't know. But I would welcome whatever he wanted to give me. I'd be his good little toy.

Mr. Bryce watched me from the other side of the table and I looked away, taking in the atmosphere of the restaurant so I didn't give myself away.

"What was in the box?"

Now I really did choke. I snapped my head to him, clearing my throat to breathe around my shock, and stared at him. "The- what?"

He nodded his head to the side, pointing out a large stained-glass wall sat between the restaurant and the reception area. Through the center of the glass, you could clearly see the desk. "The red box you were delivered."

"Oh," I stammered, trying to figure out what the fuck I was going to say as more blood pumped to my tickled clit instead of my brain. "My sister." I rushed out, coming up with something on the fly. "I told her I was in the city for the day, but she was busy, so she was just having a key to her apartment dropped off in case I wanted to stay overnight instead of returning to Hartington."

"Why wouldn't you return with me the way you came?"

Fuck, the man did not just say the word came. "Um, like I said, it was just a nice gesture. I have no intention of using it."

"Hmm." He hummed, but our server's arrival with a few dishes in his hands stopped him from questioning anything else. "Ah, here we are."

The server laid down multiple dishes on the table, each holding a different type of food that I couldn't name. "Enjoy." He said with a slight bow and then backed away.

"Holy moly." I whispered in awe. There wasn't a single plate set directly in front of me like I would have guessed, instead they created a circle in the center of the table.

"So," Mr. Bryce started, with a quick rub of his palms together and an expression of excitement on his face. "I've ordered us two of my favorites and two I've never had before. I figured we would family style it all and explore together." He handed me an empty plate and then pointed to the plates explaining the dishes. "That way, if you don't like something, you can just move on to the next."

Maybe it was the vibrations warming my clit, or maybe it was his uncharacteristic friendliness, but Lincoln Bryce fascinated me as he started dishing things onto my plate.

"Thank you." I whispered, and he paused, plate in mid air with what looked suspiciously like snails on it.

"For what?" He scowled briefly, like the words were foreign to his ears.

"For being kind." I stated plainly, accepting the plate so it wasn't stuck in mid air any longer. "For making me feel comfortable."

He sat back in a chair slightly and mulled that over in his head. "You're welcome."

# CHAPTER 17 - LINCOLN

S he ate like she orgasmed. It was a total body experience. Initially, she held back, trying only small bites of things and leaving the rest for me. And sure, I probably could have eaten the entire table clean, but that wasn't the point.

The point was to spoil her, even if she didn't know that. So I pushed more and more foods in front of her, even ordering another round of choices when we finished the first. And I refilled her glass of wine, twice. My cock was hard the entire time, watching her lips wrap around her fork and the little moans that escaped them as she savored every flavor. Well, every flavor but the escargot, she spit that out in a very unladylike way as soon as the taste hit her tastebuds. And I fucking roared with laughter.

I couldn't remember the last time I spent time in a woman's presence where I wasn't either fucking her senseless or ruining her life.

Sometimes I did both at the same time.

But with Peyton, her bubbly and often sassy demeanor was refreshing and inviting. I didn't check my hacks or data once while I sat with her. Another very uncharacteristic action for me.

We were breaking every cardinal rule of fine dining; sharing plates, spitting out snail guts, and laughing as we enjoyed our night. But not a single person dared to say anything to us.

Sometimes money gave you the power to be threatening without even having to prove how threatening you could be.

And I'd fucking destroy anyone that tried to interrupt our evening.

I was so enjoying myself; I didn't even toy with her clit vibrator too awful much as we ate. Instead, I left it on low, like a slight little hum against her body to remind her I was there. Even if she thought it was from Dane.

When I hacked her computer weeks ago, I found the toy in a virtual cart online linked to the site she searched for her primal kink obsession. And last week I ordered it, knowing I'd play with her with it, one way or another.

But as the waitstaff removed the dinner plates and placed the dessert menu back on the table, I knew my time was running out.

She reached for the menu but I held my hand up for the server to stop, "We'll take one of everything."

Her eyebrows rose in silent surprise as the server bowed and walked away.

"You can't do that." She said eventually, leaning back in her chair and picking up her wineglass. The wine was an aphrodisiac itself, thanks to the spices and chocolate in it, but watching her drink it got my cock harder than any high I'd ever chased before.

"Do what exactly?" I challenged, drinking my drink.

"Spoil the fat girl with sugar." She deadpanned, "It's too easy of a tell."

"What did you just say?" I tilted my head to the side, studying her, but the effects of the wine made her oblivious to my subtle movement.

"You know what they say," She flicked her hand around the room. "Fat girls always get dessert. And you just ordered us five of them."

"Shut up." I demanded and her eyes snapped to mine, keying in on the tone in my voice as I leaned forward on the table. At the same time, I adjusted the controller to her toy in my pocket, where she couldn't see. "Don't ever refer to yourself as fat ever again."

I upped the intensity of the toy by five clicks and she squirmed in her seat, setting her wine down like she was afraid she'd drop it. "I am though—"

"*Shut up*, Peyton." I swallowed my fury and leveled my voice. "If you ever refer to yourself as fat in my presence again, I'll fire you."

"I'm just stating the facts." She narrowed her eyes at me, "And it's my body, I can refer to it however I want to."

"Any man that has told you that you're anything but sinfully sexy is a dumbass of epic proportions." I was crossing lines I hadn't intended to cross yet. But I couldn't control the flow of words in response to her statements. "Your body is perfection, and any man, especially a real man like me, would do just about anything to have a woman like you in my bed. So don't you dare discredit yourself or your figure based on weak unimportant men and women in the world who have no class or experience with perfection." I leaned forward, once again upping the clit stimulator secretly. "Because you are fucking perfection, Peyton. And if I want to feed you five different desserts so I can watch the way you sensually eat them, I will."

She opened her mouth to say something; something that would probably break every rule established between a boss and employee, but our server returning with our desserts impeded her.

Changing the tempo on the toy, her eyelids fluttered as the server arranged the food in the center of the table and her hands gripped the edge as she fought not to come.

I was going to make Peyton come in a crowded room, as Lincoln Bryce, without even touching her.

Ignoring everyone else in the room, I could taste her pussy on my tongue as I stared at her.

"Mr. Bryce," She whispered and then cocked her head to the side as her eyes closed completely. She was so close, but she had no idea I was aware of her plight.

"Lincoln." I corrected her as I cracked the hard top of a Crème Brulé in front of me and scooped a generous bite onto a spoon. "Tonight, and from now on, I want you to call me Lincoln."

"I—" She opened her eyes and then shrieked briefly as I pressed the spoon against her parted lips. When I pushed it forward, her lips parted even more upon the creamy dessert, touching her tongue.

I was a bastard for toying with her like I was. I'd never spoon fed any other person in the world, especially someone I was trying to convince that I was an ass. But I couldn't stop myself with her.

She worked it around in her mouth and then tipped her head back slightly, still gripping the table with white knuckles, *and then she came*.

Like my perfect, angelic, dirty little sex puppet.

She didn't make a sound, which I'd give her credit for someday. But I knew she was orgasming as she dipped her chin and nodded her head like she was savoring the delicious dessert. When she finally swallowed and opened her eyes to stare at me, her pupils were pinpoints and a red blush covered her lush tits over the lace of her bodysuit.

"Orgasmic?" I teased.

"The best I've ever had." Now she was teasing me.

I took the same spoon she'd eaten off and took a bite as she stared with rapture. "Mmh, I might fight you for this one." I took another bite, leaning back in my chair as I nodded towards the other desserts between us. "You can have the éclair."

Though to be honest, if she sucked the cream from an éclair I was going to fuck her over the side of the table. I'd push her lush tits into the souffle and eat the poached chocolate covered pear straight off her ass while everyone watched.

I lowered the intensity of the vibrator but changed up the tempo as she tried each dessert, moaning and smiling like a cheshire cat with each delectable bite until I couldn't help but reach down and palm my cock through my slacks as I watched her.

I was going to make her come the entire way home; I wanted her pussy soaked and ready for my cock when we got there.

Because she was going to run for me again, even if she didn't know it.

"I can't possibly take another bite." She leaned back in her chair and then shifted her hips. The toy must have felt too intense that way for her to keep a straight face as she squirmed in her seat.

"Should we return to Hartington, then?" I nodded to the server and held my card out for him to take.

"Mmh-hmm." She nodded, nearly comatose from the food coma and the high of her sexual needs.

I signed the receipt and stood from the table, walking to her side. Our eyes locked, and I reached out my hand towards her, repeating the same gesture I had made in the car on two occasions. However, the moment her hand touched mine, a surge of arousal coursed through me, intensifying my desire. Somehow, she affected me in ways that no other woman ever had, even with a simple touch of her hand.

"I need to pee." She said, and then chuckled, "I mean, I need to use the restroom."

"Let's go." I put my hand on her back, fighting the urge to slide it down over the large swell of her ass as we walked through the nearly empty restaurant. We'd sat through two, maybe even three, rounds of patrons as we indulged and dined. And I had enjoyed every single second.

She walked down the hall to the restroom, glancing briefly over her shoulder before disappearing through the door, and I instantly pulled my phone out to check her camera. Thankfully, the lobby was nearly empty as I leaned against the wall and watched her camera go from dark to light as she pulled it out of her purse.

I watched in rapture as she propped it up on her purse hanging on the back of the door again, just as she had before, and then lifted her skirt and pulled the toy off her clit, sagging when it was free.

I typed out a message to her.

**Naughty girl.**

She used the restroom and stared right at the camera with a sexy little smirk on her face, toying with me just like I was playing with her. When she was done, she pulled up her panties and adjusted her top without replacing the toy.

**Puppet.**

I could hear the warning in my text and watched her read it, before leaning forward to whisper. "I can't. It's too much." She whined, running her fingers through her hair. "I'm too drunk. I'll come and won't be able to hide it from him if you keep playing with me."

**Put it back where it belongs, Puppet. Don't push me on it.**

She pouted slightly and then leaned forward so her tits and pretty face were on the screen. "What are you going to do if I don't?"

Fucking minx. My thumbs flew across my keyboard, typing out a response in record time as I grinned like a fucking monster.

> **I'll fuck that virgin ass of yours so fucking hard I'll rip you open and leave you broken for the rest of your life.**

She pulled back slightly and swallowed her shock. So I sent another message.

> **Now be a good girl and put it back on so I can reward you when you get home, instead of punish you. Either way, you're taking my cock in just over an hour.**

She moaned and sagged into the stall wall slightly as she read my message. "Whatever." She smirked and lifted her skirt again, slowly and erotically replacing the toy against her clit again before replacing her panties over it. "I never said I was an anal virgin." She sassed as she put her phone back into her purse, effectively freezing me out and taking away my favorite sight in the world.

Her.

I could still hear her though and as I cranked the toy up to high, her gasp and moan filtered through my phone and around the sparse lobby.

Multiple heads turned my way as I smirked down at my phone, ignoring every single one of them. I programed the toy to change and alternate different tempos and speeds before sliding my phone back into my pocket just before Peyton sauntered down the hallway.

She took my breath away as I watched her walk under the warm runway lighting of the hall, and I didn't care that she could probably read the lust on my face as she stared right back at me.

It was far easier to lust after and spoil her than it was to be an ass to her, but I still had to follow my plan.

"Ready?" I asked, sliding my mask of indifference back on my face, noting the way her eyes squinted slightly in confusion from the quick shift and then walked away toward the exit.

If I did it right, she'd be so fucking angry at me by the time I parked in my garage at Hartington, she'd be ready for the hate fuck she was going to get from Dane.

She'd be ready to let loose again and work off her frustrations in that primal way we both craved.

And if the glare she aimed my way when I ignored her car door and slid in my side as the valet rushed over to get it for her, she'd be ready to go the moment her feet hit the grass.

# CHAPTER 18 - PEYTON

THE LINE WALKERS

I tightened my hand around the handle on the door as I silently came.

For the third time since getting in the car.

I sagged into the seat when the tendrils of pleasure eased, leaving me exhausted and spent. Lincoln's warm voice broke through the fog in my head and I forced my eyes to open. "Are you going to throw up or something?"

He had been cold and silent since I left the bathroom, and the emotional whiplash *was* making me nauseous. "I'm fine." I snapped, even though I would never have spoken to another employer of mine that way. But Lincoln Bryce had messed with my head all damn day long and I was over it.

I just wanted to get home to see Dane. I didn't know exactly what he had in store for me, but from the way my panties were sticking to my entire nether region, I was officially wet enough for him, just like he demanded I be.

At least one of the hulking, bossy men in my life would find me pleasing tonight.

That thought gave me pause as I sat in the darkness next to Lincoln and mulled over the last week of my life working for him. Then, reflecting on the strange interruption in my life by Dane, and all the wild things I had done with him thus far. I thought of the up and down moods of Lincoln and how he was a recluse, yet always seemed to know everything.

Just like Dane.

"I'll drop you at the guest house." Lincoln interrupted my train of thought and I realized we just pulled onto the long, winding driveway of the estate.

"Okay." I readied myself, completely eager to be out of Lincoln's frustrating presence and back to the safety of Dane's predictable un-predictability. At least with Dane, I knew he was more than likely a psychopath. He didn't hide his crazy from me and never made me wonder if he actually liked me or not.

But Lincoln—fuck. He played mind games for selfish reasons so he could hook me and then watch me squirm. I was well aware he played with me like a toy at dinner, and I fucking hated it. Mostly because he made me want him more than I already did. And then he did what he was good at; he made me feel small.

Well, fuck him.

I told Dane that last night was a one-time thing, but as my heels touched the smooth black top of my personal parking area by the guest house, I knew I was going to play along again. If Lincoln had left me alone or even bothered to be nice consistently instead of shut-ting himself off suddenly and acting like I didn't exist or as if I had somehow disgusted him like he had that night at the hot tub or in his closet, I probably would have been strong enough to stay away from my stalker.

Instead, I walked away from his fancy car without a backwards glance. As I turned the corner around the side of the house to walk up the front walk, my phone pinged in my purse and I paused, pulling it out.

> **An Uber will pick you up in six minutes. Change into that pink sundress hanging in your closet with nothing else on under it. Leave your phone and purse at home. That way, I don't have to pick it all back up when you drop it.**

I contemplated telling him no for the fun of it. But I was too desperate for the physical release he offered me. Orgasming wasn't enough right now; I needed his touch. I needed his torment. I needed the fear and the high he gave me.

I knew he was watching me so I spoke my reply. "You're bossy." I unlocked my door and dropped my purse on the table at the entrance before pulling my heels off and gently setting them off to the side. I was willingly allowing a stalker to fuck me, but I wasn't crazy enough to damage the pretty gift he so creepily returned to me.

Even if I did abandon them in the muddy forest... oops.

Dane's deep rumbling voice vibrated through the speaker in my hand, "You enjoy following my rules."

"Should I call you Daddy then instead of Dane?" I grinned, keeping the camera angled away as I walked through my dark apartment.

His deep growl emanated, and I bit my lip to stop the moan that tried to escape in response to the primal noise. "Only if you want me to breed you to earn that title."

"Fuck." I moaned, no longer able to hold it back. "No." I shook my head as I tossed my phone down on my bed. "No, I don't want that."

He chuckled, and it sounded like he was in a car driving somewhere. "Then don't threaten me with it, because I'll hold you down and force my come deep into your womb if you want it."

"Stop it." I took a deep breath. "You're a stalker and so mentally unstable you're making me crazy right alongside of you. We'd be the worst parents in the world."

"Hmm." He hummed, "Are you on birth control?"

I snorted, "Don't you think you should have asked that before last night?"

"You didn't tell me to wear a condom, and you took my bare cock like such a good girl. I didn't hear you complain. But we didn't discuss it first, so I held off on filling you up. That's why I'm trying to discuss it now. Do you make Ty wear a condom when he fucks you?"

"Dane." I sighed, stripping out of the tight confines of my outfit and sighing as everything was free for the first time in hours. "I think this serves my point that last night was a one-time thing." I eyed the toy as it turned off in my hand and then set it on the shelf next to me. I was honestly so excited to use it again sometime, even as I tried to tell him we couldn't do it anymore.

His voice deepened even more, and all mirth was gone, "Put the sundress on Puppet. Don't make me tell you twice."

I froze, staring at the pink milk-maid style sundress he was talking about. The fact that I didn't even balk at him telling me which dress specifically, meaning that he had been in my closet at some point, should have alarmed me. It should have been the red flag I needed to use as a reason to end things. It should have been so many things, and yet, I glossed over it.

"Why didn't you wake me up when you brought my things last night?"

"Because you needed your rest after what we did. And because I knew I'd be seeing you again."

"Why won't you let me see you?" I questioned, even as I slid the dress off the hanger and put it on.

"What would seeing me change for you?"

"I don't know." I admitted, admiring the way the pink fabric clung to my bare breasts in the mirror. Normally I would have worn a strapless bra to keep my girls decent and in place, but his instructions for nothing underneath were clear. My nipples were on full display through the thin fabric and the cut of the bust enhanced the shape and weight of them. It hugged them rather than disguising them. "Maybe it would make it feel more real."

"Says the girl that tries to hide from me by walking away from the camera."

I pursed my lips and untied the string that held the front of the dress closed over my tits, letting the fabric split open and show even more of my cleavage off. "We both know you'd find me if you wanted me bad enough."

I had meant on his abundant cameras and hacking skills, but the words took my brain somewhere else.

And apparently his too.

"I'll always find you, Puppet. There isn't a place on this Earth that you could hide from me. Not now that I've had you."

I walked over my phone and propped it up on the chair along the wall, looking at my reflection on the screen as I slipped my hands up under the short skirt of the dress and pulled my panties down before hanging them off of one finger for him. My tits were exposed, and my skin was flushed from the way his toy had tormented me for hours, as I completely removed any barrier between us for when he found me.

And wet. I was so fucking wet.

"There's my pretty little Puppet." He all but moaned, and I squeezed my thighs together, desperate to come again. I'd come more in the last week than I had in the last three years with Tyson and that was so pathetic and also so telling. "Your car is outside. Be my good girl and come to me."

"Will you tell me where we're going if I ask?" I started walking toward the door.

"No." I could hear the smile in his voice. "It's a quick ride and then you'll know what to do."

I snorted, "All I've known in life are quick rides."

Tossing my phone down on the table by the door, I walked out without even bothering to wait around for his reply. I was angsty and angry at Lincoln for making me feel small again, and I was going to let Dane fuck it all better for me.

Jesus fuck, I didn't even recognize myself anymore.

And I didn't hate that.

# CHAPTER 19 - LINCOLN

I had no tracker on Peyton, and a part of me hated that. But it would be the last time I gave her the option to hide from me. She didn't know how right she had been when she said I'd always find her.

Tonight I'd prove that to her.

I'd prove just how obsessed with her I was.

I could, however, track the driver and I watched as she got to the entrance to the deserted pumpkin patch where I instructed her to drop off Peyton.

Standing at the dark gate of the closed family fun park, I could just imagine how confused Peyton would be. There'd be no family fun going on tonight.

Tonight there would be only terror.

And pleasure.

Only time would tell who got what out of the deal.

I got out of my Range Rover, parked on the backside of the grounds, and took my spot as I watched the headlights from the

Uber pulling back out onto the road. We were miles away from any neighbors, and the owners of the long running pumpkin patch didn't have a lick of security to get around besides the chain on the parking lot, that I already cut free.

Which meant we had the whole place to ourselves.

Time to play.

I entered the back of the maze, walking the path I already knew by heart until I made it to my spot. I changed out of my suit and into another dark set of jeans and a zip up black hoodie. But I didn't bother closing it up this time. I wanted Peyton to see me, to touch me.

Eventually, at least.

To begin with, I was going to torment her through the maze and make her wild with fear and panic before I even revealed myself.

I backed into the small space between stalks until I wasn't visible on either path and waited to hear her soft footsteps as she slowly made her way through.

Her angry voice met me before her sight did. "I hate you." She turned around in the path when she got to the intersection and looked each direction. "I fucking hate you." She hissed. As she gripped the skirt of her sexy dress, her hands balled into fists. Her anxiety was palpable, and I smiled behind the spooky mask as I watched her.

The mask wasn't necessary, but it went with the Halloween vibe and it ensured she wouldn't recognize me when she faced me. Because last night I was perfectly fine fucking her from behind, but tonight I wanted her on her back when I slid deep into her body. I wanted to stare into her eyes as I claimed her, even if she couldn't see mine.

"Dane!" Her shrill scream echoed off the corn stalks around us, "I fucking hate you! Do you hear me, you creepy piece of shit? I hate this!"

"No, you don't." I replied, causing her to scream in fear. She whipped around to face me, but I had already backed up through the corn to the next path and disappeared from sight.

"Wait!" She pushed through the corn but was much slower and I was two paths away before she got through the first.

"Make it to the exit before I do." I yelled, "You won't like the consequences if you don't."

"Fuck you!" She yelled back, but I heard her turn and start running towards the south wall where the exit was. Little did she know the path was full of dead ends and U-turns, though. "You're cheating!"

I crashed through a wall one path over from hers and she shrieked at the noise, running faster as I turned and ran in the other direction. She couldn't decide whether to chase me down or win the game. I could almost feel her adrenaline rushing through her veins, making her indecision and critical thinking skills run into each other.

She'd never make it in time, but that was the point. She wasn't supposed to win. She was the prize, not the victor.

I tucked myself in next to the exit as she made it closer and waited, using darkness and her distraction in my favor. It was going to feel so good to claim my prize.

I heard her footsteps as she rounded the corner, sprinting toward the opening, and saw the look of immense victory on her pretty face as she neared it.

And that was when I revealed myself. I reached out with my hand and caught her by the throat as she ran by, pulling her into the corn with her back against my chest. Predictably, she fought like a rabid cat getting carried towards a bath. Every time her nails gouged another bit of skin off my hands and arms, my dick got harder.

I took a deep breath against her hair, even though the mask was in the way, but it added to the overall vibe of the hunt. "You lose." I growled, and she fought anew.

I dragged her backward, through different paths of the corn as she kept fighting me. She reached up behind her and slashed at my face, catching the mask and trying to rip it off, but I got her where I wanted her without her succeeding.

People could find a couple of different openings in the maze, each one had benches and hint boards to use when they were too lost to find their way out. And the bench we neared made the perfect spot to play with my little toy. I forced her to the ground with her back against the back of the bench on her knees.

"Nice mask. I would have taken you for more of a Freddy fan." She sassed and then gasped when I tightened a leather cuff over her wrist, immobilizing her. She fought me for the fun of it, but I made quick work of the other one and then stood up to admire her.

Her chest rose and fell rapidly, and her tits were almost completely free of the low-cut dress. I couldn't wait to play with them either, and my mouth watered as I stared down at her. Last night I barely got to touch them, but tonight, I'd feast on them before I fucked her.

She adjusted herself on her knees, parting them and sinking lower as she stared up at me. "Well, is that why you wear a mask?" She nodded at me with her chin, "Is your face fucked up like Freddy?"

I tore my sweatshirt off and grinned under the mask when her eyes roved over my exposed chest and abs. Her lips parted as I walked away from her, showing her the expansive art on my back above my belt, and laid my sweater over the tall board with hints on it along the other side of the clearing.

"You should be more worried about what I can do with a knife." I tilted my head to her creepily as I sauntered back to her.

Her chin rose as she tried to muster up her bravery to face danger head on. "You can't use physical pain against me as a threat. You already said you'd never hurt me."

I pulled my favorite knife from my pocket and flicked it open as I neared her. Standing right over her and her eyes widened as she watched me spin the knife around between my fingers like a magician. "I don't have to use physical pain to hurt you." I stopped swirling the knife around and lowered it so the point of the blade landed on her cheek. "Sometimes the fear is enough to mimic the pain."

I gently slid the tip down her cheek, light enough not to break skin, but hard enough to threaten it with the slightest movement.

"So you're a sadist, with a conscience?" She whispered, moving just her lower jaw until my blade reached her plump lips.

"I have no conscience, Puppet." Lowering the blade, running it down the column of her throat to her collarbone. "I've killed four different people with *this* knife alone."

She shuddered, and the knife nicked her skin enough to draw blood, and I palmed my cock as she hissed. "You—" Her tongue shot out to wet her lips as real fear finally filled her eyes while she stared up at me.

"Did you think the psychopath bit was a facade?" I asked as I sank to my knees in front of her. "Did you think I was actually harmless because I vowed to not to hurt *you*?"

"Dane—" She swallowed, and I slid my hand through her long-tangled hair, "I told you last night that I don't want you to hurt me. And you agreed."

I gripped a large fistful and tilted her head all the way back until she stared up at the star filled dark sky. Lifting the bottom of the mask up to reveal my mouth, I was confident she couldn't see me as I lowered my face to her neck. I licked a trail over the nick I left in her skin, tasting the blood and sucking it into my mouth. Her entire body vibrated, as I changed to kissing, moving up her neck to her ear.

"That was before you spent all night flirting with another man." I bit her neck hard, and she gasped, flinching away from the pain. "Coming, for another man." I pulled back, lowering my mask again as I dragged my knife down lower over the large swell of her tits. "Fantasizing about another man."

"No!" She hissed when I trailed it down over the front of her dress to the hard peak of one nipple. I traced slow, small circles over the puckered flesh as she tried desperately to stay as still as possible by panting small puffs of air. "You wanted me to be wet. *You* made me come!"

"While you moaned for him and let him feed you." Indulging in her expectations, I snapped and played the angry role she expected. "I told you that you were mine!"

"That's not true!" She cried out with wild eyes as I dipped the tip of the knife into the fabric hard enough to pierce it and then slashed it quickly, ripping it open up to the neckline, exposing one delicious tit. "You wanted me to think he was interested in me!" She yelled, growing more frantic with each second. "You made up that lie about him jacking off to me and then put all the what if's in my head. And then he was almost—" She gritted her teeth when I moved to her other nipple, toying with it over the fabric. "Nice to me." She cursed between her clenched teeth. "Stupid me for letting both of you in my head, right? How could the man be interested in ugly, frumpy, fat me!"

I pierced the knife in and ripped open the other side of her dress, and pulled her head back painfully as I sucked one of her nipples into my mouth. Her scream echoed through the trees as I sucked it hard and then bit it hard enough to leave a mark.

I fought the urge to spank her ass until she couldn't sit for a week for talking so negatively about herself. But I had to keep my cover in place, so I showed her with my actions just how untrue those words were.

Her lack of confidence was one reason I orchestrated the entire split personality thing in the first place. She needed to believe in my attraction to her before she learned who I was in real life.

Nodding my head sharply to fix my mask again, I then let go of her hair to wrap my hand around her neck, holding her still as I cupped her pussy under the short skirt of her dress. "I made nothing up." I rubbed my fingers over the soaked surface of her pussy, toying with her. "He jacked off, and he came so fucking hard thinking about you."

Moaning, "You're lying." She couldn't move forward without dislocating her shoulders thanks to her hands being tied by her head, but it didn't stop her from rocking on my palm. "He hates me. He's always so cold. But it doesn't matter!" She shook her head as best as she could with my hand tight around her throat. "I don't want him. I want this. I want you."

Grinning, I pushed two fingers into her, using my palm to rub her clit, and she melted into my touch, sagging against my hold. "Why do you want this? Besides the thrill of the taboo, what do you get from it?"

She moaned, "I've already told you; I've dreamed of it and I wanted to know if it was meant for me."

"Did you dream of your monster last night?" I thrust into her and curled my fingers forward to rub her G-spot. She purred like a kitten each time I rubbed that extra sensitive spot and soaked my hand even more. "Did you dream of the fictional hunter, Puppet?"

"No." She closed her eyes and shook her head, "No, I didn't."

"Who did you dream of?"

"No one." She whispered frantically, "I slept like the fucking dead and woke up to you watching me. The moment I fell asleep, I was thinking about what we did. And then when I woke up, you were right there." She gasped and tightened on my fingers. "You're always right there. In my head, in my life."

"That's right, Puppet." I growled, rocking my hand faster as she neared her peak of ecstasy. "I'm always going to be right here. You can't escape me."

"Yes." She moaned, "I need you."

"Good girl." I praised, keeping her head tilted up with my hand around her throat. Biting her nipple again, then sucked on it as she shot off like a bolt of lightning crackling across the summer sky. "Fucking hell, Puppet." I growled when her orgasm coated my hand and her scream echoed in my ears. "Squirt for me, baby, show me just how much you love my touch."

"Yes!" She soaked the dirt between her knees and then sagged forward in exhaustion.

But I was far from done with her. I stood up and undid my belt as she lazily looked up at me, reeling from her orgasm. As soon as she saw me unbutton my pants, she licked her lips and sat up straighter. "Good girl." I praised and pulled my cock out, already rock hard and desperate for release. "Stick your tongue out for me, Puppet."

She leaned as far forward as possible and seductively did as I said, leaving her tongue flat and ready for my cock. I took my burner phone from my pocket and pulled the camera app up, blinding her momentarily with the flash as I started taking a video. "Smile for the camera baby, we're going to make another home video."

She purred like a fucking satisfied cat as I slapped her tongue with the head of my cock. She chased it with her tongue, twirling it around and then sucking on the head like my own little sex vixen. Her plump lips formed the perfect seal on me as she started rocking forward, swallowing me down. God, she was so sexy and perfect for me.

"That's it, Puppet. Take my cock all the way down, just like last time." I thrust in deeper, making her gag before she pushed forward, taking more of me with my next thrust. Her throat was so tight as I felt her lips against the base of my cock. She stared right at my camera while she sucked me down, the bright flash highlighted the shiny tears in her bright green eyes.

I cut the video, pulling out of her mouth and releasing one wrist from her cuffs. "All done already?" She sassed, licking her lips and biting the bottom one.

"Only because when I come tonight, it's going to be deep inside of your pussy." I challenged, bending down and lifting her in my arms as she squealed, grabbing my shoulders for stability. I positioned her on her back behind the bench and secured the cuffs around one of its legs, simultaneously hooking her other wrist back into it. Then I forcefully pulled her down, tightly pinning her arms above her head. "And you're going to beg me to fill you up, Peyton."

She moaned, stretching like a satisfied cat, and then spread her legs, bringing her knees up invitingly. I started the video again, and she shimmied, letting her big breasts shake enticingly for me. "Fill me up, Dane." From my view, I could see the wetness of her arousal glistening from the bright light. "You do it better than anyone else ever has."

I growled, and I lowered myself to my knees, pushing her knees back to her chest to open her up for me. "That's because you were made for me, Puppet." I slapped the head of my cock against her clit and she rocked against it. "Your pussy was never supposed to take any other cock but mine."

"Fuck me, please." She pulled on her restraints as she started getting desperate. "I need you. You've made me wait all fucking day."

I chuckled behind my mask and lined up, pushing deep in one punishing thrust and focused on her face as I forced her body to take me. Her perfect eyebrows pinched in the center as a deep, breathy groan slipped through her parted lips. "Like that?"

"Just like that." She opened her eyes and widened her thighs as I leaned forward, fucking her. "Just like that, baby."

Something about hearing her call me baby made my balls tingle and my need to fuck her hard even stronger. She was playing with fire, because the more she begged for it, the more likely I was to lose restraint and give her everything she ever dreamed of.

I pulled back up so my camera had a clear view of her body as I started rubbing her clit with my thumb, slowly circling it and adding more pressure with each thrust. "Tell me something, Puppet?" I mused dramatically as I pushed her near orgasm. "Who do you think would be more irate if they watched this video of you taking my cock? Your boss, or your boyfriend?"

"Oh god." She moaned, arching her back and pushing harder against my cock. "Stop talking."

I chuckled and then leaned over her supple body to lean the phone against the same post her cuffs were tied to, flipping the camera around so I could see us in it. "Roll over and put your fucking ass in the air."

I sat back on my heels and stroked my cock, rubbing her wetness in as she scrambled up on her knees with her hands still bound to the bench. She hesitated when she saw the camera recording her, so I helped persuade her to do what I said with a firm hand on the back of her neck and a hard slap to her ass, pushing her down onto her forearms. "Dane." She moaned, looking directly into the camera as I pushed her knees apart and penetrated her again. It was fucking hot watching her eyes roll in the video firsthand as I bottomed out back in my favorite place on earth.

"Answer my question, P." I thrust hard, making her lush tits sway beneath her as she arched her back and took me like a good girl. My fucking good girl. "Who do you think would be more mad if they saw this?"

"Dane, please." She moaned, unwilling to fall down that rabbit hole, but I needed her to imagine it. Because it was going to happen.

"They'd both jack off to it, no doubt." I mused, tilting my head to the side creepily from behind her as I fucked her. "But I think one of them would be more mad than the other, don't you?"

"No." She gasped, "And shut the hell up or get off me."

I grinned behind my mask as I laid over her back, pushing two fingers into her mouth and fish-hooking her behind the teeth as I slammed harder. With a forceful thrust, I made her moan around my fingers and confidently stated, "I bet your jackass boss would be more mad than your boyfriend if he knew you came all night long for me while you were with him." As I fucked her, she sucked my wet fingers, and I taunted, "I bet he'd be pissed knowing your sweet pussy got the leather seat in his sleek car all wet, but it wasn't for him." Reaching beneath her, I pinched one of her nipples, making her squeal and buck against her bindings. "I bet he'd wrap his hand around his cock again and jack off too, though, letting the soundtrack of your moans milk his cock for him."

"Dane!" She mumbled around my fingers and I let her mouth go. "Fuck!" She screamed when I pushed both of my wet fingers deep into her ass, stretching her open.

"Pick one to send it to."

"No!" She gasped, leaning up as far as she could to relieve the pressure I had on her neck.

"Fine, then I'll pick." I shrugged, nonchalant.

"Wait!" She screamed and tightened down on my fingers as I thrust them in time with my cock. "I'll pick."

"Good girl." I slowed my thrusts and rolled my hips, pleasuring her, pushing her closer to losing her mind. "So, who's going to watch you come on my cock?"

"Tyson." She closed her eyes and then screwed them up tight. "Send it to Ty."

I chuckled and slammed in deep, scissoring my fingers. It was exactly what she needed to crest her orgasm, and she screamed as she came. It was my cock she was coming on, but I knew the idea of her fuck wad boyfriend seeing her getting fucked by a real man pushed her over the edge. "Good choice." I kept the same punishing pace until she collapsed with her forehead in the dirt as I let go of her neck. Pulling the phone from its resting spot, I flipped the camera around and showed her tight, wet pussy with the evidence of her orgasm coating my thick cock. I twisted my fingers around inside of her ass, making her mewl and moan as I started pumping her full of my come. "That's it baby girl, milk my cock like only my perfect little Puppet can. Good girl." I slowed my thrusts, until just the head was inside coating her with come and then pulled out, letting her used pussy gape for a moment in the absence of my fat cock.

"Oh, my god." She gasped.

"Show little Ty where a real man comes." I demanded, lowering the camera until her wet pussy was the only thing in view. "Push my come out for him to see who you really belong to."

"Jesus." She complained but did exactly like I said, and then the milky opaque evidence of my orgasm dripped out of her.

I turned the phone around, showing my ridiculous mask and sweaty body mocking him further. "Don't worry, Ty, I'll keep your girl nice and satisfied from now on. She doesn't miss you at all."

I cut the video off and pocketed the phone, putting my cock away even though all I wanted to do was slide back into her heaven.

"I hate you." She stated from where she still hung her head.

I grinned and pulled my fingers out of her ass and then spanked her before she fell to her stomach in the dirt. "You keep saying that, but I haven't believed you one time."

She didn't reply as I let her wrists free. She brushed my hands off and got to her feet on shaky legs, leaning on the bench for support. "I can't do this anymore."

Anxiety bloomed in my gut like a sour feeling as I regarded her, but she wouldn't look at me. She just crossed her arms over her chest to hide her nudity from me. Dirt covered her pretty pink dress, and her wrists were red from the cuffs. "Why?"

She sniffed and swallowed, "Because it isn't what I thought it would be."

"How?" I took a step forward, but she backed up, finally looking up at my masked face. "How is it different from your dreams?"

"In my dreams he—" She hiccupped and clenched her teeth as her emotions rose, "He worshiped me."

I couldn't make sense of her words and what changed from this morning when she was playing with herself on camera for me without reservation. "I worship—"

She cut me off with anger burning in her eyes, "You play with me! You treat me like a toy. You use me for you own sick, tormented pleasure!"

"That's what you wanted!" I snapped back as she started slipping through my fingers right in front of me.

She shook her head slowly, "Maybe I don't know what I want then. Maybe I got it all wrong."

I scoffed as she spoke every fear of mine into existence. "I can't believe this." I walked away to where I tossed my sweatshirt and then held it out to her. "Put this on."

She silently accepted my shirt and covered her body with it, zipping it up and sinking into it like a security blanket. I fisted my hands to keep from ripping my mask off all together and showing her exactly who I was. If I did that, now, she'd run. And she'd never forgive me for deceiving her. I hadn't had enough time to show her everything she needed first.

I pulled my phone out and smashed the buttons, summoning the car that waited for her around the corner. Then I picked up the burner phone I used tonight and every night since I first messaged her. "Take this. Look at what's on it and try to tell yourself that you weren't worshiped by me when you're done." I pushed it toward her, forcing it into her hand when she hesitated. "Do with that information what you want."

Her eyes widened as I gave her exactly what she thought she wanted.

An out.

"Dane." She whispered, gripping the phone in her hand as she stared at me, confused.

"Your car is in the parking lot." I nodded to the opening in the maze near us. "Go home, Peyton. Go back to the mundane, and the boring, and the safe. Go back to a man who doesn't treasure you and doesn't even stay faithful to you. He's the only one that treats you like a toy." I got the cuffs off the bench to busy my hands as they shook. "That was always what you were going to end up going back to at the end of your contract at Hartington, we both know that."

"I didn't—" She stammered, taking a step toward me as my words and her feelings jumbled in her mind.

"Go, Peyton." I roared, pointing to the exit. "Go home!"

I walked away from her because I couldn't keep my hands or my mind still with all the feelings shaking around in my head. I fucked up; I fucked everything up with her. Somehow, I'd never been more wrong than I was currently, and I didn't understand how I got it so mistaken.

My boots crunched over the dry ground as I walked to my car, hidden in the back parking lot, taking me away from the only thing I'd ever wanted before.

I replayed every conversation we had. Replaying every bit of research I'd done into her world and into her mind before I even made my first move.

How did I get it so fucking wrong?

How did I fuck it up so royally?

I slammed my car door and ripped my mask off, throwing it on the floorboard before punching my steering wheel and screaming into the solitude.

As I gasped for breath and sat back against the seat, forcing myself to calm down, I realized that solitude had finally failed me. For years, it had been the only thing I longed for.

And then Peyton appeared on my desk in a stack of resumes and I thought, for just one second, that maybe I could keep my insanity in check long enough to let someone else in.

Pulling my actual phone from my pocket, I dialed a number I hadn't called in years. One I kept programed only for emergencies like this one.

Maddox answered on the second ring.

"Linc."

The familiar creepiness to his voice triggered a visceral reaction in my body. It felt like broken bones and torn ligaments righted themselves inside of my body, healing the damage and setting right for the first time in so long.

"I need a job."

"No."

"Mad."

"No. Whatever happened, whatever made you call me, it's not worth it."

"It is." I demanded, hating how fucking faithful he was, even after all these years.

"Linc, you walked away because of what it cost you. Who it was making you into. You made me promise never to let you back in."

"You either let me in, or I'm walking into the first dive bar I find and putting skulls on spears in the middle of the street."

He groaned, feeling my sincerity through the phone. Decades worth of history spoke to my level of unhinged. "So I'm talking to Dane then."

"I need to lose myself in something, Maddox. Either help me or read about it in the news tomorrow, I don't fucking care."

"Fucking hell," He sighed. "Fine. I'll send you a file."

I hung the phone up and watched headlights pull back down the road, taking Peyton away from me.

Good. It was better that way, because once I crossed the line I was about to, I'd no longer be worthy of her. I'd no longer be redeemable.

# CHAPTER 20 - PEYTON

THE LINE WALKERS

I sat in a chair on the sun deck of Mr. Bryce's pool and stared at the glittering water, lost in thought. It had been three days since my freak out on Dane in the corn maze.

Three days of absolute radio silence. And I hated every single fucking second of it.

My freak out had taken even me by surprise. I didn't plan out what I wanted to say; I didn't reflect on my feelings and what they meant. I just spoke.

And I regretted them.

He was right, of course. I had asked for every single thing he gave me. Begged for it even.

I just wasn't prepared for how getting what I wanted would make me feel. Dane probably thought I was mad or embarrassed by what we did, thanks to what I said. But that couldn't be further from the truth.

The truth was, I had finally felt free for the first time in my adult life.

For the first time since I took my first AP class in high school.

For the first time since I understood expectations and generational pressure.

The truth was, I was the first person in my entire family line to go to college. The first person to get a scholarship. The first person to have a career instead of a job. I was the first person in generations of Everett's to make something of myself.

And I just had a degree in hospitality and until I randomly took the housekeeping job at Mr. Bryce's estate, I used that degree to help design hotels for wealthy people. Hotels I'd never see the inside of as a guest in my lifetime.

But it was a start. It was the foot in the door that my parents dreamed of for me my entire life.

When I got accepted to college, it paved a way and understanding for my younger siblings to follow. A beacon in the night, guiding them towards something more than my parents ever had.

My parents were the most wonderful people in the world, our home had been so full of love and life that as a child I never understood the pressure they put on me to get *more*. What more could I want besides love? Laughter. Peace.

When I was a teenager, I started to understand that love, laughter, and peace didn't pay the bills.

It didn't give security in an ever-changing world. So I started paying better attention to the lessons my parents were teaching me and my sisters.

And I started working my ass off so I could make them proud.

But it never made me happy, at least not in the way I wanted to be. The pressure was unbearable on my shoulders.

Do the right thing, Peyton. Lead by example, Peyton. Show your sisters what they can have if they work hard too, Peyton.

And then I met Tyson. God, what a fucking idiot I had been seeing his flashy job and over the top ego and thinking it would ease some of that burden if I found a guy who could shoulder some of it.

WRONG!

Tyson was the opposite of that; he was a fucking sandbag tied to my neck that I had to carry around with me on top of everything else. The only reason I kept him around was because it made my parents happy to see me *with* someone. They didn't know the real him; the needy, controlling, manipulating, unfaithful him. But it eased their minds a little, knowing I had *someone* in the world at my side.

Now that I had been away from him on my terms instead of his, though, I knew I could never go back. Because the truth was, Tyson was abusive.

He never hit me. I think we both knew I'd probably hit him back if he tried. But he did manipulate me. He held things over my head and isolated me until one day I woke up and he was really my only option to keep moving forward. To leave him, would mean I'd have to go backwards for a ways.

I'd have to start over.

And I couldn't stomach the look on my parent's faces if I told them I needed help, after all of these years. So I stayed. At least I had, until I found the job posting for Mr. Bryce's housekeeper. In three months, I'd make enough for a fresh start.

And then I'd be truly free.

Yet, for some reason, since meeting Dane, the idea of being free from any other person in the world didn't hold the same appeal it had a few months ago.

God, I fucking missed Dane's presence in my life. Which was fucked up. That was like a prisoner saying they missed the guards, always watching them once they were free.

But it was true.

I probably would have been able to avoid thinking about him more than I had if Mr. Bryce hadn't made an emergency trip somewhere, leaving me alone with idle time on my hands.

For a man who never left his estate, according to Mrs. Straight, he had left twice since I began working for him already.

I snorted to myself at the thought. Maybe I was the problem.

The dinner fiasco had ended terribly the other night, and then when I got up the next morning, after the maze fiasco, there had been an email waiting for me, announcing his unplanned departure.

Return date- to be announced.

So I sat. And I wondered. And I worried.

I grabbed my glass of wine from the side table next to the chair and caught a glance of the phone Dane left me that night.

It just sat there, mocking me because I had yet to go through it. Frankly, I was afraid of what I'd see. Afraid of what I'd feel when he proved me wrong. It didn't help that I had zero way of communicating with him to tell him I fucked up, because the creepy messages he sent me were only accessible after he initiated the conversation. And then they'd go away when he closed them out.

The shrill ringtone of my actual phone scared me as it started going off next to Dane's phone.

"Hello, Olivia." I sighed, answering my sister's fourth attempt to call today alone.

"I'm coming to Hartington." She snapped in response. "I'm rescuing you and dragging you back home by your fucking hair for how much trouble you've put me through the last few weeks."

I snorted humorlessly as I took a sip of my wine. "You're still as dramatic as ever."

"You take a job, on a whim, two hours away from home, picking up your entire life for a *change*, and then you have the audacity to suddenly become unreachable. Every single time any of us tries, you ghost us." She huffed, "And then you end up with an actual ghost on your computer and have the audacity to call me dramatic?"

"Wait," I sat up, fighting away the warm buzz of the wine. "What did you say about my computer?"

She sighed so loud my ear ached in its wake. "You were hacked. And I don't know when the middle east started using ghosts to steal credit card information and identities, but nonetheless you're completely infiltrated."

"Olivia Everett, if you don't start at the beginning, I'm excommunicating you." I warned, already tired of her theatrics.

"Ugh!" She sassed, "I hacked your computer because you wouldn't fucking answer your phone and you left me with no choice. But when I got into it, I hit a fucking wall so thick I couldn't even break through the system I had installed on it in the first place." I could hear clicking in the background as her words swirled around in my head. "At first anyway. It actually took me three days of constant work to get in, and once I did, I was stuck in ghost land. Someone hacked you and used a completely untraceable system to do it. But they can see everything. Literally everything. Even your computer camera was hacked, on multiple occasions."

"I know. Hold on, are you telling me you hacked me?" I replied, attempting to grasp the significance of her revelation. I stood up and started pacing, "You installed a system on my computer?"

"You knew someone hacked you that wasn't me and you said nothing?" She argued over me, "Do you have any idea how sophisticated a ghost program is, Peyton? It's essentially giving someone full remote access to everything in your life. Social medias, bank accounts, login information, camera footage, I mean come on! I thought you knew better than to click on fishy email links!" "Stop," I barked in my best older sister voice. "Stop talking and listen for five seconds. I didn't click on anything stupid, so shove that idea right up your ass. And yes, I knew that someone had hacked into my computer, and I know the person responsible. It's fine. But now I want to go back and talk about you and what you're doing hacking me. How do you even know how to hack people, Olivia? I thought you worked at the bank!"

"You know them?" She screeched, "Peyton, the only people who can run ghost programs this effectively are the kind of people who go bump in the night! They don't exist in the real world because they're too fucking dangerous to mingle with normal people!"

"Oh my god," I groaned, rubbing my forehead in exasperation. "Explain yourself first, and then I'll go."

"Fucking hell," She replied and sighed, "I don't work at the bank."

"Obviously."

"I do IT work for a freelance company. They work in cyber security, so I've learned a lot over the last year. I put a program on your computer when I was first starting out, like a practice run. I never had to use it because you live the most boring life possible and you were always right down the road. But then you went completely AWOL, moving away and shutting us all out, so I tried to take a peek into your life through your cyber footprint. But someone else locked it down tighter than Fort Knox."

I tried to figure out why Dane would not only hack me, but make it impossible for anyone else to do the same in return. Maybe to prevent me from kicking him out of my cyber world? As if I'd have any clue how to do that. Apparently Olivia did, though.

"Say something!" Olivia snapped through the phone.

"I'm very disappointed in you, young lady." I deadpanned, trying to buy my brain more time to come up with an answer in response to her information throw up.

"Now tell me about the hack."

I sighed and sat back down in the chair, "I can't in a way that will make sense to you. But I met someone, and he was the one who hacked my computer or whatever it was he did."

She paused, and I could almost imagine her mouth opening and closing. "You met someone?"

"Yes."

"So that means you've finally kicked Tyson to the curb? That slimy degrading piece of shit deserves far worse than just that, but I'll take it as a start."

I snorted and rested my head in my hand. "Not exactly. But I will."

She sputtered, "You cheated on him? Peyton Rosa Everett, I didn't think you had that kind of bad-ass-ery in you!"

I rolled my eyes, "It's complicated, but I am going to end things for good."

"When?" She rushed on, "Wait, the guy you met, who is he?"

"I--," I paused, physically unable to tell her anything about him. "I'll tell you about him if it lasts. It's complicated." I repeated, "But please just know that I'm fine, just busy with work and you don't have to show up at Hartington to double check."

"Hmm." She hummed, not convinced. "Tell me one thing, P."

"Maybe."

"Does he treat you the way you deserve to be treated?" she asked, all serious now. "Does he worship you?"

The word attacked my memories from when I threw it in Dane's face three days ago. Shame and guilt filled my stomach. "He's treated me better than Ty ever did."

"Well then," She whistled, "He gets my seal of approval. Cyber stalking aside, because that's just weird."

I chuckled lightly, "Believe me, I'm actually kind of into it."

"Ew." She cringed and shuddered, "I'm going to go now."

"Bye, I love you."

"I love you too, P. Don't be such a stranger, okay?"

"Okay." I grinned, relaxing for the first time in days. "I'll call you in a day or two."

"Better." And then she hung up.

I sat there contemplating what I said about Dane to her. I didn't lie; he treated me better than Ty ever did.

Even if it was in his own secretive and creepy way.

I picked up the extra phone he gave me and powered it on, holding it like a precious jewel that was going to give me the answers to every modern-day mystery.

Hopefully, at least the mystery of Dane.

The background was generic, and I opened the contacts list, surprised to find it completely empty. Text messages, the same. There weren't even any apps visibly downloaded. One icon sat on the screen beckoning me.

Gallery.

The very first picture in the camera roll looked like a screenshot of another other, of me. After examining it, I realized it was during a video chat with a friend a few weeks ago. I was in my apartment that I shared with Tyson. I was packing my suitcase to move to Hartington.

I was grinning as I packed a pair of fuzzy sleep pants for when the weather started getting cooler.

I looked happy.

Was I happy in my life back then? No.

Was I smiling so broadly because I was making moves to get out of it? Probably.

Dane had hacked into my phone before I even made the move to a new city, it looked like that was the first time he watched me. He said he saw a picture of me and that led to him searching me out, but how would he have seen one when I still lived two hours away? None of it made sense.

I scrolled to the next photo, and the next, and then the next. They were all screenshots of my screen as I talked on the phone. My brain rapid fired back through those different conversations as I tried to remember what I talked about with friends, but it was all just useless information about what I was looking forward to with my move.

Nothing stood out as important.

The next photo, though, made my chest ache.

I was crying.

I knew instantly, looking at it, that I hadn't been on the phone when the photo was taken. No, Dane had hacked my camera without me using it to take that photo. It was the night before I left when Tyson didn't even bother coming home to say goodbye to me.

I sat on the couch with all of my comfort items around me, all the pieces of things that made me, me, on all sides. Yet I felt alone and alien in my own home. I never felt peace inside of that apartment like I had expected to. It had always felt suffocating.

Because it was Tyson's.

That was the night I told Tyson that I wanted to take a break while I was gone. I didn't want to be with him anymore because he didn't even bother to show up and say goodbye to me. It had been the final straw that broke the camel's back.

Or maybe it was the last drop of water that broke the dam and let all the water free to flow where it wanted to for the first time.

I scrolled past it, wanting to move past that night altogether. The next photo was of me from my computer screen the first night that Dane contacted me. I could see the arousal in my eyes as I stared at myself and my body warmed instantly, remembering that night.

The night that started it all.

I flipped through the next few until one in particular stopped me in my tracks. It was a video, but it wasn't of me.

It was Mr. Bryce, standing in his closet with his hand on the center island in a tight fist. The camera must have been up in the corner, like a security camera. How had I missed it all the times I'd been in there?

I clicked the play button and leaned in close to see it clearly as Mr. Bryce's fists clenched and opened multiple times on the center island before he let out an animalistic groan and reached down into the waistband of his pants and pulled his cock out.

"Oh, my god." I paused the video, feeling like a voyeur and looking out over the pool deck as I tried to calm my breathing down. "The panties." I whispered to myself, recognizing his outfit from that day he caught me in his closet with my panties off, taking a picture of them for Dane.

Dane had said that Lincoln had jacked off after that, and I didn't believe him. Could he have been telling the truth?

I chewed on my bottom lip and looked back down at the screen. Before I could think better of it, I hit play.

"Jesus fuck." I moaned when Lincoln's head tipped back as he stroked his cock. He was big. Like *really* big. I shouldn't watch his private moment in his own home, but I couldn't tear my eyes away from it either as his hand circled the head of his cock, twisting it.

His voice flowed through the speaker of my phone and my body tingled when he moaned my name.

"Peyton." His warm voice echoed in my ears as my name fell off his lips. "Fuck yes, baby." He had his eyes tightly shut as he pleasured himself. My fingers slid over the soft fabric of my shirt absentmindedly as I watched the most erotic thing I'd ever seen before. Before I knew what I was doing, my fingernails traced small circles over my nipples, making them hard as his moans turned me on. He was so vocal as he jacked off, I found myself wondering if he made that much noise when he fucked a girl.

I bet he was a dirty talker when he was deep inside of a woman.

"Take it, Peyton." His voice deepened as he got closer to his orgasm and for a second I half expected him to say Puppet instead of Peyton. There was something so familiar in his moans and growls as he stroked his cock faster and faster.

I licked my lips, pinching my nipple and watching him as he tipped his head back and roared. He grabbed a clean shirt off the island and came onto it with a massive cry and I watched as each shot of come coated the dark fabric, aching to know what it tasted like on my tongue.

And then the video ended, going black and leaving me feeling like the worst kind of creep as I realized how wet I was from watching my boss jack off for me.

And then I remembered why I had the footage at all and felt even worse.

Dane had given it to me to show me just how much he worshipped me, and I got wet for my boss while watching it.

"Jesus." I panted and forced myself to scroll away from the dirty video and instantly found myself back on the screen.

This time, though, I was on my knees, taking Dane's thick cock into my mouth as he praised me. The camera angle was from somewhere on a tree around us. I couldn't see the front of Dane's body, he was angled away just enough, but I was on full display in the black mesh bra and nothing else as I greedily sucked him down.

Dane's gravely voice flowed over my body like a caress through the video, *"I already told you, P, I'm the only one who will ever give you everything you need."*

God, he had been so right.

I pushed my fingers down the front of my loose shorts and played with my clit as I watched me suck his cock. Fuck, I missed him.

"Dane." I groaned when the video ended and I flipped to the next one. It was another video I'd never seen it before. But I knew instantly what it was.

It was that same night, as he snuck into my place, returning my dropped items to me. He videoed himself, creeping through my place, setting my shoes and purse down by the mirror after silently walking into my bedroom. I couldn't see him, of course, just the tops of his shoes as he crossed the room to my bed. I laid in the center of it on my back with my arms thrown over my head.

I looked like a mess, with my tank top barely covering my boobs and my hair in a cluster.

He stood over me, watching me after putting my phone on my charging stand and then leaning over my body. His fingers danced lightly over the side of my face as he pushed my hair back off of it.

And then he leaned down and pressed a gentle kiss to my temple as I slept. I leaned forward, trying desperately to see any part of his face, but all I got was his lips as they briefly touched my face. That was it.

"Fuck," I groaned, rubbing my clit faster as he watched me. Why was it so erotic to me knowing he had broken in and watched me sleep?

That was creepy, yet there I was, wet and aching for him as I watched.

"Dane!" I hissed, begging him to hear me somehow. I never knew when he was watching me through my phone, but he always answered me when I called.

Until now.

Only silence found me in response.

I flipped through the camera roll, finding more photos and videos of myself. Most were of just me, videos of the morning after as I came for him with my toy, and then dressing for my afternoon with Lincoln.

God, even as I dressed sexily for another man, he still wanted me. There was something so much more powerful between us than just play, like I had accused.

The last video was of that night, in the maze. I watched as he fucked me on my back, legs spread and tits out, begging for his cock.

Never in my life had I ever felt more sensual than I did watching myself with him. He made me feel bold and wanted. Lust, like no other, covered my body as he flipped us around and put the phone against the bench so I could actually watch us both on the screen.

Fuck, he was so sexy. His body, covered in intricate tattoos and designs, was as if cut from stone as he thrust into me from behind.

And that mask.

Jesus, Mary, and Joseph. The Ghostface mask was so hot.

His abs rolled as he rocked his cock into me, and the look of pure pleasure on my face made me nearly unrecognizable.

He did that.

He made me feel that good. And then he made me choose who he was going to send the video to.

And ruined it all.

I was a people pleaser and having that kind of pressure on my shoulders made me both hot sexually but anxious and when the high of the orgasm faded; I imagined Tyson getting the video and what he'd do with it.

He'd show anyone who would watch it.

He'd tell everyone what a whore I was.

He'd tell my parents what I was really up to here, and they'd be so ashamed of me.

It wasn't like it'd be the first time he used videos against me.

And of course, instead of telling Dane that, I panicked and lashed out at him. It wasn't his fault, exactly, but he had to have known that you couldn't do things like that in the real world and get away unscathed.

Sure, he had a mask on and could hide his identity from everyone in the fallout, but I wouldn't have had that same freedom.

I would have burned for it.

Ty would have ruined my life back home for it. I never would have been able to return to life as it was, and maybe that was Dane's plan all along.

I closed the gallery and opened the camera. With no other means to contact Dane, I was desperate to talk to him. So I hit the record button and told him everything I needed to say, not even knowing if he'd ever see it.

I needed to at least say it all to get it off my chest, so I no longer felt weighed down by it.

And then I needed to ride the jet in the hot tub because I was hornier than ever and alone to take care of the problem myself.

THE LINE WALKERS

I dreamed of him.

Dane.

My monster had a name, and a voice that I recognized as he chased me through the woods. He had for the last few nights, which made the divide between me and Dane even bigger in real life.

But when I heard his voice in my ear, purring with that deep gravel that I craved when he pushed deep inside of my body, I leaned into him, grasping at him to keep him forever.

"Did you miss me, Puppet?" He growled, and I moaned.

"Dane." I called out, digging my nails into the back of his neck as he thrust deep from behind. He always fucked me from behind, but tonight he held me to his chest while he did it. My voice sounded unfamiliar than it usually did in my dream, like it was groggy in sleep. I cleared my throat and Dane sighed in my ear as his thrusts stilled.

"Remember who you belong to, Puppet." He growled and then bit my neck hard enough to make me scream out and flail in his arms.

But when I swung my arms out, they hit the softness instead of his bulky body or the damp earth around us.

I ripped my eyes open and stared up at the ceiling in my bedroom, hissing in frustration as my dream time with Dane was cut short. If I couldn't see him in real life, I should at least be afforded a few hours in dream land to ride his cock.

It was the very least the universe could do.

That was when I heard it.

The sound of someone walking through my living room.

I froze in place as my heart rate skyrocketed into my chest as I fought through the fight-or-flight urges burning my limbs.

A shadow crossed the doorjamb of my bedroom entrance and I realized instantly that it wasn't Dane.

He was too tall, if that was possible. His head nearly brushed the top of the doorway as he walked through it.

And I fucking screamed bloody murder.

# CHAPTER 21 - LINCOLN

## THE LINE WALKERS

I stepped out of the shower, running the towel over my head to dry my hair as I sighed, exhausted.

I'd been up for almost three days straight, and the shower I just took was the first time I stopped moving that whole time. The fatigue in my bones was so intense that I almost fell asleep standing up.

My brain finally stopped spinning too, it was so tired, I could no longer obsess over her.

*Peyton.*

I left Hartington three nights ago on a mission to wash her memory from my skin and replace it with blood. I never craved bloodshed anymore, I was a different person than who I used to be when I ran wild with Tamen.

But her rejection burned in my gut in a way that would have eaten me alive if I didn't find another outlet for it. So I reached out to an old contact, who has a reputation for being the most unhinged man in the game.

Maddox 'Whisper' Renner was the worst kind of psycho out there. He had so many screws loose he had no conscious or moral compass anymore. Which served him well in his life, hunting down the worst of the worst and taking them out. He was a mercenary essentially, only taking jobs that promised to be hard for him for the fun of it.

Which meant the jobs he gave me over the last seventy-two hours should have been damn near impossible for me, thanks to being out of the game for so long.

But the level of unrest I'd become in the wake of Peyton's rejection left me just crazy enough to get them done.

But I was done. I was empty and fulfilled at the same time.

I was calm.

With her back within reach, just a few hundred yards away from me even at that very moment, I didn't know how long it would last. But I couldn't stay away from her anymore.

I had made sure she made it back safe after our time together at the maze, and then I went black. I couldn't look in on her without losing my resolve to stay away.

*"Maybe I don't know what I want then. Maybe I got it wrong."*

Her sweet voice echoed through my brain nonstop since I walked away from her, and it wreaked havoc. She said I wasn't what she wanted after all. Which meant she didn't want me, as me.

If I was a normal man who gave her niceties and flowers instead of hand-necklaces and dirt stains on her knees, she'd want me. But that wasn't *me*.

That was why I came to her as Dane first, instead of Lincoln. If I had pursued her as Lincoln, she never would have understood the depth of my tendencies and tastes, she'd see the polished businessman and fall without understanding the risks associated with it.

Never mind her own emotional hang-ups, thanks to her family always demanding perfection from her so she could be the pride and joy of their storytelling. Regardless of her own happiness, they expected her to be perfect.

I studied her parents extensively when I started recon on her before I hired her. To be honest, I didn't think they were bad people. They were simply obsessed with giving their kids more than they had, even going as far as working their own fingers to the bone and breaking their backs to give their kids every chance as success.

It took no time at all to realize that wasn't what Peyton wanted, though, and I couldn't understand how they never saw it. Or maybe they did, but they turned a blind eye in the name of greater good for everyone, I don't know.

Peyton loved them more than her own happiness, that much was clear, so she did as they expected, crafting the perfect life her parents could brag about to their friends. Silently dying a little more inside each day.

That was why I allowed myself to infiltrate her life. Between that and her closet desire for the dark and depraved, it felt right to break her out of the mold of perfection for a little wrong and dirty.

But I was wrong.

I had gotten it all so fucking wrong.

I slid a pair of sweats on in my closet, looking away from any surface she may have touched while I was gone and then pulled a sweater on. Avoidance was only serving for so long, and I had responsibilities to see to that I couldn't ignore any longer.

Even if all I wanted to do was crawl into bed and sleep for the next week straight.

I walked down the hall to my office, fighting the urge to look out the gigantic windows across the grand living room below that looked directly at her guest house because I didn't know what I'd do if I actually saw her. Thankfully, she was probably asleep, given that it was after three in the morning.

As I neared the locked door to my office, an alarm from inside piqued my ears and I froze, trying to get my sleep deprived brain to place that particular tone as I pushed my finger to the biometric scanner on the knob.

And then it clicked.

Perimeter Breech Alarm.

I ripped the door open and looked at the chaos of alarms going off on my screens as I tried to make sense of what they all were.

> *Perimeter Breech Alarm- South Quadrant- four minutes ago.*

"Fuck." I scanned to the next one, trying to assess who was fucking stupid enough to cross my property line. Four minutes was a long time, they could already be—.

> *Guest House Alarm- Forced Entry- Main Entrance- one minute ago.*

"No!" I roared, grabbing two firearms and tearing out of my office at a dead sprint for Peyton. "Fuck!"

As I jumped down the five steps to the concrete patio, a shrill scream pierced the air and my heart seized completely in my chest as I fought through the fear and fatigue in my brain and focused my thoughts into that deadly calm space I found before a kill.

Because I was going to kill whoever dared to touch my girl.

The locked side door off the pool deck was no match for my kick, as I sent it splintering out of the jamb. Barefoot, I entered the house, hardly noticing the pain. Another scream ripped through the air, followed by a crash of something glass from her bedroom.

"Peyton!" I roared, and lifted my guns as a dark figure came out of her room, backing up with his arms over his face as another large object flew through the air and hit him in the head.

"Fucking hell, woman!" The intruder cursed exactly one millisecond before I pulled the trigger on both guns aimed directly at his head.

"Tamen?" I paused as Peyton's voice carried through the dark house.

"Get the fuck out of my house!"

"You belong in an insane asylum!" Tamen yelled back, turning around and stopping short when he saw both guns aimed at him. "Oh, he *is* home."

"Lincoln?" Peyton's shaken voice floated seconds before her head popped out of the doorway that Tamen had thankfully moved away from. "Oh, my god." She dropped her arms, lowering the footrest she clutched as a weapon as her wild eyes locked onto mine.

I could hardly fucking breathe seeing those green irises again after three days away. "Are you hurt?" I asked her, finally lowering my guns from my brother's face. She quickly shook her head and wrapped her arms around her indecent body. Because, of course, she wore only a light blue nightgown that hugged every single inch of her lush curves to perfection. I looked away from her and glared at my stupid idiot brother, directing him to the door with one pistol still clutched in my hand. "Get the fuck out!"

He raised his brows at me and smirked, "Who am I speaking with right now?" He squinted his eyes, "Lincoln or—"

"GET OUT!" I roared, taking a step at him, herding him toward the door so I was between him and Peyton.

"Definitely not Lincoln." He mused and glanced behind me to where I felt Peyton still cowering at the entrance to her bedroom. "Interesting."

I fired a shot, aiming directly over his right ear and hitting the wall behind him as he flinched slightly with an amused look on his face. Peyton's scream of fear cut through the gunpowder before my vision even cleared. "I said get out." I repeated in a lethal voice I didn't even recognize.

He held his hands up in surrender, after quickly dabbing at the blood dripping down from the graze I gave him on the top of his ear. "I'll be in your office." He looked over my shoulder once more to where Peyton was, "My apologies, Ms. Everett."

His use of her name only made me want to pull the trigger all over again, this time aiming at his heart. He was my only blood relative left on Earth, but I would put him six feet into it if he even dared to come near Peyton.

When he was out of the house completely, I lowered my gun and forced myself to turn around to look into the eyes that had haunted me since I left her in the maze. "Peyton."

"You shot him?" Her eyes were as wide as saucers and she still cowered behind the door frame into her bedroom.

"I should have done far worse for him invading your space, like he did." I slid the guns into my waistband, careful not to let her see my ink under my shirt, and scrubbed my hand over my face.

"Who is he?" She carefully stepped around the broken remnants of the lamps she used as projectiles and came out into the living room, flicking a switch and bathing the room in warm light.

I glossed over her question, fighting every urge to pull her against my body. *She doesn't want you, Linc.* "Are you okay?"

"I think so." She rubbed her hands over her arms. "He didn't touch me. He just scared me." Her shoulders shook as the weight of it all came crashing down. "I woke up to him walking into my bedroom and I—" She stared off at the wall, remembering her fear, "I guess I went into fight-or-flight mode."

"You went into fight mode, Peyton." I nodded to the broken shards of glass and porcelain on the floor of her bedroom. "Rightfully so."

"Sorry." She sank in on herself slightly. "I'll pay for the broken stuff."

"Stop it." I shook my head and took a step toward her, with my hand fisted to keep from actually pulling her into my arms like I wanted to. She didn't know me as Lincoln, only as Dane, and she didn't want Dane. And I couldn't separate the two anymore, so I was hopeless. "Stay right here."

She sank down on the couch and watched me as I went into her bedroom. "What are you doing?"

I took her duffle bag from underneath of her bed, not even pretending not to know where it was, and started putting some clothes into it for the next day or two. "You will stay in the main house until I can repair the door."

I caught her glance over at the side door as I moved to her bathroom, grabbing her toiletries and putting them into the bag too. "Oh, dear." She stared at the wrecked splinters of her door and then stared up at me as I came back out to the living room. "You did that?" She looked down my body, "To get to me?"

I put her bag over my shoulder and tried to convince myself to stay silent, but I couldn't. "I'd do far, *far* worse to get to you, Peyton." While helping her up, I abandoned my attempts to avoid touching her and reveled in the way the bare skin of her arm felt against my palm. I held out her bathrobe from the back of her door and pushed it onto her arms. The sooner her hard nipples were covered up, the sooner I'd be able to think straight. "Come on, let's get out of here."

She let me put my hand on the small of her back and lead her across the pool deck into my home in a trance. When we got to the bottom of the staircase, her steps faltered, "You don't have any guest beds." She chuckled lightly, looking up at me as I herded her up the steps. "I know, because I clean all the empty rooms."

"That's so I don't get any visitors."

She mulled that over for a moment, no doubt taking longer than normal because of the events that happened and the ungodly hour.

When we got to my bedroom door, though, she snapped out of the haze. "Wait." She turned and faced me in the now open doorway. "What are you doing?"

"Getting you settled in my room so you can get some rest." I walked forward, forcing her to go into my bedroom, and shut the door behind us. Her eyes were wide and her lips parted as she licked them, looking up at me.

"Your room?"

I grinned for the first time in days, setting her duffle bag down on the footstool at the end of the bed, and then pulled the blankets back. Twenty minutes ago, I couldn't wait to slide under those blankets and sleep for the next few days. Yet there I was, welcoming her into my bed while simultaneously trying to convince myself not to join her.

*She doesn't want you.*

"As you stated, I have no spare beds in the entire house." I walked back over to her and she held her ground, staring up at me. She probably hated Lincoln as much as she hated Dane after how I treated her at dinner the other night. Or better yet, right after dinner. "Get into the bed, Peyton."

"What about you?" Her eyes roved over my face as she stared up, unmoving. "Where will you sleep?"

"I won't cross boundaries with you, if that's what you're worried about." I stepped back, indignation burning from her recent rejection aligned with the new one.

Her hand shot out and grabbed mine before I could back away completely. "I didn't mean that." She licked her lips again, and I fought the urge to growl and take a bite of them. "I mean, you look dead on your feet. You obviously need to sleep too."

I took a step forward. "Are you worried about me, Peyton?" I tilted my head the way Dane always did, tempting fate to burn my hopes and dreams at my feet just so I could get out of the perpetual limbo I got myself into.

Her green eyes parted wide and her breath hitched, before she blinked and let go of my hand. She opened her mouth to say something, but I stopped her.

"Go to bed," I moved around her tempting body, gripping my doorknob with enough strength to crush it in my palm. "I'll sleep on the couch in my office."

I didn't wait for her to agree or not, closing the door behind me and heading into a conversation I didn't want to have.

When I found Tamen behind my desk with his feet up, he was staring at the screens and observing Peyton standing in my bedroom, who was lost in thought and not moving.

I clicked the kill switch, effectively locking down every screen so he couldn't see anything else. "You've got five seconds to explain yourself before I leave bits and pieces of you on the floor."

He grinned in his usual asshole way and dropped his feet when I shoved them off my desk and dumped his ass backward out of my chair. I knew he could have deflected my move, always one to be fast as a cat, but he fell to the ground with a thud. Laughing, he got up and exaggeratedly brushed off his clothes before choosing to sit on the couch across the room instead of going back for my chair.

"Hello, dear brother. I missed you too." His thick English accent grated my nerves like it usually did, when I first spoke with him after a long time apart. It reminded me of everything he got that I didn't.

It reminded me of the life he lived that should have been mine.

"T."

"Fine." He cocked his head to the side in the familiar Bryce family mannerism we didn't discuss and rested his elbows on his knees. "I heard on the wire that you went back underground."

I scoffed, righting my chair and sitting in it, depositing both guns back in their holsters under my desk. "If I was back underground, I wouldn't be here right now."

"Thirty-seven." He raised one brow at me, mocking me like I didn't know the final number from the last three days. "You eliminated thirty-seven contacts in one run. What else would you call it? The chatter is going wild about the Ghost's return to the game, out from behind his computer screens for the first time in years."

"I'm not in the game, Tamen." Leaning back against the chair. "I simply distracted myself in it for a moment."

"Because of her?" He challenged, "Peyton Everett?"

"Careful," I leveled a death glare at him, "That's your only warning."

He snorted and pointed at his red angry ear, "This wasn't a warning? Has your shot gotten that bad in retirement?"

"What are you doing here, Tamen?" I snapped, tiring of his antics.

My brother held my stare and relaxed, "No one has heard from you in too long, Linc. And then I hear that you not only hired someone new, even temporarily, but also went back into the darkness that nearly fucking killed the both of us last time." He sighed, "I'm checking in on you."

"Welfare check complete." I turned away from him to face my computer screens, already itching to see Peyton on my screens without him lurking. "Only your welfare was in jeopardy."

He stood up with a groan and shook his head, "She doesn't know, does she?" I didn't look at him, hoping he'd leave as I stared blankly at the black screens, but he didn't drop it. "That you're the masked man she's been fucking?"

I slowly turned my head to face him, leveling him with a glare only my enemies saw right before I ended the lives of their dearest loved ones. I was too irrational to kill my enemies for their crimes; it hurt them more to make them watch the ones they loved most suffer first. "If you so much as utter one word to her, I'll eradicate your entire branch of our bloodline."

He raised his brow at me and nodded solemnly on his way to the door. "That's something you've wanted to do for decades now, Linc. Next time threaten me with something new, or I'll start to wonder if you've gone soft on me."

I didn't reply as he left my office, but I pulled my security system back up and watched him go to the home theater I never used and make himself a bed in one of the recliners. I should have kicked him out instead of locking the door remotely, caging him in so he couldn't do something stupid or harmful to Peyton as I got some desperately needed sleep.

When Tamen heard the lock click on the door, he smirked to himself and flipped off the sky.

He knew I was watching. I was always fucking watching.

# CHAPTER 22 - PEYTON

## THE LINE WALKERS

I woke up, groggy and disoriented, as I tried to remember what happened, and then I sat up ramrod straight, looking around.

Lincoln.

I was in his room, in his bed. After he obliterated my door to save me from an intruder in the middle of the night. And then shot him!

I blinked away the fitful sleep I managed to get, groaning when I saw it was half-past eight already, making me officially late for work.

Did I have to work after watching my boss blow off a stranger's ear in my living room four hours prior? That seemed insensitive.

I still didn't know who the devastatingly handsome Englishman was that broke in, stumbling his way through my messy living room and groaning as he reached my bedroom like he couldn't wait to—sleep?

I shook my head, none of it made sense, of course, because Lincoln had been zero help in answering any of my questions as he shoved me into his room, and left.

*"Get into the bed, Peyton."* His thick honey voice saying my name would play on repeat in my fantasies for years to come. And that made me sick to my stomach because I felt guilty for lusting at my mysterious and infuriating boss, even as I longed and ached to feel my monster's body on mine again.

I looked over at my phone where I left it after finally crawling into Lincoln's bed, hoping to see a message from Dane on the screen waiting for me. But it was black.

"Are you there?" I whispered, just like I had every morning, praying he'd respond someday.

But still more silence. I was really starting to think I would never hear from him again. What if I fucked it all up when he pushed me out of my comfort zone and freaked out? Wasn't him pushing me out of my comfort zone the whole point of fucking a stranger in the woods like a good little slut? I just didn't know I'd have a minor freak out until I did. And now I didn't know how to make it all better.

Last night when the man broke into my temporary residence, I imagined Dane following him in and saving me. He was always watching beforehand, but he wasn't watching last night.

No, Lincoln was the one who saved me last night, not Dane.

Lincoln was the one who broke down a solid ass door with his bare foot and shot the intruder, even though I was pretty sure they were related. There was something about the man, Tamen, as Lincoln called him, that was like my boss.

They looked nothing alike, unless you count their dark handsome features, but that was it. Their eyes were different, their body structures, even their continental residences. But something was familiar between them.

I rolled over, allowing myself one last selfish inhale of Lincoln's pillows, taking in that expensive masculine scent that embodied him, and then forced myself to get out of his bed. I'd never allow myself back into it, so there was no point in allowing my body to get comfortable in it. After dressing in a casual outfit, considering he didn't pack me anything work related, I took my bag and vacated his room.

My bare feet didn't make a sound as I looked up and down the empty hallway, trying to figure out what exactly I was supposed to do. Would it be wise for me to head back to my place and start cleaning up the mess? Should I go about my normal work day even if I was late and under dressed? Should I find Lincoln and ask him exactly what he expected from me.

Never mind, I was a grown ass woman who fought off an attacker in the middle of the night, I could go home if I wanted. I slipped from the still quiet house and down the patio steps to my place. The door from the patio sat askew in the frame and I grimaced as I remembered the ear-splitting noise it made as it shattered under Lincoln's foot.

"Sorry about that, by the way." A voice called out from behind me and I jumped and shrieked as I swung on the man.

It was *the* man from last night. The intruder.

I backed up as he sauntered across the pool deck toward me. Why did he have to look so yummy?

He wore just a pair of black jeans and no shirt or shoes. And he didn't fucking need them either, for they simply covered the beauty of his body. He was muscular with a perfectly defined six pack and a drool worthy adonis belt right above the low riding jeans. And ink.

A new unlocked kink for me, thanks to Dane apparently.

I stared at him, holding my bag in a death grip as he got closer. He didn't seem intimidating, as he strolled, with one hand in his pants pocket and the other wrapped around a pink coffee mug with a picture of Mrs. Straight and her kids on it.

"The door," He nodded behind me and stopped a few feet away. I had been right when he walked through the dark last night, he had to be six and a half feet tall. "I apologize for my brother, at least. Since he's the one who kicked it down."

"Broth—brother?" I stammered like an idiot as I tried to imagine tight laced Lincoln Bryce and the tattooed dark and dangerous man in front of me having the same genetics. I mean, I guess when I allowed myself to remember that Lincoln Bryce pulled not one but two guns and even shot one of them at the man in front of me last night, the dark similarities were noticeable.

The man grinned and took a sip of his coffee. "I tend to bring the worst out in Linc. I always have." His hair was the same dark chocolate color as Lincoln's, but their eyes were opposite. My infuriatingly sexy boss had eyes so dark you couldn't even differentiate the pupils most times, but his brother had bright blue ones that somehow made his features seem even darker in contrast.

I glanced at the guest house behind me and then back to the man, "Is that why you came in last night?"

He nodded, "I usually stay in there when I visit. I didn't know he'd have you all the way out here, though I should have guessed." He grinned again like there was something deeper meant to his words, and then he closed the gap between us and held out his hand. "I'm Tamen Bryce."

"Peyton Everett." I shook his hand, ignoring the way the large thing completely dwarfed mine.

"Has my brother been a terrible bear to deal with in Mrs. Straight's absence?" He tilted his head to the side and for half a second, I imagined him as Dane. The mannerism seemed so natural to him, and goosebumps broke out over my skin. If it wasn't for the simple fact that his accent was so thick, I would have nearly believed that he was my anonymous stalker turned lover.

"He's manageable." I said, after a long pause. "If you don't mind, though, I need to get started cleaning this mess." I motioned toward the mess of my living space and took a step back.

"Say no more." He bowed gracefully, it was odd how natural it looked compared to the creepy head tilt he gave me a moment ago. How did he master both? "I'll see you around."

"You're staying?" I asked, dumfounded. Mrs. Straight said no one ever visited, let alone anything about a long-lost brother staying for a while.

He shrugged with an amused glint in his eye, "Someone has to keep Lincoln on the straight and narrow." He turned away and casually tossed over his shoulder, "He's been known to get himself into trouble when he's been bored in the past."

I didn't reply as I watched him walk back across the pool whistling a tune on a cherry sunny morning like he didn't have a worry in the world. "Fucking wild twilight zone." I whispered, and then walked around the front of the house to use the undamaged front door.

As I worked, cleaning up the remaining evidence of the entire ordeal, my mind wandered to Dane and how I was going to get him to talk to me again. I mulled over different tactics than just yelling at my phone, hoping he was watching me, including seeing if my secretive sister Olivia could hack him back. But that would open me up to so many questions I wasn't ready to answer, so I had to figure out another way.

I was adjusting a picture on the wall that had been knocked askew at some point when I noticed a hole in the wall.

The bullet hole. From the gun Lincoln shot, that made my ears ache with the vibrations.

With a gentle touch, I pressed my finger against the rough, exposed drywall mess, a clever idea coming to mind to grab Dane's attention.

A sinister smile pulled my lips up as I imagined how terrible the entire thing could blow up in my face if I wasn't careful, but I was just desperate enough to try, anyway.

First, I needed to go back into town. Next to the post office where Dane sent me my dirty gifts, I noticed a store front with metal bars and cages on the inside of the windows.

I was going to lure Dane back after a stop into Larry's Sporting Goods and Gun Shop.

THE LINE WALKERS

"You can do this." I whispered to myself, trying to make myself feel as brave as I had been earlier when I hatched my *Get Dane Back* plan.

My hands shook as I grabbed the handle and opened the door. I couldn't back down though, I was too far in. Hell, I'd even sent Olivia a location pin and told her if I didn't check back in within three hours to send the authorities. I wouldn't be surprised if she showed up in place of the police long before the three-hour window, though, given how she already threatened to drag me back home after finding the hacker bug Dane left on my computer.

So I had to keep going. One foot in front of the other, my favorite red bottom heels that Dane bought me clicked against the sticky brick floor as I walked deeper into the biker bar he sent me to the first night he chased me.

My dress was so indecent; I belonged in a centerfold instead of surrounded by dirty, disgusting men who were just stupid enough to take what wasn't theirs. I really hoped I hadn't overestimated whatever invisible barrier held them back from actually touching me last time.

If I did, then the new toy I bought earlier at the sporting goods store would get used without a second thought. But I didn't think I'd need it.

I was banking on Dane breaking his silence.

Didn't mean my asshole wasn't puckered tight with fear as the whole place fell silent as I walked across the place to the bar. I kept my head high, ignoring the whistles and leers as I slid onto the same barstool I sat on the night I met Dane.

The same female bartender from that night came over right away and leaned over the polished surface. "Are you nuts?" She hissed, leaning over the top. "You need to go."

"I need a strawberry margarita, please." I said back, trying to be polite, because she wasn't wrong. Placing my phone on the top of the bar, I hoped Dane was getting an eyeful of my surroundings.

"He's not here." The bartender widened her eyes.

"Who?"

"The Ghost." She whispered, looking at me like I was dumb when she was talking in tongues. "The only reason you made it out last time was because he orchestrated the entire thing, sitting right there to make sure no one stepped out of bounds." She nodded to the corner of the bar and I looked over my shoulder at a dark booth along the edge.

He would have had a perfectly clear view of every inch of the place from there.

One time, I'd asked out loud if he was watching me as I stared at my phone. He had texted back almost instantly, *Always Puppet.*

Which was obviously a lie. Because I had told him I changed my mind. God, what I wouldn't do to take those words back in the heat of the moment.

"They're rough tonight." She tried once more, setting down a drink in front of me. A coke. "Rougher than normal, and that's saying something. So drink your drink if you must and then get the fuck out of here before something happens that you won't survive." She looked down at my dress and shook her head.

I nodded to her, grimacing at the chiding. She wasn't wrong. I wasn't either, though. I had no other way to get Dane's attention besides throwing myself into the literal lion's den and hoping he showed up before they tore me to shreds.

"Well, well, well." A man took the seat next to me, sitting with his back against the bar and leaning toward me as the smell of sweat and cigarette smoke assaulted me. "Look at this pretty kitty all alone in the dog pound."

I glanced up at him briefly and then turned my attention back to my drink, no longer interested in it.

"Pretty little kitty didn't bring her escort with her tonight." Another man sat on the other side of me. They were the two that sat down beside me that first night too. The first man had a patch on his leather vest that said President under his name, Blade. I'd watched enough Sons of Anarchy to know he was the leader of the group.

I also knew if anyone in the place was going to call the shots, it'd be him.

"How do you know?" I looked over at the other guy, noting the VP patch on his vest. "Do you always see him when he's around?"

I didn't have a fucking clue what I was saying, but I had to think on my toes to keep myself safe long enough to give Dane a chance to figure out what I was up to. If I ran with my tail between my legs in the first two minutes, I may not make it out alive.

I kept my face forward, but noted the way the VP looked around me to Blade, like what I said wasn't farfetched.

"You do call him the Ghost, don't you?" I tried to be as non-chalant as possible, using the tidbit of knowledge the bartender had given me.

"I don't call him anything." Blade gruffed, leaning his elbow on the bar so his hand brushed against my bare arm. He was an ugly mother-fucker, and he smelled even worse, and as he leaned over to intimidate me even more, I nearly threw up in his lap from the disgusting color of his teeth. "I will call *you* something though," He rubbed his knuckles up my upper arm. "Kitty."

"That'd be silly." I scoffed and turned to him. "Because I fight like a fucking bear." I slid my hand into my purse on my lap, gripping my new toy tight in my palm in case I needed it. I knew for a fact I wouldn't get out of the crowded bar with just it defending me, but I was sure it'd shock the fuck out of whoever tried to stop me first and maybe even second, no pun intended.

Blade grinned and opened his mouth to say something when his phone rang loudly in his pocket. At the very same time, my screen lit up on my phone laid on the bar.

My heart raced when I recognized the same inconspicuous text bubble front and center.

**Get the fuck out of there. NOW!**

Dane!

My fingers shook as I picked up my phone, acutely aware of Blade growling as he brought his own phone to his ear. I wasn't a rocket scientist, but I knew it was Dane.

I pulled a five-dollar bill from my purse and laid it on the bar as Blade simply listened to whatever Dane was saying on his end and turned to stand up. Before my heels could touch the floor, though, the VP wrapped his meaty hand around my upper arm and stopped me. He squeezed my arm so tight a soft whimper escaped through my clenched teeth before I could stop it.

"Not so fast, Kitty." He sneered, "No fucking way are you walking out that door twice without letting me take a taste."

I had my phone in one hand, and the other wrapped tightly around my only way out of the place, ready to use whatever means necessary to escape his tight clutches.

"Let her go." Blade sneered, pocketing his phone again and standing up over the top of me.

"What?" His VP snapped, and I tried pulling my arm free, but he stood up, yanking me off my stool with him as he disobeyed his boss. "No fucking way, Blade. He can't call the shots. This wasn't scheduled!"

"I said let her go." Blade thundered, and the entire bar fell silent for a second time since I walked in. "Unless you want death himself on your fucking doorstep."

"He ain't fucking shit!" The man yanked me again, putting more distance between us and my exit. I tried pulling away again, and he somehow tightened his hand even more on my arm, making me wonder if I'd hear a crack if I even took a deep breath.

My phone buzzed again, and I glanced at it.

*Back exit. Just like the other night. Run and don't fucking stop until you're home.*

I didn't think I just acted. I shoved the pointed heel of my stiletto into the man's calf and shivered when I felt it pierce skin and then cut its way down through the muscle. His painful howl echoed in my ears as I tore away from him, passing by stunned on lookers and ran for the back exit.

As my feet twisted in the gravel, I instinctively kicked off my shoes and abandoned them. Leaving one shoe now stained in blood, I ran barefoot through the darkness towards the woods I knew were located diagonally across from Lincoln's estate.

I wasn't sure what exactly would stop the bikers from following me, but I sure fucking hoped something would.

"You fucking cunt!" The VP roared from the back door to the bar, "Don't ever come back here again!"

I didn't stop, I just ran for dear life. Thankfully, I'd used a ride share to get there, or I would have abandoned my car for good, there was no way I was going back again.

Suddenly, my foot snagged on a low branch, causing me to lose my footing and tumble onto the forest floor, landing on my hands and knees.

My phone and purse scattered into the bushes around me and I quickly lost track of them in the darkness. "Fuck." I hissed and then froze when a shadow moved beyond the trees behind me and a figure stalked toward me. "Fuck."

# CHAPTER 23 -
# LINCOLN

"So," Tamen took a long drink off his whiskey. "I'm offended you went to Maddox instead of me when you needed an outlet."

I rolled my eyes as I worked at my computer, trying to pretend my brother hadn't barged into my office uninvited, like there wasn't a state-of-the-art biometric scanner on the door to stop him. Which apparently it hadn't.

"Seriously, Linc. Talk to me."

I had avoided him most of the day, burying myself in work I'd ignored while I worked out my frustrations on unsuspecting bodies of flesh and bone. At least they had been whole before I got ahold of them. But now it was getting late, and he had me cornered. I was so determined to avoid Peyton that I refused to leave the safety of my office, fearing I might run into her around the main house.

So I was stuck.

"How'd you get in here?"

He scoffed like it was obvious and rolled his eyes when I glared at him, unimpressed. "I have a copy of your fingerprints."

I sighed, changing the scanner on the door to a two-step feature including a passcode.

"Rude." He deadpanned when he watched me change the process.

"For one of highborn English descent, you're the rude one." I threw back. "Peyton could have been hurt last night."

He raised one brow, clearly happy that I was willing to speak of her, and I groaned inwardly. "Well, since you've mentioned her, I've got a list full of questions." He leaned forward with his elbows on his knees, "Did you know what she looked like before she got the job or after?"

"We're not discussing her looks."

"Oh, so you're going to pretend she isn't fucking sexy as sin?" He questioned, but I kept my face stoic, aimed at my screens. "Or better yet, you don't care if I take her for a spin?"

The key on my keyboard creaked under the weight of my fingers as I fought to remain impassive. "If you go near her again, I'll murder you. I already told you that."

"Hmm." He hummed and sat back. "She couldn't get enough of my ink this morning. Has she seen all of yours?"

"Tamen." I warned, but my brother had no self-preservation and only desired to tempt my life expectancy by threatening his. A true fight between us would leave an impressive mess of bullet and knife holes in its wake.

"Does she know about Dane?" He cocked his head, "Or better yet, has she met Dane?"

"Leave it alone."

"She has, hasn't she?" He hummed and ran his fingers over his bottom lip in contemplation. "I didn't think she had it in her, to be honest. To tempt the biggest monster out there and walk away unscathed."

"She didn't." I paused, staring aimlessly at my computer screen as her words from the maze played again through my head.

"Did she get hurt?" He asked calmly, knowing my past.

"No." I shook my head, "But she regretted it."

"Because of her boyfriend?"

I glared at him and rolled my eyes, going back to what I was doing.

"What?" He scoffed, "I may not be as good as you on a computer, but I can search a name on Facebook and do some sleuthing."

"I read the situation wrong. She said she wanted one thing and then back peddled when I gave her everything she asked for."

"Ah." He nodded, "And let me guess, you walked away without even a backward glance." I gritted my teeth, "Hence the break from darkness being broken and you eliminating names off of lists even I didn't know existed. Got it. It makes sense now."

"Whatever."

He snorted and rubbed his hands together. "I can't remember the last time you've tried and failed to act so unbothered by something before, Linc. Not a single time."

"Like I said, it doesn't matter, she regretted it."

"And you'll never allow yourself to be what someone regrets again." He stated quietly. "Like our father did."

I clenched my teeth to keep from blowing his brains all over the wall behind him.

But he wasn't done with me yet, "Tell me something, Linc. When are you going to stop letting the actions of a small man dictate your actions as a much fucking bigger one?"

I once again chose not to respond.

"Interesting." He rose to his feet and put his hands in his pockets as he faced me. "Don't let him be the reason she lets someone else give her what she wanted. I'm guessing if she asked you for it, then she still wants it, even if she doesn't recognize the part of her that does."

He wasn't wrong. I knew that. But I didn't know how to give her another chance to deny me. Rejection stung so fucking deep into my soul, fracturing it beyond recognition each and every time.

"You know I'm right, and I wouldn't wait too long before you get your head on straight and make her see that, too. Especially not when she's going out looking as sexy as she did right before I came up here."

My eyes snapped up to his and my blood boiled as his words sank in. "What do you mean?"

He shrugged and opened the door to the hallway, "She was looking for trouble when she got into an Uber on my way up. My guess is she's going to find it in the little clothing she had on when she left."

He departed, already knowing he had said enough to bait me into acting. Before the door to my office was closed all the way, I pulled up the location tracker that I put on her phone and swore when I saw where she was.

Eight Ball Bar.

"Fuck!" I roared, grabbing my guns and tearing from the room.

THE LINE WALKERS

I pushed my way through the bar and fired a shot before I even cleared the door, landing one bullet directly into the VP's head. He had just come back inside from screaming at Peyton as she ran for her infuriatingly stupid life toward my house, and he landed on his back before anyone else even dared to pull their guns.

I bellowed out as I crossed the room toward Blade, and everyone froze when they saw who fired the first shot. "The next one goes into your old lady's face after I break every single bone in her fucking ugly ass body for what you allowed to happen tonight."

He clenched his jaw but held his hands up, "She came in here, without warning."

"And they should have given her the same treatment as last time," I barked as I stepped over the VP's dead body, putting two more holes in the zipper of his jeans for good measure.

"That wasn't—" Blade started, but I aimed my gun to my right, at his third in line.

"Keep talking and you'll find yourself sorely out of members tonight!"

He pursed his lips and nodded to the back door. "She left, unharmed."

"I'll be back to chat about that." I spit on the floor at his feet. "Maybe you'll see me coming, maybe you won't." And I followed Peyton, not trusting that some loner biker wasn't chasing her down from the parking lot for the sick fun of it.

I cleared the back door and took a deep breath of fresh air as I caught sight of her white dress as she moved deeper into the woods. And I did what I did best, I let my fucking wild side free.

She wanted to be chased down by a madman; she was going to get her wish.

She wanted Dane's attention after I went dark on her, she'd regret her words from that night.

I'd make her fucking eat them. And then I'd make her come on my cock to prove just how wrong she'd been.

My boots thundered through the underbrush as I chased her, feeling my pulse slow and my adrenaline hyper fixate on her body as she sprawled out across the forest floor. We were deep enough to be obscured from the bar, but not safe from any lurkers or intruders.

She caught sight of me as I moved through the trees and she cursed, scrambling across the ground on her hands and knees, searching for something in the brush. I didn't warn her it was me; I didn't even toy with her. I simply pounced, landing on her back and trapping her under the weight of my body.

Without a mask or a hood on, she would see me if she looked over her shoulder. The real me.

Lincoln. So I kept my hand buried in her hair, forcing her to stare at the dirt as I pulled my shirt off over my head.

"No!" She hissed, grabbing for the bushes like she was going to get away from me with the help of the twigs.

Silly girl.

I wrapped my shirt around her face, lifting it so she could breathe, but blocked her sight and quickly tied it behind her head, blindfolding her. Gasping for breath, I could feel the throbbing pain in my cock for her while she continued to resist, despite her blindness, desperately attempting to escape from me. I flipped her over onto her back and looked down at her silk dress, covered in dirt and absolutely fucking perfect even still.

Unable to resist her sexuality and beauty after four days apart, she entranced me. Instantly, I tore the front of her dress down, revealing both of her sexy, lush tits to the chilly night air.

My obsession with her would always be my fatal flaw, though.

I just didn't know that when I let go of her arms to grope her tits, she'd prove it to me.

I didn't see it coming, but I heard the hum of electricity a nanosecond before she hit me in the abs with the spicy lightsaber she wielded. "Puppet." I groaned and collapsed forward onto her as searing pain encapsulated every cell in my body.

Stun gun.

Fucking checkmate, Puppet.

# CHAPTER 24 – PEYTON

## THE LINE WALKERS

I gasped when Dane's voice hoarsely called my name as he collapsed on top of me, taking the wind out of my lungs under his bulking form. "Oh, God."

I tried dislodging him, but he was so fucking heavy I couldn't move him off my chest. I also couldn't breathe. Or see.

His arms draped over mine, preventing me from reaching up and lifting the fabric he put over my face when he caught me. At first, when he jumped onto me and took me to the ground hard, I was fucking scared. I thought maybe it wasn't him after all, and that perhaps a biker had followed me out into the woods. But as soon as his skin touched mine, I knew he was *my* monster.

And then I got angrier. Because fuck him for making me endanger myself before he bothered to respond to me. He said nothing as he manhandled me, but I could tell he was barely holding back his own anger at finding me in the bar at all.

Turned out, we were like oil and water when we were both mad. As soon as I got my hand in my purse where it was trapped under the bush, I knew I was going to use the stun gun on him to teach him I wasn't some defenseless little toy to be played with after all.

I just didn't expect it to be so effective at subduing him. And now, I found myself trapped under his two hundred and fifty pounds of muscle, and even the exuberant amount of anger coursing through my veins couldn't lift him off my body. I tossed the stun gun down, trying to use both arms to push him off.

"Come on!" I hissed, trying to shift my hips, so he'd roll or slide off me at least.

"That hurt." He slurred against my cheek as his hot breath teased my ear. The way he said it sounded so much like Lincoln's voice, I froze until he turned his face into my neck and bit me.

Hard.

"Ouch!" I screamed, trying anew to buck him off as he started to get his arms and legs underneath him. I frantically reached for the stun gun, fully intent on using it again if he fucking bit me another time, but he grabbed my wrist and pulled the thing from my fingers as the electricity cracked between us. "Don't you dare!" I hissed when I felt him pause with the gun in his hand, and then the thing jolted to life right in front of my blindfolded face.

"Don't what, Puppet? Don't do exactly what you did to me?"

"You're a brute! You can handle it!"

I heard him toss it on the ground away from us as he pushed his knees between my legs and spread them apart to accommodate his lower body. I couldn't help it, but my ankles locked behind his waist, holding him tight to me for the first time in days.

He had both of my wrists in one hand above my head again as he leaned down and kissed my neck. "Why did you lure me here if you were just going to attack me? Why risk your safety to be so stupid?"

I arched into his touch, desperate for more of it. "I didn't plan on using the taser on you."

"Did you think it would stop a bar full of men from raping you and then killing you for the fun of it?" He hissed against my ear and bit it, gentler than the one he gave to my neck but still enough to hurt. "Was that your plan?"

"I didn't have a plan, exactly!" I cried out, rocking my hips under him as his hand came down to my breast, sandwiched between our bodies and mewled for him when he played with my nipple.

"Then why did you do something so stupid?" He demanded, moving to my other breast and lowering his lips to my burning nipple after pinching it to suck it into his mouth.

"Because you left!" I cried, "You left me!"

"You didn't want this." He moved back up my body and laid his forehead against mine and even though I couldn't see him through my blindfold, it was the most intimate moment I'd ever shared with a man before. "You regretted *this*."

Shaking my head, I heard the vulnerability in his voice, finally understanding why he went silent on me for the last few days. I hurt him. "I was wrong, but not about us. I was wrong about how I thought it would make me feel."

"Puppet." He growled when I humped him from beneath. I didn't care what I looked like or what he thought of me acting like that. My need for him to know how much I craved him far outweighed my dignity.

"I thought I'd feel empowered and strong if I let you have me. I thought it would make me feel in control of my life for the first time, like I was making the decisions finally. That was what I thought I wanted." I leaned forward when he lifted his forehead off mine and sank my teeth into the muscle where his neck and shoulder met, dragging him back to me as he hissed, but his cock twitched against my clit when I showed him the raw intensity I felt for him. "But that wasn't what I felt. When you forced me to choose who you'd send the video to and when you showed me just how fucking deeply you knew me, inside and out, that wasn't what I felt."

As I attempted to seduce him by licking his neck, even though I was restrained and blind, he growled and tilted his head to the side, offering me more of his sensitive flesh.

I went on, laying it all on the line. "It wasn't what I wanted to feel after all." I bit his neck and moaned when his fingers found my wetness between our bodies as he ripped my lace panties off. Finally, he was going to fuck me. "But you knew that, didn't you?"

"Tell me anyway." He growled and freed his cock from his pants to rub it through my soaking arousal, teasing us both. "Say it."

He pushed his cock in deep and I arched my back like a cat, taking his thickness in my restrained position.

"I felt taken care of." I moaned, rocking against him as he pulled out and pushed back in, giving me everything I needed. He always gave me what I needed. "I *feel* cherished. Even if you only ever fuck me in the dirt."

He thrust harder and let go of my hands as he slid both of his under my head to cradle it. "I'd fuck you in the middle of a bed made of the world's finest silks, if it was what you wanted. But it isn't."

I grinned, bringing my hands down and wrapping them around the back of his neck to hold him to me. I could have pulled the blindfold away and seen him for the very first time, but my eyes didn't need to see his face to feel connected to him. Instead, I ran my nails up the back of his head, teasing the skin of his scalp before grabbing a handful of his hair and pulling his face to mine. "Kiss me."

"With pleasure, Puppet." His stubble burned against my lips as he consumed them with his. I opened for him the second his tongue teased me and he pushed it in deep. Every time his hips thrust against me, his tongue matched the motion, and I clung to him and my sanity as I dared to let it go in the name of ecstasy. The fact that it was the first real kiss I'd shared with him felt so perfect for the moment.

It felt new.

It felt right.

"Dane," I moaned, gripping his hips with my legs, "I want you to fill me up again. I couldn't fully enjoy it last time because of my confusion, but I want to feel you there again."

"Mmh," He growled, biting my neck again and then my ear. He was so aggressive tonight with his mouth, but also the gentlest he'd been while fucking me yet. "My pretty little Puppet wants my come?"

"More than you can understand." I tilted my head back when he sucked on my neck, marking me, and I fucking welcomed his brand. In order to dispel any doubts in the morning light, I wanted to wear proof of him, so I wouldn't question if any of it was real. "I shouldn't want you, I shouldn't want this, but I can't stop. Dane, I've never wanted someone like I want you."

"You never had me before, Puppet." He laced his fingers through mine and held both of my hands down next to my head as he rolled his hips. "I'm the only man you'll ever have again, no one else will ever make you feel like this."

"Yes." I moaned, losing my grip on reality as I chased the pleasure he promised. "Make me come. Please Dane, come for me and give me what I need."

Dane grunted, slamming hard into me and rolling his hips on the bottom of each thrust. "Always. No one can fuck you like I can."

"Yes!" I cried out as I started coming and his resounding roar as he orgasmed in sync settled any doubt I had about our connection at that moment. I collapsed into the dirt as tears sprang to my eyes from the intensity of the entire interaction. I was hooked on Dane, and I never wanted to let go.

He kissed me again, resting his forehead against mine as we both gasped for our breath in the silence of the trees. "Peyton." He whispered, showing that he, too, was overwhelmed.

"I'm sorry." I whispered back, dragging my nails up and down his bare back, memorizing every powerful muscle and dip in his skin. "I don't regret us."

"You should though." He sighed and dragged himself from my body, but didn't get off me completely. "I'm a dangerous man, Peyton. In ways you can't comprehend."

I paused, feeling the trails of fear trying to climb my spine as his words sank in. But something warm filled my stomach at the almost sad tone of his voice as he said it. Tyson was a clean cut, soft handed businessman who never hurt a fly because he was too weak to stand up for himself, yet he hurt me more than any man ever had. I knew even a man as dangerous as Dane clearly was, he wouldn't use it against me. "Will you ever hurt me?" I lifted my fingers to his face, letting his whiskers chafe against them as he rubbed into me like a cat desperate for human touch. Was my monster desperate for my touch?

"Never." He growled forcefully, "That's one of the few things I can promise you."

"Will you ever leave me again? Will you ever ignore me when I call out your name?" Asking for it made me feel vulnerable and small, but I needed to know.

"I tried to stay away from you to protect you, Peyton. You said you didn't want me and I tried." He hummed deep in his chest, "I tried to busy myself in other ways, to stay away. But I can't, and I won't ever again."

My chest seized as I imagined what he did with his time. "Other women?" My voice shook as I asked, fearing the answer. I didn't know him. Not the way he knew me, but still the idea of him with other women made me shake with rage.

"I haven't fucked another woman in over a year, Puppet. Fate knew you'd be mine eventually, and it left my appetite unfulfilled by anyone but you. No one drew my attention in at any depth, so I went without. I was waiting for you."

"Dane." I cried and then gasped when he rolled us so I was on top of him, straddling his still wet cock. "Then how did you distract yourself?" I couldn't see him, but I'd never felt sexier. My dress was in tatters down to my lower rib cage, my tits were exposed, and my skin was no doubt a mess of dirt and debris, yet again.

Even so, I felt like a goddess. Dane did that.

He was right, I could have a bed full of silks if I wanted it, but the last few times I wanted him just like this. Maybe next time I'd beg him to fuck me like a normal person, but this time, I wanted my monster, not a man.

"You don't want to know that answer, Puppet." Dane lifted his hips and his cock slid through my wetness, rubbing my clit as it went. He wasn't fully hard, but he was still hard enough to give me pleasure.

So I took it. I ground my hips forward and back, rubbing my clit up and down the length of his cock. "Why don't I? Did you do something terrible?"

I remembered his comment about killing people with the knife he cut my clothes off with and my pussy clenched at the level of danger and darkness I teetered on in Dane's embrace.

He sat up and bit one of my breasts, pulling another shriek from my lips before he used his tongue to soothe it. "Everything I do is terrible."

"Not this." I gasped and moaned as I selfishly neared another orgasm. "Tell me you don't think this is terrible." I rocked faster, and he groaned, fisting my hair and tilting my head back.

"You're right, Puppet. You may be the only good thing I've ever done in my life." His lips latched onto my exposed neck, biting, sucking and marking me all over.

And I fucking loved it. I clawed my nails into his bare shoulders and neck, leaving my own marks as I reached my peak once again. "Tell me." I slowed down as euphoria crashed over me and left me limp and exhausted. "Good or bad, tell me anyway. Tell me *anything*."

He smiled against my neck and wrapped his arms around me, holding me to his chest. Once again, the urge to remove my blindfold tried to overcome me, but I resisted. I would let him keep his secrets for a little while longer. But *just* for a little while.

"I broke a vow I made to myself a long, long time ago." He admitted, taking a deep breath in. "A vow not to spill blood for others."

I froze as my ears rang with his words. "You killed someone again?" I asked, remembering the way he taunted that information out when he used his knife to cut my dress off last time.

"Not just someone, Puppet." He tightened his arms around me like he was afraid I would bolt at is confession. "A lot of people."

"Because of me?" I whispered, feeling guilty and something else all at the same time.

"Because of me." He replied quickly, "Because it is who I am. Even if I do not want it to be."

"Would you have done it if I hadn't freaked out last time?" I pulled back like I was going to see him, even though I was still blind. "Would you have broken your vow if I didn't push you away?"

"Shh," He soothed, sensing my anxiety crawling up my throat as I started feeling responsible for the lives of 'a lot of people' suddenly being cut short at Dane's hands. "They weren't good people, Puppet. I don't harm innocent people."

"Death is still death." I rested my forehead against his, "You still darkened your soul because of me."

"Worried about my soul, Puppet?" He smiled against my lips.

"How else will you be stuck with me for the rest of forever if we end up in different places?" I smiled, trying to find the calm he had when talking about such a foreign thing. People I knew didn't just kill other people because they were bad, yet somehow, I wasn't repulsed by the image of Dane playing the role of vigilante.

He groaned and tightened his hold around my back again and I leaned into his warmth, "Planning forever with me, P?"

I tilted my head and kissed my way down his neck, nibbling the salty skin as I went. When I got to his chest, I slid my hips back so my knees were on the ground between his and I pushed him back onto the ground. He obliged with a slight 'oof' as he hit it, but he didn't stop me. "You told me the first time you fucked me, I could either accept you and come to you willingly, or you'd come to me." I slowly kissed my way down the center of his chest and stomach, familiarizing myself with his skin as I went. "This is me, coming to you willingly, Dane." I reached the spot where his jeans were undone and bit the sensitive skin right above his cock, which grew harder with each press of my lips against his skin. "I want you." Whispers escaped my lips as I ran my tongue up the length of him, and I moaned at the combination of our tastes. "I want my monster in real life."

"Peyton." He moaned, burying his fingers in my hair and guiding my head as I pleasured him. It was such a power trip, making the man that was always in control lose a bit of that authority to me. "Fucking hell, Puppet." He groaned when I spit on his cock and took him deep. "That's it."

"I love the way you taste when you're covered with me." Wrapping my hands around it, I stroked him as I teased the head of his cock with my tongue.

I was a whore, there was no other way around it anymore. I was in a situationship with a man I thought I once loved because I was too much a people pleaser to just rip the band aid off and leave him. While simultaneously sucking the soul out of the man who hacked me and then stalked me to get into my life. Oh yeah, can't forget how I imagined my stuffy asshole of a boss, Lincoln, laying under me while I sucked Dane's cock twice already too.

Yep, I was unredeemable.

"That's it, Puppet." Dane groaned, tightening his hand in my hair and pushing me down harder onto his cock. I hated when Tyson tried to force my head down on his cock, but with Dane, fuck, it made my already pleased kitty purr for more as I widened my knees and arched my back to take him further down my throat. "Fuck, Peyton. No one has ever sucked my cock like you do. You're a goddess, bowing on your knees to me right now, and I'm unworthy."

I hummed, playing with his tight balls as I ached for his release so I could feel as powerful as I did the last time I got him to come like that. But tonight, I wanted his come in only one place.

"Jesus," He grunted, "I'm going to come so fucking hard." He tensed and I knew I had to move if I was going to get what I wanted. "Peyton!" He growled when I pulled off him and then scrambled up his body, impaling myself onto his wet cock and drawing a roar of release from his throat as he started coming deep inside of my pussy.

"That's it, Dane." I moaned, feeling him pumping me full as I kept riding his thick cock. "Fill my pussy up, baby. Come for me." I slowed my hips as he came off his high and smiled to myself, knowing I did that. I made him lose his mind and chase after the ecstasy that I promised him.

He rolled with lightning speed and I landed in a fit of giggles under him as he pushed my legs wide and kneeled down between them. "Are you sure you don't have a breeding kink, too?" He asked and ran the tip of his tongue over my clit, flicking it.

"No promises." I giggled and moaned when he growled against my sensitive spot. "I don't want kids right now, but the act of taking your sperm is a tremendous turn on for me, I won't lie."

He chuckled and sucked my clit into his mouth as I bowed up off the ground. "That's exactly what a breeding kink is, Puppet. The pregnancy isn't even the biggest reward." He lowered himself down between my legs and chuckled when I gasped as he pushed his tongue into my wet pussy. "Now it's my turn to familiarize the taste of both of us together, just like you've been doing."

"Oh, God." I clawed at the earth beneath us. "This was not on my BINGO card."

# CHAPTER 25 -
## LINCOLN

I was in the kitchen before Peyton was that next morning. She wasn't late, I was just eager to see her again. I hated leaving her last night after the earth-shattering declarations she made to me in the blinding dark, but I had no choice.

Even with her baring her soul and begging me to keep her broken pieces safe for her, I couldn't tell her who I really was. If I did, she'd run from me. Not because she wouldn't still want all the things I could give her, but because she'd feel like she had to leave to make me pay for lying to her.

And I couldn't risk her leaving me before I won her over as Dane and Lincoln both, but I knew I was running out of time to do that. I had to prove to her that the day-to-day man that I was, Lincoln Bryce, could worship her just like Dane could.

Letting another man in emotionally would test her boundaries and morals, especially when she was convinced that Dane was the perfect man for her. But I needed to show her both sides of me, because I wouldn't be able to hide them when she was in my life full time.

And she would be in my life, full time. Sooner rather than later, I just had to convince her to stay.

I flipped the pancakes, making sure they did not burn, as I heard the patio door open and close in the other room.

*Game time.*

I listened to her modest little flats click across the marble floor and then falter when she saw me in the kitchen, at the stove no less. I didn't look over my shoulder, but I knew she'd look at her watch next, to make sure she was in fact not late, and then smooth a hand over her hair and clothing, to make sure she looked perfect before she announced her presence.

As if I could not sense her, even if I didn't hear her.

"Good morning, Peyton." I called, forcing her to step into the space before she could bolt. The last time I saw her as Lincoln was when I left her in my bed after shooting my brother for breaking into her guest house. We both had kept our distance from each other yesterday. But while I was giving her space, she was apparently hatching out a plan to draw Dane out of hiding.

I smirked at her stupidity in the name of desire.

Peyton cleared her throat and started walking into the space. "Good morning, Mr. Bryce." She walked into the kitchen and lurked when I continued on with my task. "Would you like me to take over for you?"

"No, but you can get two plates out of the cabinet behind you." I nodded her way, finally looking at her and even though I had stalked her, watching through her phone as she got dressed for the day, just twenty minutes ago, my cock still throbbed in my sweats when I saw her first hand. She had propped her phone up and painstakingly dressed, piece by piece, sensually for Dane to watch before she came to spend her day with me, but for once, the digital view I'd had didn't do justice.

She was fucking sexy as hell, turning to reach into the top of the cabinet for the plates I requested, while I stared at her thick legs, wrapped perfectly in a pair of white pants. God, her ass made my mouth water as I remembered how good it looked bent over the first night I took her in the woods, slamming into her deep and hard. The boating style blue and white striped shirt she wore had me imagining what she'd look like laid out on an over-water hammock of a large sailboat, naked and sunning herself with no one else around for miles. And when her hair brushed over her shoulder just right, I could make out the markings I left on her neck that she'd tried to cover with makeup. But they were there, and they were mine.

I barely looked away as she turned with two plates, offering them to me. "Is your brother staying for long?"

My cock softened instantly at the mention of Tamen's presence in my home. "Not if I can help it." I had not told her he was my brother, so they must have talked when I was still actively avoiding hacking into Peyton's alluring camera. A mistake I would never make again after what trouble she tried to get herself into last night.

Her lips parted and her eyebrows rose briefly as she leaned her hip against the counter. "He apologized to me, if that makes it any better." She held my stare briefly before looking away the way she normally did. "He explained how he normally stayed in the guest house when he visits. I'd hate if he was in the doghouse because of me."

"You aren't at fault for anything he did." I waited for her to look back up at me. "We don't like each other, and that's been decades in the making."

She pursed her lips and swallowed, watching me as I flipped through the pancakes. "Then who's the other plate for, if not for him?"

I set one plate in front of her and put three large cakes on it. "You." I passed the butter dish to her and nodded to it as I plated my own heaping breakfast. "I figured I'd feed you this morning."

She froze with her knife half swiped across the first pancake and I grinned to myself as I reached over her for another knife. "Scooch." I pushed my hip into hers, scooting her down the counter so I could stand next to her and butter my pancakes. "I made bacon too."

Moving to open the oven and pull out the pan I had warmed in there, she watched with an unreadable look on her face. "You didn't have to—"

I waved her off, putting a couple of slices on her plate with my bare fingers and then licking the salt off them as I grabbed my own. I could feel her eyes burning a hole in the side of my face as I moved around the space like a domesticated house-husband instead of the closed off and grumpy asshole she thought I was. "Come on," I shrugged toward the kitchen island where I ate breakfast every morning, "Let's eat before all of my hard work gets cold."

When I sat down, she slowly finished buttering her pancakes and then took a seat two spaces down from me, even though I had put her coffee cup down in front of the one next to me. I'd let her have that one, but she'd pay twice for the next defiance.

I hid my sinister grin behind my coffee as she took hers and added a splash of cream to it.

She broke the silence, "I think you have the best coffee in the world." She took a sip and sighed into it. "I've never been big on coffee, but since starting here, I'm addicted to this fancy stuff."

I took a sip of my black cup of Joe and bit back the comment I wanted to make about her never having to stop drinking it now that she was mine, and instead went the safer route. "I'm glad you like it. Help yourself to it whenever you want."

She smiled softly and then cut a piece of pancake, dipping it into her syrup and taking a bite.

I knew it'd happen. It wasn't like I hadn't seen her eat before, but the result was still the same. Absolute enthusiasm exuded from her entire being as she savored the taste of Mrs. Straight's famous recipe that I stayed up most of the night looking for.

Two hours of sleep was worth it to see Peyton savor the food in her over-the-top way. It was the same way she ate dinner with me at the restaurant last week. It was the same way she took a cock, moaning and savoring each and every delicious inch she took.

Last night, I ate her out and made her come two more times, before I finally walked her back to the clearing from the first night, blindfolded. The urge to rip the damned thing off had nearly overcome me so many times while I was with her, but I resisted. I had to be sure she was ready for me first. All of me.

But as we shared a mundane experience like breakfast at my kitchen bar, I knew she was the only woman who would ever truly accept me for the good and bad inside of me. Just as she had last night when she rode me to orgasm after learning I'd killed people in the wake of our fall out. And then sucked my cock like a goddess and took my come in her favorite place.

Fuck, I was hard again.

I turned back to the bar, trying to hide my erection as Peyton took a sip of her coffee and moaned with a happy little smile on her face. She would not make it easy on me with those noises, either. "Tell me something about yourself." I broke through the tension.

She covered her mouth with her napkin and finished chewing. "What do you mean?"

"I mean, you've lived here for two weeks and I know little about you." I held her stare and went on, "Tell me something."

"I- uh," She stammered and adjusted herself on the stool, "I grew up a few hours from here. My parents have lived in Massachusetts their entire lives."

I held my hand up and shook my head, "Not your LinkedIn bio, Peyton. I asked about you." Leaning forward and staring at her, I pushed on, "Tell me something important about you."

"You go first." She challenged bravely as she took another bite, "Show me what you mean."

Oh, the things I'd gladly show her, but she'd have to settle for words for now.

"I'm allergic to raspberries." I said and her eyebrows rose slightly as I kept going, "I've never been to a professional ball game before, but I've watched every game the Patriots have played since I was born. My guilty midnight pleasure is ice cream, and I have an incredibly irrational fear of heights."

Her lips parted as she listened to me ramble on, divulging useless information, and then she snapped them shut when she realized I was done and waiting for her to go.

I wasn't sure what I expected her to say, but it sure wasn't "The Patriots don't stand a chance without Brady leading them." She ginned finally and added, "Go Bills."

I rolled my eyes, scoffing at her. "I thought you said you were a lifelong Masshole."

She shrugged, taking another bite, "I went to college at UB. And besides, Josh Allen is a total hottie."

I audibly gagged, and she giggled, tipping her head back and letting the seductive sound surround us both. And I fucking smiled.

I only ever smiled for Peyton.

She adjusted herself on her stool and contemplated her response dramatically before giving it.

"I'm obsessed with everything Fall themed, from pumpkin patches and apple picking, to jumping into leaf piles and sitting by a warm fire with a cup of hot cocoa." She pursed her lips as she thought about what else to share, but I was stuck in a memory of chasing her sexy ass through a corn maze and then ravaging her like a wild animal tied to the bench in the middle of it.

Fuck it, my cock was harder, and I was done trying to convince it to soften.

Luckily she didn't notice as she went on, "I hate the smell of vanilla but I'm addicted to vanilla cupcakes and I once thought I wanted to be a doctor, until I had my tonsils out in high school and passed out when they put my IV in." She giggled, "Apparently I have a fear of needles." She shrugged and widened her eyes comically, "Who knew?"

"Not you, apparently," I joked, and she giggled.

"I do now." She sighed, "I quickly changed my degree aspirations to something more realistic."

"Hospitality?" I questioned, remembering her impressive resume filled with years of hotel chain climbing up to management.

"Yep," She nodded, with a little less enthusiasm than before, "It was practical, and the job availability was plentiful. I could go anywhere to work with a degree like that."

"And it brought you here, to me." I replied, feeling the thickness in the air between us growing as her eyes flicked up to mine.

"It did." She replied, holding my stare before blinking it off like she was breaking a trance. She took another bite of her pancake, "To be honest, it's a nice break from reality."

"The job or the location?" I questioned.

"Both, I guess." She shrugged, "Managing a hotel is no simple thing to do, but in the same sense it gets boring day in and day out. And the city," She rolled her eyes, "That gets old even faster."

"You don't enjoy living in the city?"

"I hate it." She replied openly, "It's suffocating. But there aren't many opportunities for a young hotel manager in a beautiful location like this," She nudged her nose toward the enormous windows overlooking the vast forest around us. "So I'll have to soak in as much of the scenery as I can while I'm here." Her smile widened, "Especially because Fall is here and I can't resist indulging."

"Hmm." I hummed watching her. "You're welcome to go hiking out in the woods anytime you want. There are multiple trails that are marked and easy to traverse."

Her cheeks reddened almost instantly, and I fought back the grin that wanted to show, remembering the way her tits reddened when she came on my cock and face last night. "Okay." She hid her face as she took a bite of her bacon.

Since I had already finished mine, I stood up and walked away from her. "Just don't go out too far to the east, there's a biker bar on the edge of the property and they're a rougher kind of crowd." I heard her audibly swallow and looked over my shoulder at her even redder face. "But don't worry, my entire property is lined with motion sensors and cameras. I see everything."

"Everything?" She whispered, and I put my dish into the dishwasher and turned to face her. Putting my hands on the island between us, I leaned forward, so we were staring at each other over the space.

"How do you think I knew Tamen had entered your space the other night?" I cocked my head to the side, "I always see everything."

"Lincoln," She breathed, and I silently begged her to admit what she'd been up to in my woods like I didn't already know.

But my brother's annoying pompous accent broke up our moment as he entered the kitchen, "It smells delightful in here." He walked in shirtless, again, and sauntered over to Peyton's side, glancing over her shoulder to her empty plate. My fists clenched tight on the island as he invaded her space and Peyton's eyes flicked down to them before snapping back up to my face. I held her stare silently as my brother chatted on. "Are those Mrs. Straight's famous pancakes?" He took her fork and stabbed a piece before eating it and groaning, "I'd let that woman do dirty things to me if she promised to feed me afterwards."

"Tamen." I growled, finally looking away from Peyton's bright green eyes wide with shock and focused on the man I wanted to choke to death while she watched. Would she get as turned on as she did last night as she rode my cock and talked about who I killed in her absence? "Enough."

"What?" He grinned with his stupid charismatic bullshit persona on and looked between the two of us. "Like you wouldn't fuck your employees if they gave you something you were missing out on like I am." He scoffed, taking the last piece of bacon off her plate and eating it. "I'm missing out on good home cooking from a beautiful woman. Speaking of which, want to come work for me instead of my boring brother?" He winked when Peyton looked up at him and I couldn't help the monster inside as I grabbed my empty coffee cup, ready to throw it at his face.

"No! Don't." Peyton put her hand on mine, stilling me and silencing the rage in my head as she stood up, keeping her hand on mine. "Please don't, Lincoln."

Tamen's face lit up as he watched over her back and I almost shook her off to chuck it at him, anyway. "Yeah, *Lincoln*. Wouldn't want you to get hurt poking the bear or something."

"There are extra pancakes over there," Peyton interrupted, squeezing my hand once before letting go and facing Tamen head on. "And I'm more than satisfied with my current arrangement here with Lincoln, thank you. Find someone else to cook for you."

My heart did a weird skipping in my chest as I starred at the majestic woman who not only told my brother off, but also defended me in the process.

Not once in my entire life, had someone chosen me in a fight against Tamen. Not even our father.

Tamen grinned, knowing exactly what she just did, and then busied himself getting his own breakfast while all I could do was stare at Peyton.

She ran her hands down the front of her shirt and stiffened her spine. "I have laundry to fold." And she walked out of the room without a backward glance, completely unaware that she had just rocked my entire world.

Fucking hell, Puppet, that deserves a present.

# CHAPTER 26 - PEYTON

## THE LINE WALKERS

> **Congrats Puppet, you've earned yourself another gift.**

I smiled the entire way to the post office in town on my afternoon break, like a lovesick puppy. And I couldn't care less. I was happy.

It felt a little foreign and kind of like at any moment it was going to be taken away from me, but I tried not to dwell on the foreign feeling. Because then I had to acknowledge how being happy was a new feeling for me.

And that would make me sad for all the years I wasted up to this moment. So instead I drove with a goofy grin on my face to the quaint little town for another round of Secret Santa from Dane. I tried getting out of him what exactly I had done to earn the gift, but he just chuckled darkly through the speaker on my phone in my guest house and said, "You'll find out, eventually."

As I parked in the parking lot of the post office, I looked around the quaint town with a different view as I tried to envision living in it from now on. Was Dane from this town, or did he come to me for our encounters from somewhere else?

He couldn't have been far away, given how quickly he made it to me at the bar after I tried to sacrifice myself for his attention. Admittedly, a stupid idea. But I'd gotten what I wanted in the end. So I was going to mark that one down as a win.

The bells on the door rang as I stepped inside of the deserted post office and the little old lady looked up from her book at her desk and grinned. "Ah, Ms. Peyton." She stood up and pulled her glasses down her nose as she came to the counter. "I see you survived the last few weeks, I kept watching the news for a missing person's poster with your face on it like you asked."

I smiled, feeling foolish for involving her now that I knew Dane. "I'm fit as a fiddle. But thank you for watching out for me."

"Ach," She waved me off, "All I do is watch. I watch who comes and who goes. Who leaves with who and who goes about it on their own."

I squinted and leaned on the counter. "Any more info on my secret admirer?" I asked, hoping she knew something more about Dane this time.

She chuckled, "Besides the fact that he has superb taste in cars and, I'm guessing, presents?" She reached under the counter and pulled out a smaller gift box in matte black with a velvet bow on it. "And the fact that he is still devilishly good looking." She shrugged, "I unfortunately didn't get to take him for a test drive on the counter this time either, though."

I snorted and took the box from her. "Bummer." I winked and stepped back toward the door. "Because that man knows how to turn a woman wild for him."

Her wrinkly face pitched up in excitement as a shit-eating grin broke out on her face and she whooped out loud. "That's my girl!"

I chuckled and started to open the door when she stopped me.

"If you know how he is in bed, how is it you know nothing else about him?"

I shrugged and contemplated my answer for a moment before giving it. "Sometimes it's nice not to worry about names, social standings, or future plans when you want to forget about everything else in the world, too."

"Anonymity." She nodded, "I like your style, girl."

"Until next time." I lifted the box in goodbye and walked out.

THE LINE WALKERS

O nce again, Dane's instructions were simple regarding his present. I had to be free from distraction and available only to him before opening it. So when I walked back into my guest house, via my brand-new door that Lincoln had fixed sometime yesterday, I was eager to ignore the rest of the world for Dane.

"Oh monster, where art thou monster?" I called out loud as I kicked my shoes off and walked through my dark guest house toward my bedroom.

I expected Dane's deep voice to flow through my speakers to me like usual, but there was nothing.

"Dane?" I called out again as I got into my room, pulling my shirt free of the waistband of my pants. "Hello?"

I laid my phone down on the table by the door and pulled my shirt off over my head, eager to be free of the constricting fabric.

"Puppet."

"God!" I screamed in terror as Dane's warm body pressed against mine from behind. He wrapped his gigantic hands around my bare waist and pulled me tight to his massive chest. The fabric of his shirt was soft like a well-worn cotton and I melted into his touch. "Dane."

"You should be more careful Puppet, if you say my name too many times, I appear like Beetlejuice." He growled against my ear as his hands wandered over my body.

"Mmh," I moaned when one of his hands glided over my chest and up to my neck, pulling my head back against his shoulder and looking away from him as he laid sensual kisses along my neck. "Then why didn't you appear when I played with myself earlier? I called out your name on repeat the whole time."

"Minx." He chuckled against my skin. "Liars don't get rewarded with sexy gifts and orgasms."

"Okay, fine," I smiled as his fingers skimmed over the lace of my bra. "I didn't play with myself earlier, but I really wanted to. Instead, I had to go into town to get my present."

"Do you want to open it?" He pulled the cups of my bra down, freeing both of my breasts and instantly took them into his palms, thumbing my nipples.

I could look over at him if I wanted to. I could just see the outline of the hair hanging over his forehead out of my peripheral vision.

"Do I get to see you?" I whispered and then pushed my ass back into his body, where his hardening cock pushed back against me.

"Do you feel me?" He hummed, pushing his cock harder against my back, bending down slightly to rub it up the entirety of my ass.

"Yes." I moaned, leaning into him.

"Do you hear me?" He pressed his lips against my ear and growled as he toyed with my nipples.

"Yes." I knew where he was going with it, and I was only slightly disappointed with the distance he kept between us.

"Do you smell me?" He slid one hand up my throat and over my mouth so I could smell his skin and his familiarity burned deep when my senses were consumed with all things Dane.

It was just dark enough that if I turned to look at him, his face would be hard to see clearly. But I was tempted to try, anyway.

"Yes." I admitted when he dropped his hand to my throat and tightened it, drawing a breathy moan from my lips.

"Then you don't need to see me right now."

"Please." I whined, and he chuckled.

"You want to beg me tonight, Puppet?"

"Don't I always end up begging you for something?" I hissed when he pinched my nipple and pulled on it.

"Because you're my good little girl."

"Mmh, then reward me already." I challenged, reaching behind me and cupping his cock in my hand, stroking him. "Give me what I obviously ache for."

He chuckled and pulled me back to the chair next to my bed and sat down, making me land in his lap. I hated sitting on laps because I was too big, but Dane positioned me until I was settled right on his legs with my feet on the floor between them.

I huffed when he was no closer to impaling me on his cock, and he chuckled. "Open your present, Puppet. So I can get mine."

"Hmm, I don't remember getting you anything." I deadpanned as he laid the black box on my lap and then gasped when he bit my neck directly over the mark he left last night. I had to use makeup tricks I hadn't used since high school to cover it so I could face Lincoln.

My pussy throbbed, remembering the way Lincoln had hovered around me all day long, feeding me breakfast and then kind of lingering like he wanted to spend time with me. It didn't make any sense.

"Distracted?" Dane hummed, bringing me back to him and the present.

"Around you? Always." I giggled when he gripped my hands and started pulling the bow open on the gift.

When I had the bow free, I lifted the lid, but Dane reached over next to us and clicked the small reading lamp on and I froze. "I'm trusting you, Puppet." He laid wet kisses over my shoulders and I stared down at the present in my lap. "Be my good girl, baby."

"Okay," I whispered and finished opening my gift. It'd be so easy to look over my shoulder and see his face for the first time, but as he laid his cheek on my shoulder looking down at the gift, I forced myself to be good for him. "Oh,"

In the box was a black satin pillow of sorts with three very precarious items cushioned on top, and my body tingled as I looked down at them.

"Pick the one you want to explore first." He stated, rubbing his hands up and down my thighs in a comforting yet teasing way. It was the first time he freely touched me when we weren't fighting for control or power in the dirt like a couple of animals.

"Well, I know which one I'm not going to start with." I whispered, grabbing one that probably wasn't safe either, but felt safer than the other one.

It was two things, actually. A delicate black ribbon choker with a gold jewel closure and a matching bracelet in the opposite coloring. I noticed that the gold bracelet had a beautiful sparkling chain instead of ribbon, and when I lifted it to inspect it, the black closure on it seemed slightly scary. And sure enough, the black gem was a skull with emerald stones in the eyes, giving it an eerie yet painfully beautiful appearance.

I lifted the choker to examine the jewel closure closer, and it was a matching skull with dark black gems for eyes.

"What are these?" I whispered, noting the way the different colored gems reminded me of us. True, I'd never seen his eyes before, but I imagined they'd be dark. Just like Lincoln's were. There was just something about his personality that said his eyes were dark, like his soul.

His fingers traced over the black ribbon choker and he responded, "Some people would call this one a collar."

An image of a woman in a sex dungeon locked in a cage with a padlocked chain around her throat came to mind and I shivered at how unappealing that was. "What would you call it?"

"A token of commitment." He said, taking the seemingly harmless ribbon from my hand and using both of his hands to bend the skull at the center. Right before I thought it'd break in his large hands, a seam appeared down the middle of the face and the token parted. "It's something to be worn no different from a promise ring or something more conventional to prove to the person you're with that you're theirs."

"That seems serious."

"It is. It's not meant to be taken lightly. I wouldn't take it lightly if you were to wear it."

I felt overwhelmed, so I shifted my attention to the glittering golden bracelet with a matching skull with glowing green eyes. "Then what is this one?"

He smiled into my hair and put the black choker back into the box. "This is the training wheels edition of the necklace. Something more normal with the same meaning. But this one represents a commitment to yourself." He ran his fingers over the glowing green jewels and opened it, the same way he opened the choker. "This one is a gift to yourself, linking you to no one but you. Because if you accept my necklace or not, I want you to accept this bracelet as the first step to regaining your individuality and autonomy."

"I don't understand." I whispered, but that was a lie. Despite not being the one to disclose that part of my life, I knew what he was referring to.

"Choose yourself, Puppet, if nothing else. Choose your own happiness and your own path and stop doing it for everyone else."

Tears burned my eyes as I felt the impact of his words on my heart. So instead of telling him how right he was, I held my wrist out, welcoming his brand and the vow it carried for myself. His fingers gently clasped the skull back together and then he reached into the box, pulling out a pin key. "If you lock it, it won't come off without this key."

"Lock it." I whispered, watching as he twisted the small lock and I looked down at the symbol of me and him intertwined. "This is the same skull you have on your back."

"Is it selfish of me to want to be a part of your happiness, even if it isn't with you choosing me?"

"No." I smiled to myself. "Not at all."

"We'll hold on to this one until you're ready for it." He took the key and tucked it back into the box with the necklace.

"Fair." I ran my fingers over the bracelet and felt the warmth in my soul at the gesture he gave me. And then I remembered the other things in the box and groaned to myself, pushing my emotions to the side. "And the other parts of my gift."

He chuckled darkly, lifting the black leather like blindfold that had cushions in the eye spaces with a tight elastic band to go around my head. "This is so I can fuck you face to face like last night without worrying about you suffocating with my shirt over your face."

I snorted, "Or you could just reveal your identity to me. And end the whole charade."

"Soon, Puppet." He kissed my neck again.

"Okay, and the last one?" I eyed the last *gift*.

He snorted, "I thought that one spoke for itself." I stared down at it in the box atop the satin cushion. "Pick it up."

I tentatively picked up the silver item, testing the weight of it. I turned it over and ran my thumb over the green gem that matched the ones in my skull bracelet and snorted at the beauty within such an obnoxious object. "A butt plug."

# CHAPTER 27 - LINCOLN

"I told you that you'd take me there sometime." I slid my hands up her bare chest and then undid her bra. "Now be a good girl and put your blindfold on so I can play with my Puppet."

She snickered, and I saw her eyes instinctively dash to the side like she was going to look at me. "And if I don't?"

I growled, feeding on her bratty side as I took both of her wrists in my hands and pulled them wide, leaving her vulnerable. "Then I'll leave you tied open like this somewhere incredibly," I bit her shoulder and then pulled her arms behind her back, "inconvenient."

"Mmh," She hummed, leaning her head back against my shoulder. "Is that supposed to be a threat?"

I grabbed the blindfold and slid it over her head, tightening it around her head so I knew she was completely blind, and then I stood her up between my legs. Having her so close to me, as me, was invigorating and terrifying all in one. But I was ready to have her at my mercy without worrying that she'd kick me out the second she saw who I was.

I undid her pants, sliding them down her legs, followed by the pathetically useless pair of panties that were already wet with her arousal until she was naked before me.

Wearing only my gold chain around her wrist. *Fuck*.

The first time I saw her wear the black necklace would be my undoing. That would be when I knew she was mine. Truly, unconditionally, mine.

Until then, I'd settle for my brand on her wrist, linking us together in even the slightest way.

I stayed seated behind her and ran my hands over her plump ass and down her thighs. She sighed like she was in a dream and I leaned forward to kiss the small of her back. "Tell me Puppet, have you dreamed of me lately?"

I could hear the smile on her face as she sighed again, "Only when you stay hidden from me. Then I have no choice but to find you in my subconscious."

"Then fear not, because I'm done hiding from you. I'm never staying away again, whether you like it or not."

"Mmh, promise?" With a dreamy expression, she turned her head and looked over her shoulder, as if expecting to see me there. "Because I'll do something stupid again if that's what it takes to get your attention."

The fact that she couldn't see it coming made the sharp crack of my palm on her ass cheek even more rewarding for me, paired with her shrill squeak of surprise and soft moan of pleasure on the end. I stood up, melting my body against hers and consumed every inch of her with my touch until she was panting and clawing at me as I teased her nipples and pussy lips.

"Please, Dane." She moaned, leaning into me.

"What do you want, Puppet?"

"You." She dug her nails into my arm and guided my hand lower until my fingers finally brushed up against her clit. "I need to feel you inside of me."

"You want my cock, baby? You want to feel me deeper than anyone else has ever been?"

"Yes," She nodded her head in delirium, "I could take you every day and never tire of the way it feels when you first push into me. That second of overwhelming fullness and then pure ecstasy that follows like I've been empty my entire life until that moment."

"Then be a good little Puppet and bend over. I want your hands on your ankles and your legs spread wide so I can play with you."

"Turn the light off." She whispered after hesitating a second too long.

I grinned, knowing she was about to get her first lesson in just how fucking sexy she was to change the way she viewed herself. And it was going to push her so far out of her comfort zone.

Kicking the inside of her right foot with my shoe, her feet spread further apart. "You're blindfolded, what do you care if it's bright or not?"

"You're going to be staring at my asshole." She argued, "I'd appreciate if there was a bit of darkness to buffer out my flaws while you do it."

"Wrong." I put one hand on her hip and the other around the back of her neck, forcing her to bend down as she tried to resist. "I'm going to be eating your asshole, not staring at it." Pushing my groin into her exposed pussy, I spanked her ass once more for the fun of it and then sat down behind her. "Hold on to your ankles, baby." I slid both hands over her ass cheeks and shook them, growling, "You're going to forget your own fucking name by the time I'm done with you."

She protested, simply because she thought she should, but ended on a gasp when I spread her cheeks further and licked her from front to back. "Ah!"

I buried my face between her cheeks and ate her pussy and ass so well, she'd never worry or be self-conscious again. I fucking hungered for her, every inch of her. "That's my good girl," I praised and hooked my toe under the ottoman, pulling it over to her. "On your hands and knees, Puppet. So you can take my toy, and then my cock."

She fell forward on it, bracing her knees on the tufted top, and then arched her back, presenting to me perfectly. "I want to come."

I grabbed the heavy metal butt plug with the green gem on the end of it and the small bottle of lube from the box and started prepping it. "Not until I'm inside of you."

"Dane." She whined and then froze when I stood up behind her, silencing her with cold lube dripped onto her virgin ass.

"Do you want this?" I used my fingers, rubbing in the lube, and smirked when she moaned and pushed back against them. "Do you want to wear my toy while I fuck your pussy so you can come harder than ever before?"

"Yes." She whimpered and moaned when I pushed one finger into her ass. I went slowly, but not as slow as she probably would have wanted me to. She feared the unknown, and it was my responsibility to guide her to the pleasure I knew she'd find.

"Do you want my cock right here someday?" I twisted my finger around and thrust it. "Do you want to give me something you've never given to another man?"

"Yes, God, Yes!" She spread her knees wider, nearly falling off the ottoman, eager for more.

"Good girl." I pushed the head of the toy against her ass with my finger still inside and started adding it, removing my finger so she was never closed completely to feel the burn of insertion again. "Push back on me, Puppet. Let me in."

"Fuck, goddamn." She groaned as her ass swallowed the plug. My first urge was to pull it out and push it back in again so she could feel it more, but I was so fucking hard I couldn't wait another second to be inside of her.

"Does my girl want to come?" I pulled my shirt off and kicked my boots off before stripping bare for my Puppet. I needed to feel her skin on mine tonight, every single inch.

"So much, please Dane. I want your cock."

"You got it, baby." I ran the head of my aching dick through her wetness while I pushed the flared end of the plug in and twisted it. "Take it, Puppet."

I slammed into her wet pussy and she mewled, with her head hung between her arms as I fucked her. Her voice thickened, conveying a mixture of pleasure and pain, as she said, "That's so good, baby. Fuck me harder, Dane."

I grabbed her hair and pulled her up, suspending her in midair as I fucked her wildly. She cried out in ecstasy as the change in angle pushed her over the edge. "Mmh, you're milking my cock, Puppet. You want my come, don't you?"

"Please," she begged, reaching behind her, digging her nails into my hip and screaming out when I fucked her harder and neared my orgasm. "That's it, Dane. Mmh, give me all of it."

I opened my mouth to tell her just exactly how I was going to give it to her, when an alarm sounded on my phone, forcing my hips to still completely.

After Tamen broke into Peyton's house, I activated all perimeter alarms on my phone, no longer counting on being locked away in my office at all hours to see them there. And the alarm that rang out on my phone was a high class one, meaning person or vehicle detected.

"Why'd you stop?" She gasped, falling forward when I let go of her hair. "Dane?"

I pulled out of her and walked across the room to my phone, opening the alert.

> *Perimeter Breech Alarm- South Driveway- thirty seconds ago.*

"Fucking hell." I groaned, vowing to murder Tamen if he was driving up the driveway, and setting off the alarms, making me neglect my dire need to come. But as I pulled up the camera feed, I saw it wasn't my brother at all.

No, the man driving the piece of shit old model Benz like it made him look important was about to derail more than just my orgasm.

Tyson.

"Dane?" Peyton called again, "I'm going to take this off if you don't answer me. What is going on?"

"Get dressed, P." I barked, fighting the fiery rage burning in my gut at the idea of her boyfriend showing up tonight of all times.

Did she know he was coming?

No, I knew she didn't, thanks to how far into her digital life I'd inserted myself. But that didn't answer why he was showing up to her work unannounced.

"Dane." The tone in her voice caught my attention, and I froze as she pulled the blanket from her bed around her naked body, still blindfolded. "You're scaring me."

"Your boyfriend is pulling up the drive." I snapped, angry with myself and that piece of shit.

"Tyson?" She gasped and froze. But we didn't have time to freeze because she couldn't answer the door blindfolded, and he sure as fuck would not see her naked. Never again.

Which meant I had to get her dressed and get out before he got to the door.

"Here." I pulled her thick black bathrobe from the back of her bathroom door and put her arms into it.

"Just ignore him," She started, reaching up to her blindfold, but I pulled her hands away and she started wringing them together in front of her. "I have to get dressed."

"You don't have time." I pushed my legs into my pants and did them up, followed by my shirt and boots. As I stood back up, I heard the slamming of his car door out front.

"I'm not answering it." She grabbed me as I moved by. "I can't, Dane."

Her fear was palpable, and I stopped, staring down at my Puppet. She was terrified.

"Why are you scared?"

Tyson chose that time to start banging on the front door, making his presence known.

"I can't—" She stammered, "Don't make me open that door."

"Has he hurt you before?" I growled, and she shrunk even more into herself. "Peyton, answer me."

"Please be quiet," She whispered, "Maybe he'll leave."

Tyson's puny fist hit the door again, and she shook, wrapping her arms around her body.

I pulled her into my arms, and she clung to me like a raft in a hurricane as Tyson started ringing the doorbell on repeat, echoing the noise through the space. "Go into the bathroom." I took her by the elbow and led her into the bathroom. "Lock the door behind you."

"Dane, no." She gripped my shirt, trying to pull me inside with her. "Please don't leave me."

My chest erupted in agony at the proof that was written through her body language suddenly that I had somehow missed. She was afraid of Tyson and it didn't have to do with physical violence. Not with me standing next to her.

No, something else was amiss. And suddenly, her freak out in the corn maze when I forced her to choose to send a video of her being fucked to him made so much more sense. Fuck, I was so stupid.

Over my fucking dead body would he ever go near her again.

"I'm not leaving this house or opening the door," I pushed her back and then leaned down to kiss her forehead, tapping the blindfold. "Take this off when you lock the door."

"Please," She cried, but I shut the door behind me, and almost instantly she locked the bolt. She was that afraid.

I opened my phone and hit the only person I both trusted and hated, as he was my only option.

"Peyton!" Tyson's voice rang out through the house and I fought the urge to go break his fucking face in. But I couldn't do that without revealing myself to him and exposing the fact that Peyton had been with me. And for whatever reason, she was terrified of that, so I had to find a way out.

So I called the next best thing. "Bro," Tamen's voice echoed through the phone as soon as he answered. "Who is he?"

I could hear the alarms in my office going off in the air around him through the phone, no doubt drawing him into my space.

"Peyton's ex. Get rid of him."

"Like permanently?" He asked, and I could hear him running through my house toward the guest house, "Because I'm itching for some bloodshed in the woods, it's far too boring here."

"Not permanently, but feel free to use physical persuasion to get him to fucking leave."

He chuckled as he shut the house door behind him. "Let me guess, you're saving that pleasure for yourself."

"T." I growled, hoping Peyton couldn't hear me through the door. I'd blow my whole cover.

"Is she safe?" He asked.

"Yes."

"Got it, Boss." He said and then I heard him yell out, "Yo, wrong house pizza boy."

I hung the phone up, opening the cameras to watch as he walked up behind Ty from the darkness and rolled my eyes at how absurd Tamen looked. He had on a pair of his signature black dress slacks and shoes but no shirt, and his pearl-handled gun stuck out of the waistband.

He looked insane, which he really fucking was. And Tyson was about to figure out just how much.

"Do I look like a fucking pizza boy?" Tyson adjusted the collar on his cheap shitty suit and squared up to Tamen. "You Lincoln Bryce?"

"Do I look like a self-made billionaire?" Tamen threw back, pulling a cigarette from behind his ear and put it in his lips.

"You look like his thug." Tyson sneered and looked back at the door. "I'm here to see my girlfriend."

"She's busy." Tamen blew smoke directly into his face and grinned.

Tyson bristled. "Doing what? It's after her work hours, and her car is here."

"Well, had you not interrupted, she might have been doing me by now." He shrugged, "Guess she'll have to settle for just the big boss's cock tonight."

"You piece of shit!" Tyson spit and turned to bang on the door again, "Peyton Everett, you whore! Open this fucking door or I swear to God-"

Tamen slammed his face into the solid wood door, cutting off anything else he was about to spit out for Peyton to hear, causing his teeth to lodge themselves into it. "Now see, you're a fucking mood kill, man." Tamen growled, pulling him back by a handful of his hair. "And I'm in the fucking mood to kill, *man*."

I rolled my eyes as Tamen ripped the now crying punk's keys from his hands, popped the trunk to his cheap ass car and shoved him into it, punching him a few times for good measure and slammed it shut.

My brother glanced up at the camera that he knew was discreetly tucked in the corner of Peyton's porch, offered a salute, whistled a silly tune, and hopped into the driver's seat. He skillfully reversed the car, disappearing down the dimly lit driveway without uttering another word.

I had no clue what his plan was, but I knew Peyton's piece of shit ex wasn't going to be a problem anymore tonight.

I clicked off the one light that was on in her room, blanketing the room in darkness once again and then leaned against the door frame outside the bathroom door.

"He's gone, Puppet."

The lock turned, and the door cracked open, yet she stayed hidden behind it. Like such a good fucking girl. "He didn't leave on his own, did he?"

"Does it matter?" I replied.

The sound of her swallowing was loud. "I'm sorry."

"For what, exactly?"

She sighed, and I hated the feeling that noise gave me in my chest. "This was never supposed to be complicated." She sighed again and that same feeling tightened in my chest. "It was supposed to be fun—"

"Were you not having fun?" I growled, remembering how well she was taking my cock and my plug before everything went to hell.

"No! I mean yes," She groaned and thumped her forehead against the door. "I don't know."

"Put your blindfold on." I demanded, pulling my shirt off over my head again and kicking my boots back off.

She hesitated, so I made sure to let the noise of my jeans hitting the floor vibrate through the air between us. "Or you could just tell me who you are." She whispered, "I know you, don't I?"

I pushed the door open and found her standing behind it with her blindfold on like my good little girl and I pulled her out into the bedroom. "You know me better than most, Puppet."

I undid the sash on her robe and pushed it down her arms as I backed her up to the bed. "But I *know* you. It's the only thing stopping you from revealing yourself, isn't it?"

Turning her, I pushed her down onto her stomach on the bed and guided her knees up toward the head of the bed until she was bent over, exposed for me. I pulled the plug out of her ass without warning and she screamed, bucking from the sensation like she forgot she had it in at all. "You're the only thing stopping me from revealing myself." I replied, pouring the icy lube into her slightly gaped hole before stroking my fingers into her, drawing incoherent pleas from her lips before replacing the toy.

Her fear from Tyson's visit had dried her up, so I lubed my cock up and pushed in deep drawing a moan from her lips.

"I don't understand." She moaned, reaching back and digging her nails into my bare thigh as I slowly fucked her.

"You're not ready for me to reveal myself." I growled, spanking her ass and then bottoming out inside of her heavenly body again.

"Yes, I am!" She all but screamed, digging her nails in until the skin broke. "I'm ready!"

"Tell me what your pathetic boyfriend did to make you afraid of him."

Her fingers went lax against my thigh and I grinned sinisterly, knowing I had her.

"He's just an ass." She lied.

And I spanked her ass again for it.

"Puppet."

"No." She hissed, pushing back against me. "You don't get to demand things from me while giving me nothing in return. My answer is no! So either fuck me and make us both come, or get out!"

I grabbed a handful of her hair and pulled her up so she was sitting on my lap as I fucked up into her wet pussy. "I love it when you pull your strings on your own, Puppet." I growled in her ear. "I can't describe the way your defiance makes my cock ache."

"Then show me, baby." She reached behind my neck and ran her nails up the back of my head as I slowed my thrusts. "Because I want to feel you lose control for me."

I bit her shoulder and started playing with her clit as she rocked in my arms. "Hold on tight then, Puppet. Because I want your pretty little claws leaving their marks tonight."

She buried her nails into the back of my neck and started coming on my cock as I grinned into her hair.

*That's it Puppet, brand me as yours just like I did you.*

# CHAPTER 28 - PEYTON

"**W**hat the hell happened?" Olivia's angry voice snapped at me through the phone the next morning.

I blindly made a cup of coffee as my tired brain tried to catch up. It was just after five in the morning, and I had barely gone to sleep before three.

I was dead on my feet.

And also incredibly at peace.

Dane had that effect on me.

I reached for the cup and saw the shiny gold bracelet on my wrist and smiled to myself, remembering the way it made me feel to watch him lock it on me.

It felt final. Like it wasn't something he could take back.

"Peyton!" Olivia snapped, "What the hell is going on?"

"What are you talking about?" I sighed, "I'm not even awake."

"Tyson called mom and dad a half an hour ago." She urged on, and my blood ran cold. "With some *wild* tale about getting assaulted by a thug at Hartington Estate."

"What?" I shook my head.

"He told them he showed up to surprise you with dinner reservations and caught you cheating on him and then he got beat up by *one* of the multiple men you were with!" She shrieked, "Now, I'm one hundred percent in support of you sleeping with whoever the fuck you want to, and however many at a time. But mom and dad aren't so impressed by your wild activities."

"Olivia." I interrupted her tirade, "I'm not sleeping around. There were no *multiple* men, Jesus Christ. I never even answered the door."

She paused, and I could almost hear her disappointment after dispelling her tale. "Then how'd he get beat up?"

Flashbacks assaulted me of hiding in my bathroom as Dane 'took care of him' last night. But he never even left my guest house either, I was sure of it.

"Did you actually see evidence of a beating?" I asked, "You know how over the top Ty is."

She hesitated again, "Well no, but he sounded like he was talking around a mouth full of cotton." She sighed, "But he did show up? What happened?"

"Uh," I cracked my neck, trying to figure out what exactly to tell my sister. As much as I loved her, she had a tendency to over involve herself in my business sometimes. And I wasn't ready to let her opinion darken my happiness now that I was finally living for myself and putting my happiness first.

"Peyton," She groaned, "It was the hacker guy, wasn't it?"

I popped my bottom lip from between my teeth, "What do you mean?"

"The one who put the ghost track on your computer. He was the one who beat Ty up."

"No, he wasn't." I groaned.

"How do you know?" She fired, "He's willing to invade your privacy, I'm sure he knew Ty showed up and probably wanted to keep you all to himself, so he attacked him. Not that Ty doesn't deserve a good ego burst—"

"Olivia!" I yelled, stopping her tirade. "He didn't touch Ty."

"How. Do. You. Know?" She argued. "P, hackers are known to be mentally unstable."

"You're a hacker." I droned.

"Exactly." She fired back instantly, "And I'm crazy."

I rolled my eyes, ignoring her self-deprecating humor. "I know Dane didn't touch him, because he was with me when Ty showed up. Neither of us ever left the house."

There was a long pause and then a low whistle, "Look at you fucking the psycho. Get it, girl."

"Oh, my god." I threw myself down onto the couch, already tired of her shit. "He's not a psycho."

"He's not sane either, is he?"

I hesitated, because the answer was easy. "No. Not exactly."

"Those guys are always the best in bed." She snorted, "Far better than frat boy Tyson, I'm sure."

I snorted, "How would you know how insane men are in bed?"

My sweet innocent little sister chuckled, "Because you're not the only one who likes to invite monsters into bed."

"Come again?" I stuttered. Olivia had always kept things casual with men, choosing to keep them at a distance and use them for the fun she wanted and then move on. She never settled down with anyone specific, so to hear her say there was one in her life caught me off guard.

"I usually do." She snorted and then chuckled. "It's nothing serious, but it's fun."

"Is he sane?" I questioned, not that I could judge her if he wasn't.

"Mostly." She admitted. "But we're getting off topic. Back to Tyson."

"Ew." I cringed, "Even hearing his name makes my skin crawl. How did I date him for years?"

"Because you were doing it for everyone else but yourself."

I sighed, "Yeah well, I think I'm done living like that."

"What are you going to tell our parents?" She asked, "They're going to want answers as to why the answer to their prayers was beaten to a pulp by their perfect daughter's new boyfriend."

"I'll have to get back to you on that one." I took a sip of coffee, "Because I don't know if telling them the truth about Tyson or telling them the truth about me will hurt them more."

"Tell them the truth about Ty." Olivia replied instantly. "You deserve to let yourself off that hook. He's not the one for you."

"I know." I looked at the clock in my kitchen and groaned, "I have to get ready for work."

"How's that going, by the way? We've talked about your personal life more than the one that took you to the middle of nowhere to begin with. Is the old billionaire nice at least?"

I hesitated, remembering the way Lincoln cooked me breakfast the other morning after breaking into my space, guns blazing, to protect me. "I think he's as nice as he knows how to be."

"Oof," She cringed, "He's one of those types then? The kind that is so used to being alone, he doesn't know how to let the sweet, sexy woman he's trapped with, past his sky high walls and protections around his heart?"

I snorted, "You've watched too many Disney fairytales, kid."

"Beauty and the Beast always was your favorite." She hummed, "There was something you loved about the big, unlovable monster worming his way into her heart. So misunderstood by everyone else but her."

I stared off into the distance as she spoke and realized that Lincoln Bryce was exactly like the Beast. He was guarded, angry, and full of misunderstood motives and mystery.

And I was just like Belle, ready to face him on to prove he was just a big fluffy kitty under that fur.

I just wasn't sure where he fit in, with my own dark and dangerous shadow, who actually was a monster, lurking around every corner.

Wouldn't it be a fucking wild world if I could somehow have them both?

THE LINE WALKERS

I eyed my phone on my two-hour break in the middle of the day and squinted in disbelief. Not one mean or threatening text, email, DM, or phone call had come through all day.

Tyson was silent.

Which was terrifying. My ex boyfriend was many things over the length of our relationship, but silent was never one of them. And I still wasn't sure what happened exactly to get him to leave, considering Dane refused to even speak about him after his interruption. But the longer his silence stretched, the more worried I got.

And then there was the awkward conversation with my mom that I had right after Olivia's call, explaining that Ty and I were no longer together and anything he said was probably just out of spite.

I shuddered remembering the barrage of questions she threw my way before six in the morning about my future, my eggs, and my internal clock. Ick, I was only twenty-nine after all.

Olivia's words fluttered back into my brain as I took a bite of my sandwich.

Ty claimed someone beat him up when he came over last night. But Dane was with me the whole time.

My body froze as I imagined Lincoln coming out, like he had the other night when his brother showed up unexpectedly. What if Lincoln Bryce beat up Tyson?

"Holy shit." I whispered, suddenly wet at the idea of him once again defending my honor physically.

I expected that kind of behavior from Dane, yet I had made him promise not to leave the house.

Which left only Lincoln.

And Dane had told me that Lincoln had a state-of-the-art security system, with cameras included. What if he got a security warning and beat the shit out of Ty, thinking he was trying to rob the place or break in?

"Dane?" I called out, picking my phone up and laying it against my bottle of water so I could see the black screen. "Hello?"

"Puppet." His deep vibratory voice echoed a moment later, "Miss me?"

"Are you blocking Tyson from reaching out to me?"

There was an annoyed sigh as I waited for his response, "Why?"

"Because he's radio silent." I stated plainly, treading carefully with my volatile man. "And that's scary."

"You don't have to worry about him. He can't hurt you."

"Not physically," I mused, setting my sandwich down, "You proved that last night."

"Then why are you worried?"

Sighing, I tried to explain. "Because he's a vindictive man who won't just move on silently."

"Meaning?" He prodded.

"Meaning he'll try to ruin my life if he doesn't get his way. And he has the tools to do that."

"Explain that to me, Puppet."

I opened my mouth to divert and brush it off, but I stopped myself. Since the first time I met Tyson Lane, I had covered for his behavior and made excuses for the dynamic between us. But I was so tired of it.

*"Puppet.* Tell me what he has over you."

I swallowed and then tipped my phone down so I wouldn't have to see my pathetic reflection in the screen as I bared my most embarrassing secrets and failures.

"The same thing you have over me." I whispered and closed my eyes, hating the similarities between Dane and Tyson. "Videos."

There was a long pause, and my anxiety grew with each long second of time. "Did you know he took them?"

"Not at the time." I replied, "I wasn't—" I stared up at the ceiling, fighting through the shame. "Completely conscious."

"You were drunk?" He asked, "Or--?"

"I don't know." I whispered, feeling that same disgraceful burn in my chest. "I don't know how it happened. All I know is we were at his friend's birthday party, where I only had one drink, and then I woke up the next morning with only fuzzy snippets of the night."

It didn't take a wise man to figure out what kinds of things could happen to a girl at a party when she was passed out. Or drugged.

I'd never spoken about that night out loud before. Yet after breaking that seal, a part of me wanted to scream all the other horrors I'd endured at Tyson's hand to anyone who'd listen.

Dane brought me back, "I'm going to make him pay." I opened my mouth to tell him no, but no words would come and he could tell. "Aren't you going to tell me not to? Aren't you going to beg me to spare him, Puppet?"

I shook my head as a tear broke over the line of my lashes and rolled down my cheek. "No. Because I think I know what happened." I sniffed, wiping away at the trail, "And I wish I could do it myself."

"I'll get the videos back for you." He vowed, "And I'll make him pay for what he did. Whatever it was."

"Promise me you won't watch them." I took a shuddered breath, "I can't stand the thought of you watching any of them."

"I'll get the videos back, Puppet." He growled. "The nightmare will die there."

I didn't ask if he meant the blackmail or Tyson. That wasn't something I needed verbal confirmation of. I didn't even care as long as he eliminated the secrets Tyson held over my head.

Tyson had made his bed. And Dane was going to make sure that he laid in it.

# CHAPTER 29 - LINCOLN

I could have wiped out Tyson's entire digital footprint remotely. It would have taken zero time at all to infiltrate, expunge, and then destroy everything from the comfort of my home office.

But it wouldn't have fed the monster inside of me demanding blood for what was done.

That justice was going to be served painfully by hand.

"So explain to me again why I'm suddenly appropriate for baby-sitting duty?" Tamen groaned from the couch in my office as I grabbed the last of my things and put it in my bag. "You didn't even want me here a week ago."

"I still don't want you here." I deadpanned, "But if you insist on taking up space, you can earn your room and board while you're here."

"Ah," He dragged the tip of a knife under his fingernail. "Blood labor is how I earn anything these days, brother. Not babysitting."

"Well, if anything happens to Peyton while I'm gone, you'll be paying in blood." I put my bag on my shoulder and faced him head on. "Behave."

He grinned sadistically. "I never promise suitability. But I promise she won't be harmed while you're gone."

"Good." I walked out, and he followed me into the hallway.

"When are you planning on coming clean to her?" Tamen asked, and I rolled my eyes. He had no specifics about what was going on between Peyton and I. But he could tell she wasn't involved with *me*, romantically. He has spent the entire first two days watching our interactions in the house and could see the divide there.

"When the truth no longer matters." I kept walking. Had Peyton not been in her guest house, I wouldn't have been so open with our conversation.

Successfully reaching the garage door without any further interference from him, I believed I had made it out unscathed. But his voice called out one last thing right before I stepped through the opening.

"He was wrong, you know." I glanced over my shoulder, trying to figure out what he was talking about, and stopped when I saw the seriousness in my jackass brother's eyes. "Dad." He said and my blood raged into an inferno with just the utterance of our father's existence inside of my home. "You were never weak or forgettable. He was the weak man who couldn't own up to his mistakes when he got caught with two families.""It doesn't matter." I shut it down before his words could fester.

"It does matter, Linc. Because if it didn't, you wouldn't be hiding your true self from Peyton." He tilted his head to the side, "You wouldn't use secrets and darkness to get her to love you."

"I'm not." I bit out bitterly, "I'm using blood and vengeance to do that." Leaving as I had intended, I got into a black Aston Martin that Tamen had gifted me years ago on my birthday and burned rubber on my way down the driveway.

His words were too close to home, and I needed the ache they caused in my chest to go away. And I'd get that calm peacefulness by avenging Peyton's nightmare.

She once dreamed of monsters and things that went bump in the night, like they were a bad thing. But her monster was going to right every wrong done to her.

No one could heal my pain, so I'd heal hers and live in her happiness second hand.

THE LINE WALKERS

I walked across the dark parking lot, taking my place in the shadows where I belonged and waited.

And watched.

The apartment that Peyton and Tyson shared was on the third floor of a mid-range building on the outskirts of the city. The apartment had a lack of security, and their living room windows were conveniently connected to a fire escape.

It was too easy, really.

Ripe pickings, if you will.

I just had to time it right.

Not that Tyson would be any bit of a fight against me, I was just hoping to avoid drawing a crowd. Because if there was a crowd, I'd have to work fast.

And I wanted to take my fucking time with the limp dick prick.

Before I could move from my spot in the shadows, I sensed movement to my right, though there was no disturbance to the shrubs I was standing in. It was too dark to make out the way the dark somehow got darker, but I knew what that meant.

"Maddox."

A sinister grin broke through the darkness and I rolled my eyes as his dark creepy silhouette took his place next to mine.

"Who are we hunting, Linc?"

Fucking psychopaths.

"Leave."

"Aw come on," He pushed his shoulder into mine and looked at the building. "It must be good if Tamen risked his life to contact me."

Tamen and Maddox had a feud deep enough to bleed them both dry before they wised up and saved themselves. It was more than likely going to cause their actual deaths someday. I knew exactly what kind of sour taste it must have left in Tamen's mouth to reach out to my only other ally.

"I don't need any help." While gazing at my target window, I noticed the light inside turn off. Tyson was milking a serious set of wounds to his face, which apparently made him decide to stay in tonight and go to bed early.

That was perfect. It would give me more time to draw out his torture before daylight crested the skyline.

"This isn't about help, Linc." He turned to look at me and I glanced over at his face. "I know the Ghost doesn't need my help." Maddox looked back up at the building, keyed into where I was looking at Tyson's window. "But a little company never hurt."

"I work alone." I picked up my bag from the ground and walked out of the tree line.

His silent footsteps followed. I knew if I looked behind me, he'd be impossible to see in the shadows. The man didn't exist unless he wanted you to know he did. "I remember a time when you would have been so excited for a chance to work collaboratively that you would have foamed at the mouth. Which means this one must be special."

"Yeah, it's fucking special." I broke the cheap lock on the fire escape ladder and pulled it down. How fucking unsafe was Peyton while she lived here if I could get the ladder down that led to her window that easily. Not anymore. She'd never come back to the place. "Which is why I'm doing it by myself."

"Fine." He followed me up the ladder silently. I was always in awe of how he moved without a trace. Especially for a man as big as we were, even I couldn't move that quietly. "I'll just watch the show. Maybe they have snacks."

"You're a fucking nutcase." I barked, climbing to the third floor.

"Duh." He chuckled. "Normal is boring."

I scoffed but stayed silent as I made it to the landing outside the apartment I was after. Maddox edged up next to me and watched as I tested one window; it opened without any effort. I shook my head, even more frustrated that Peyton had lived with such a lack of security around her, and then silently crawled in.

"It's no fun if you don't have to work for it." Maddox whispered, sliding it closed behind us as I looked around.

Peyton's scent hit me like a brick wall the second I stood tall. She was everywhere.

Yet Tyson didn't deserve to live in her aroma, even if she was physically with me. Something I'd rectify by the time I left.

I took the edge of my gloved finger and pushed a lamp on the end table until it fell to the floor, crashing into a million pieces.

"Original." Maddox rolled his eyes as he walked into the kitchen and opened the fridge. The fucker was *always* hungry.

"Peyton?" Tyson's nasally voice called out from the bedroom as he clicked his light on. "Is that you?"

He came rushing out into the living room like he was about to rush her when I stuck my foot out and tripped him, sprawling him out onto the floor.

He caught the sight of Maddox first raiding his fridge, and then rolled over, gasping in fear as I stood over him. I dropped my bag onto the floor, letting the clanking of its implements rattle around and fray his little bitch boy nerves further. "What if I told you that you would never *see* Peyton, ever again?"

# CHAPTER 30 - PEYTON

## THE LINE WALKERS

A s soon as my feet hit the floor, I knew my stalker had visited overnight. But he snuck in and out without waking me.

Or fucking me.

*Rude.*

I stretched, shaking off the dreams of my monster, and wrapped my robe around my body before starting my search for coffee. If he had come to me last night while I slept, like I hoped he would, I wouldn't have dreamed of him.

When he was near, my dreams were empty. Like he could only exist in one reality at a time.

But he didn't wake me when he snuck in, and I was going to figure out what he did while he was lurking.

As soon as I made it out to the living space, though, I figured it out.

"Oh, my god." I whispered when I saw the pile of various electronics piled on the kitchen table. And then I saw the rest of the things laid out around the living room.

*My* things.

My clothes, pictures, keepsakes. All from my apartment that I shared with Tyson. Things I wasn't sure I'd see again if I ended things with him while I was staying at Hartington Estate. "Oh, Dane." I ran my fingers over the blanket I always cuddled under when I read on the couch in the middle of the night to avoid going to bed.

"You rang, Puppet." His baritone voice tingled my ears as it flowed through some invisible speaker somewhere. I left my phone in the bedroom when I got up, so I knew he was watching me on the cameras he hid somewhere.

It should have bothered me, but I didn't hate it one bit. I loved being the center of his attention.

"What did you do?" I asked gently, trying to curb the fear building inside of me as I saw every last piece of my existence removed from that apartment and hand delivered to me. All the things that mattered to me returned.

"Nothing." He replied dismissively.

I kept walking around and stopped when I got to the table with the electronics on it. A laptop, tablet, cell phones, two to be exact, external hard drives and thumb drives all littered the top. I picked up the cell phone I recognized as Tyson's but gasped and dropped it back into the pile when I felt something sticky on the thumb print sensor.

I looked at my finger and saw a crimson stain on it. "Is that—"

"No."

I backed up from the pile, looking around the belongings with a darker shadow over my joy. "It's blood." I scrubbed my hand up and down the side of my robe, trying to get the physical burn of Tyson's blood from my skin. "Oh Dane, what did you do?"

"Puppet." He growled, "I already answered that question."

"What am I supposed to do with all of this?" I shrieked, waving my arms down to the electronics. "What if someone comes looking for them?"

"No one is going to come looking for them." He replied. "I'll take them back if that's what you'd like and I'll dispose of them. I just wanted you to know that it was done. Your videos and pictures are gone."

I froze, staring at all the stuff, and remembered the real reason he went there at all. "Did—" I stammered, and then looked up at the ceiling, "Did you watch them?"

There was a pause before he answered, "You asked me not to."

"That doesn't answer my question." I whispered back, already knowing the truth.

"Go into your bedroom." He replied, and I shook my head in confusion. "Now, Puppet."

"Why?" I spun around, not exactly knowing where the cameras were.

"Because you need to take a deep breath and relax." He stated, "And you're going to do it in your bedroom."

"I don't—"

"Now, Puppet!" He bellowed, and I turned, walking away from the blood coated stuff and went into my room. "Good girl." Dane's voice echoed through my phone speaker. "Now lay back down in bed."

"Dane." I whined, trying to control the panic that was burning in my stomach. I moved on auto pilot and laid down in bed, even covering myself up with my blankets like I hadn't just peeled myself out of it all a few minutes ago.

"Close your eyes, baby." He instructed and my eyelids drooped as I did as I was told. "Take a deep breath."

I filled my lungs and slowly exhaled it as the lights in my house all clicked off remotely, cascading darkness over me again like a warm blanket. "Why didn't you wake me last night?"

"Because I needed to rid my mind and my skin of what I did. I couldn't touch you with that darkness."

My heart hurt for my monster. He had done something dark for me. "I need you."

"I'm right here." He growled, and I could feel the need in his voice as he said it.

"No," I shook my head, "Here. I need to feel you."

His voice cracked, "I can't. I'm not around."

"Where are you?"

"Handling something. I'll come to you tonight."

I sank into the comfortable bedding around me and forced myself to be a big girl and wait for him to be available for me. And then an idea came to mind.

I tossed the blankets back, and he growled, "I didn't say you could get up yet."

"Just wait." I frantically tore the end table drawer open next to my bed and pulled out the item that had mocked me for days now.

"Puppet." The ice in his voice raced through my veins. What I wouldn't have given to see his face as he watched me. Could he see what I was doing?

I picked up my phone and propped it against my lamp as I turned on the single light. Instantly, the camera blinked to life and my reflection lit up the screen. He was watching.

I ran my fingers over the black onyx jewels in the eyes of the skull and then bent the closure, opening it.

The black ribbon necklace that Dane bought me slid through my fingers as I wrapped it around my neck. I leaned forward toward my phone to see it clearly in the camera as I lined the skull back up and then closed it.

"Peyton." He groaned, and I could hear his deep breathing crackle through the speaker.

"I'm yours." As I sat up, I couldn't help but admire the way the entire thing looked on my neck as I fingered the closure. I had been so intimidated by it when I first asked him what it was. But then he slayed my biggest demon. He gave me back all the pieces of *me*.

And I realized that there was no one out there I wanted more than Dane. So I wrapped his collar around my neck to hold all of those pieces together so they'd never break apart again.

"You can lock it when you come to me." I picked up the pin key and laid it down on the end table, staring at him through the camera. "Because I'm yours."

He growled an animalistic noise, and I shivered. It didn't matter that I didn't know his last name or what his face looked like.

He was mine, and I was his.

And I was committing myself to him because he was the only one to ever actually be honest with me. He never lied. He never tricked me. He was perfect. My perfect dark stalker.

THE LINE WALKERS

L

incoln and Tamen were gone when I got into the main house for work. A note left on the counter told me they'd be gone all day and to take the day off.

As if.

I couldn't spend the day in my guest house with all of Tyson's electronics taunting me from the kitchen table. I didn't ask Dane if he was alive or dead. That wasn't information I wanted right at the moment.

I did, however, strip everything off except for the skulls that Dane had bought me and put on a show for him. I leaned back and spread my thighs for him as I played with myself for him, thanking him for what he did for me the only way I knew how.

He wasn't the type of man who would appreciate a thank you. I had to show him just how fucking much I needed him after what he did.

God, the growls and moans he rewarded me with through my speakers while he watched would play on repeat in my head all damn day long.

I stood in the upstairs den, dusting the window frame, and eyed the pool deck below as I tried to stay busy. Maybe I'd take a dip in the hot tub to entertain myself with my *day off*. It was too cold to go for a swim in the pool now that fall was officially upon us thanks to the bitter northern east coast weather. But the hot tub would feel—invigorating. I grinned to myself, remembering how fucking good that jet had felt on my clit that very first time I took a swim.

As I stared out the window unseeing, I traced my fingertips over the clasp of my choker while I remembered the way Lincoln had stood over me as I orgasmed for a second time. Even as much as I tried to pretend he didn't actually see anything; I knew deep down he had watched me come the first time with my tits out and my head tipped back as I rocked back and forth on the jetted seat.

Guilt washed over me as my body warmed from the memory. I didn't feel guilt for lusting after another man when I was newly committed to Dane. I felt guilty because a part of me felt sad knowing I'd never feel the sensation of Lincoln's touch on my skin the way I had fantasized about after watching the video of him jacking off to finding me with my panties off in his closet.

It was Dane's fault actually. All of it, really. But nonetheless that seed had been planted and my body craved the unknown.

I shook off the daydream and walked away from the window, already feeling the tingle in my blood as I solidified my plan to go for a dip. So what if Lincoln or Tamen came back and found me? I was told to take the day off, after all.

When I rounded the corner to leave the den, I stopped in my tracks when the door to Lincoln's office caught my attention. It was at the end of the hall and I never went down there because of his strict instructions to stay away, but from my position, I could see the faint glow of light coming from around the door.

It was ajar.

Did they return earlier than I expected? Was my plan to orgasm in the hot tub foiled before I even got in?

"Hello?" I called, standing in the main hallway. "Lincoln?"

I waited, but there was no response. Without thinking, I took a few steps closer to the plain black door that always intrigued me. It festered that old saying, *don't touch what isn't yours*. My instructions were explicit from day one; Do not enter the office for any reason.

Yet as I stood outside of it, a mere foot away, my fingers burned to touch the metal handle and open it. "Tamen?" I called, one last time trying to convince myself to stop. Beyond the point of no return, the color of the lights inside captivated me, and with just one finger, I pushed the door open, almost as if I didn't want to leave behind any trace of my presence.

As I entered the dimly lit room, the mesmerizing rainbow kaleidoscope effect of LED lights glowing immediately captured my attention, making me feel like a moth being drawn to a flame.

Just as my foot touched the threshold, the key lights slowly intensified, revealing the room in a comforting, radiant glow, as if it was unveiling its secrets to me. Along one wall of the enormous room was a massive desk, but instead of facing out into the room, it faced the wall.

At least I was sure there was a wall somewhere under the dozens of computer monitors that created a reflective surface covering every inch. The LED lights wove between each monitor and left a psychedelic effect on the black screens.

"Wow." I whispered, imagining all the tech stuff that Lincoln controlled from those monitors. It was how he made his fortune, after all. I turned from the captivating electronic wall and took in the rest of the space. I wasn't sure what I was expecting exactly, but it seemed far more normal than what I would have thought the mysterious space to look like. Two massive couches created a seating area and a wet bar adorned the other wall, lined with liquor bottles and snacks like a high-end movie theater.

Was that snack bar why Lincoln rarely left the room for nourishment?

I shook off the thought, a smirk playing on my lips as I pictured his blood thickening like syrup, a result of the copious amounts of sugar on the shelves. "My, my Mr. Bryce, what a sweet tooth you have." I needed to leave, since I assured myself there were no dead bodies or anything in the off-limits space.

Fictional images of an office lined with dead bodies and Dane standing amongst them in the center assaulted me and I leaned on the door to a built-in cabinet across from his desk, disturbing the door enough to open.

"Shit." I pushed the door shut, trying to close it back to how I found it, but something fell when it opened, getting wedged in the way. "C'mon." I whispered, leaning down to pick up what fell and pulling it free.

When I stood up with it in my hand, my blood ran cold and my stomach dropped into my toes as I stared down at it.

A Ghostface mask.

Just like the one Dane wore.

With shaking hands, I opened the door wider and dropped the mask when I saw what was inside.

Clothes. Not just any clothes, though. A dark, hooded sweater and black jeans I recognized from the first night Dane chased me through the woods. That didn't make any sense.

"No." As I pushed the hooded sweater to the side, a wave of panic washed over me when my fingers grazed the leather cuffs that had once imprisoned me on the bench in the corn maze. "No." I cried out silently, backing away from the cabinet like it would burn me if I touched anything else. The desk behind me, adorned with colorful LED lights, provided the perfect setting for the only photo Dane had ever sent me.

I was in that very office.

Lincoln's office.

Dane's office.

I bumped into the desk in my rush to get away from the closet, and suddenly all the screens jolted to life as I jumped and covered my mouth. My eyes flicked from screen to screen in disbelief as they revealed themselves to me.

I was on every screen.

Every. Single. One.

In some sort of way, I covered each screen. The inside of my guest house was on one, live streaming it. A still image from earlier today when I sat on the edge of my bed, fastening the choker around my neck, covered another.

My skin crawled when I looked from each screen to another, seeing myself on them. It was the same thing on all of them, like a shrine to me. I was the focus of everything.

I covered my mouth with my hand to stifle the scream that tried to rip from my lips as I realized what it all meant.

Dane was Lincoln Bryce.

Lincoln was my monster.

My stalker.

He lied. God, he lied about everything. I was so fucking stupid.

I couldn't tear my eyes away from the images on the screens, trying to figure out how extensive his reach was into my life when one image I didn't recognize caught my eye.

It was of me.

But not recently. I leaned forward, trying to see the background better and realized that I wasn't standing like I thought I was, but laying down on a tan surface and my eyes were half open.

Every vein in my body froze to ice when I finally figured out what I was looking at.

It was of me *that* night. That horrifying, painful night that I couldn't remember, no matter how hard I tried. "God, please." I grabbed the mouse and rolled the cursor over to that screen and died a little inside when a play button popped up in the corner.

It was the video.

The video that Tyson had alluded to enough to hold over my head for three years straight. Before I could think better of it, I clicked play and fell into the chair as the shaky cell phone video started playing. As it played, I dragged it from the edge monitor to the largest center one.

The background noise was so overwhelming that it was difficult to discern the actual number of people in the room, but when I figured it out, I wished I could forget already.

Four men loomed above me as I lay mostly unconscious on a bed in the center.

*"Fucking lightweight,"* Tyson's sick voice called out above everyone else as he kneeled on the bed next to me. *"She didn't even finish her drink."*

Tyson's actions caused the group to become rowdy, as he started unbuttoning my shirt, and amidst the commotion, another voice called out. *"It means she wants it! She didn't even need a full dose to get easy for dick."*

My heart pounded in my chest, escalating with each passing second, and I watched in horror as Tyson slowly undressed me, followed by himself. With his friends cheering obscene things, he pushed my skirt up and climbed on top of me.

*"Choke her."*

*"Open her legs wider, I can't see!"*

*"Bend her over so you can fuck her harder!"*

And they just got worse the longer I watched. I couldn't move. I couldn't close my eyes to stop the images from burning a permanent scar into my brain as Tyson raped me for his friend's enjoyment.

Similar to that night, I felt frozen and powerless to stop the torment. That night, as Tyson used me, I was trapped, and I could barely lift my arms to stop the assault.

Watching the video, I felt a surge of adrenaline. Memories of that terrifying night came rushing back, and I watched as I instinctively swung my arms at Tyson, but my attempts were feeble and powerless. Because even in my drugged state, I knew my boyfriend wasn't safe. I knew it wasn't okay.

Apparently, I was the only one in the room that did, though. The longer I watched, the more apprehensive I became about what else I might see if I kept on.

Just as my stress reached its peak, the volume of the party suddenly increased, providing a momentary respite. Then, a voice pierced through the commotion, announcing the arrival of the police. We were all of age, but noise disturbances were still illegal, apparently.

I cried out silently as the torment stopped.

In a hurried motion, Ty pulled my clothes back over my body, slung me over his shoulder, and grumbled about the unexpected interruption, all before the video abruptly cut off.

Did the arrival of the cops prevent me from being assaulted by everyone in that room that night?

I guess I'd never know, because there was nothing else after that video. Just a still frame of me looking up from Tyson's shoulder as everyone complained about missing out on their chance to rape me.

It felt like my brain was short-circuited, and I acted without thinking.

Grabbing a glass paperweight that sat on the desk, I slammed it into the large center screen, shattering it.

Shattering the image of me on it.

The glass broke in my hand and cut my palm, but I hardly felt it.

Blood slowly dripped from my fingers onto the desk, as I reached a state of numbness and my eyes blinked in disbelief at the multitude of images flashing on the screen.

I begged him not to watch it. I begged him to spare me the shame of knowing he saw what happened to me that night. But he just couldn't let my fragile heart heal from it. He had to know just how broken I really was.

Leaving the mess in my wake, I turned and walked out of the office, with blood roaring in my ears. I couldn't think as I walked through the house, trailing a crimson track behind me all the way to my guest house.

There was no doubt in my mind that I had to go.

I had to leave.

I had to scoop up the pieces I thought were all picked back up already and leave while I still could.

Before Lincoln returned.

*Dane.*

Before Dane returned.

I packed my clothes up in the two suitcases I brought for my stay and loaded them in my car. As I gathered the items Dane had fetched from my apartment, the familiar scent wafted up to my nose, reminding me of home, before I tossed them into my trunk. As if I could lock them and my memories away and never think of them again.

When I realized that my entire life could fit into the small confines of my car, an overwhelming sadness washed over me. I couldn't name the feeling exactly, but I guessed it felt a lot like grief.

Shame.

Disgrace.

Before I left, I let my phone slip from my grasp and crash onto the floor of the guest house foyer, fully aware of Dane's watchful eyes and ears through my electronics and the cameras in the house.

As I was about to step out, I caught sight of my reflection in the mirror behind the door. The vacant expression in my eyes held me captive for a moment.

I didn't even recognize myself.

I saw only a distorted person in the mirror, a mere shadow of who I thought I was that morning. My eyes fell to my neck, immediately captured by the skull, its haunting black eyes seeming to peer into my soul like *he* was seeing everything, too.

With my blood covered hand, I forcefully tore the black ribbon from my neck and let it fall onto the floor next to my phone.

The girl who put the collar on that morning, eager to let someone claim her, was dead.

The girl I forced myself to be for years, bending myself into smaller pieces of myself to appease those around me, was dead.

Peyton Everett was dead.

I would never be the same.

# CHAPTER 31 - LINCOLN

## THE LINE WALKERS

With every step I took through the house, my feet seemed to sink deeper into the floor, as if invisible anchors weighed them down. I was bone fucking weary and just wanted to crawl into bed beside Peyton and sleep with her wrapped around me.

*My* Peyton.

She put my necklace on. Witnessing her carefully clasping the skull pendant around her neck, a surge of electricity coursed through my chest. Something that felt a lot like what I imagined love to feel like, though I wouldn't know. I had never loved or been loved before.

But I was ready to lay it all out for her.

At first, there would be complications when I revealed myself to her. I was sure of it. She'd balk at it simply because she was going to feel duped. But she'd come around to it eventually, I'd make sure of it.

I'd also make sure to lock the fucking necklace first, reminding her of her vow to me.

"So you think she's going to freak when she finds out what you did to her fuck boy?" Tamen asked, following me up the stairs, and I looked over my shoulder to glare at him.

The tracker on Peyton's phone confirmed that she was in the guest house, but I couldn't let my guard down. I needed to ensure that he didn't expose me before I could make my move and come clean first hand. I was so busy cleaning up messes and putting out fires today that I didn't have a second of time to check in on her since our morning fun without Tamen looking in over my shoulder. And knowing my pretty little Puppet, there was no guarantee she wouldn't be doing something naughty if I randomly opened my cameras and I wouldn't give him the privilege of seeing that.

I'd hate to have to remove his eyeballs, too. Two sets in two days was a bit much.

Turning back around at the top of the stairs, I stopped, with one foot in midair, as something caught my eye on the floor.

Crimson.

"Is that—?" Tamen asked as he nodded to the trail across the floor leading down the hallway. "Blood."

"Peyton!" I pulled my gun and walked down the hall, following the trail as my stomach turned violently. I could feel it in my gut that she was hurt, like a new sense that had just revealed itself.

As I turned the corner, my chest seized up in agony when I saw the trail disappearing into my office, where the door was ajar. "Oh, fuck." Tamen groaned, following me as I took off running toward it.

"Pey—" As I pushed the door open all the way and walked in, a chill ran down my spine and I couldn't help but shiver at the sight in front of me.

The mask I wore during our chase in the corn maze ended up abandoned on the ground, right next to the cabinet where I stored

Dane's clothes. The door was open and the cuffs I used on her hung askew off the shelf.

I turned and my attention was drawn to the computer screens at my desk. Most of them were dark, but the one in the middle stood out with its cracked glass, resembling a spider's web. The glass orb paperweight laid on the desk covered in blood with jagged broken edges.

I shook the mouse to wake up the system and died inside when the video of Peyton's assault lit up the broken screen. "No." I whispered, haunted by what I knew happened.

And then I ran.

"Peyton!" I bellowed as I tore through the house, desperate to get to her. She knew who I was. And she knew that I had seen the video. Fuck!

I shoved the back door open to the guest house and froze right inside the doorway.

She was gone. I could feel it in my bones.

Her things were gone from where I left them when I gave them back to her the night before. The clothes, blankets, pictures, and other meaningful possessions; gone. There wasn't anything of hers left in the now cold and vacant space. All of Tyson's electronics still littered the kitchen table, but that was it.

"Baby, please!" I screamed as I searched the house anyway, pleading with any power above to make her show up in one of the rooms. But she was gone.

As soon as I ripped the front door open, I noted her car had disappeared as well. Her absence washed over me, and my knees buckled as I fell backward into the wall, ripping down a meaningless picture on my way down. I landed in a heap on the floor, staring unseeing at the wall as I tried to form a plan to find her and make it all right.

All I had to do was locate her and explain, regardless of her where she was, I had to find her. She said she was mine! She put the fucking necklace on and promised herself to me!

"Linc." Tamen spoke softly from where he crouched next to me. I blindly looked over at him, hardly able to make out the shape of his face as he held something between his fingers to me.

Blinking and forcing my body to sit upright and focus, the object finally became clear and my heart completely died inside of my chest, once and for all.

Her bloody black necklace hung limply from his fingers, with the skull closure broken and useless.

"No."

# CHAPTER 32 - PEYTON

## THE LINE WALKERS

I couldn't get over how different the landscape was here. It was early December, but there wasn't a single snowflake to be found in sunny Miami, Florida. It made me miss home.

Massachusetts never felt like anything spectacular when I lived there my whole life, but since being gone for over three months, I ached for its familiarity. I ached to smell the crisp winter air with each breeze and the age-old Christmas scents lingering from the trees and decorations as I prepared for the holidays.

My new apartment was bare. No tree. No stockings. There wasn't a lit string of lights to be found. It was bare.

Like my heart.

Every single day that passed since I left Hartington made my heart a little more unrecognizable. I couldn't feel *anything*.

It was as though I was on autopilot, surviving with the little pieces of myself piled in my arms. I was no closer to putting them back together again, because I couldn't move forward when I was stuck in the past. Instead, I just carried them around with me, balancing them precariously so I wouldn't drop one of them, losing it forever and getting that much further from repairing myself back to what I was before.

Or better.

God, I just wanted to be better than I was before.

I wanted to be who I thought I was with Dane.

I wanted that brief glimpse back of the girl that his attention, affection, and dedication had blossomed into.

Before I learned the truth.

Before I saw the video.

Before I walked away from the one thing I wanted, because he was all made up in my head.

The worst part of it all was I missed Dane. I missed him with every single ounce of myself. And part of me missed Lincoln too, now that I knew he was the man I'd fallen for as well. I just couldn't convince my heart to stop hurting every time I thought of him.

And then I'd remember that he hadn't reached out once. Not that I exactly left my forwarding address or anything, but still. For a man of his abilities, I thought he would of at least... I don't know, *called me*. Maybe thrown in a *I'm sorry* or twelve.

But there had only been radio silence. And the longer it went on, the longer I had to believe it was for the best.

Because if I didn't, Olivia was the first one to remind me I was better off without his lying, manipulating, overbearing ass.

Her words, not mine.

She was my savior in the whole thing, actually. Without her and her own tech skills, I wouldn't have known where to turn when I walked away from Hartington for the last time. She scooped me and my little pieces up and hid me away from the world and Dane's watchful eyes while we made a plan. My whole life I had protected and guided Olivia, but she was there to do the same in my moment of need and I'd never be able to repay her for that.

After a few days of mental breakdowns and pity parties, I had to get another job and another plan. Because tears and self-pity didn't pay the bills.

And since I didn't have my apartment or savings account with Tyson anymore, I had a lot of fucking bills to pay.

Tyson.

Oof.

I didn't know if I'd ever know the full story, but according to the news reports, a freak car accident on a rainy night outside of Boston left him permanently blind. I'm talking the kind of blind where they had to remove his actual eyeballs, blind.

I shuddered just thinking of it. Which I didn't do often, because then I'd have to acknowledge how deep down I knew his loss of sight wasn't from a car accident at all.

It was Dane's doing. For what Tyson did to me.

And if I thought about Dane physically blinding a man for me, I got warm and fuzzy all over, in some warped sense of commitment and loyalty from him. Which wasn't true at all, given he'd lied about something that was so much more important than Tyson.

He watched the video.

He saw my attack and didn't tell me.

A part of my soul would never heal knowing he saw firsthand how broken I was. How all my little pieces fell apart in the first place.

No man could love someone through that. Not entirely. There would always be darkness around something that was supposed to be built in beauty.

So I ran.

Then I hid.

Until I just existed.

Working in a popular tourist hotel in Miami gave me enough mental stimulation to not want to stab a fork into my thigh to make sure I was still alive, but just barely. I used a fake name, thanks to Olivia, to get the job, and got a small studio apartment where I slept in between wild shifts. But that was it, that was the extent of my life, post Dane.

Or Lincoln.

I didn't even know how to refer to him. So I didn't.

I had just worked a double at the hotel, managing the night shift and staying when the day shift manager called in sick. The only benefit to doing doubles like that was I was so bone weary tired after it, there wasn't much energy left to think in the end.

So as I slowly climbed up all four flights of stairs to my apartment, I didn't have the energy to miss him. Or hate him. I didn't even have the energy to think about him.

But when I started down the hallway toward my door, though, I noticed something laying on the ground outside my door, and I instantly saw his face in my mind. I saw the packages he had delivered to me in secret when I was right next to him in real life.

At first, I wasn't sure it was at my door, thanks to the long row of apartments, but as I got closer, I realized it was.

And that's when I stopped walking, afraid to get any closer to the large brown box sitting on the ground. My heart started racing in my chest as I stood immobilized.

Did he find me?

How?

I looked up and down the hallway, but it was empty. There was a bit of hope burning in my chest that as I looked behind me, he'd be standing there, watching me. But he wasn't.

Would I feel awful embarrassment if I picked up the box only to realize it was meant for one of my neighbors and he still, in fact, didn't care that I was gone?

I rolled my eyes to myself, intent on proving that it was, in fact, at my door by mistake, but as I leaned down and picked it up, it was my name on the label, with no return address.

My real name, not the one I'd been using for the last three months, either. Again, I looked up and down the empty hallway. Anxiety crawled up my spine as I undid the three locks on my door and rushed inside, with the box of uncertainty clutched in my arms.

I set it down on the small table and walked away from it, almost as if it would blow up at any moment if I stayed too close. Or maybe that was just my erratically beating heart that could blow up any second.

Part of me wanted to tear into it right away, and the other part of me wanted to throw it down the garbage shoot without cutting the tape open at all. So instead of making a rash decision either way around it, I walked away and busied myself with a steaming hot shower.

I stripped down, ridding my body of the clothes I wore for the last almost twenty-four hours straight, and turned the water on. And as with most days, I stared at the gold bracelet still wrapped around my wrist when it caught my eye.

The only piece of Dane I allowed myself to keep, because it had been about me. The jewels in the eyes of the skull matched mine. When he gave it to me, he told me he wanted me to wear it in honor of choosing myself above everyone else for the first time in my life.

Yet when I was alone, it reminded me of him. And that was one minor reason I kept it on.

Additionally, it was locked, and I would have needed to break it in order to take it off, but I wasn't prepared to destroy it. Not yet, at least.

I scrubbed every inch of my body even though it wasn't hair wash day to stay as busy as possible while I wrote out a pros and cons list in my head.

To open it, or to not.

To know if I was crazy, or to not.

"Fuck." I sighed, staring at it thirty minutes later after avoiding it as long as I possibly could. I *had* to know!

I grabbed a knife and slit the tape open, but instead of setting the knife down, I held onto it, like I may need it for whatever was inside.

Though when I pulled out the carefully packaged mass in the center, nothing at all made sense.

It was a tablet and a cell phone.

My hands shook as I eyed up the technology I hadn't afforded myself since I left Lincoln's house three months ago. I didn't want him to have free access to me like he did when I lived there, so I went without.

I was the only almost thirty-year-old in the world without a cell phone. And I didn't hate it.

But eying up the fancy block in my trembling hand, a shiver ran down my spine, knowing he could have been watching me again already through it. That familiar excitement of being the very center of his attention bloomed in my lower belly.

A folded piece of paper sat between the phone and the tablet, and I hesitated before pulling it free. My hands shook so hard I nearly dropped it twice before I could get it open.

Almost instantly, my heart fell to my stomach when I saw the manly script written across the entire piece of paper.

Dane.

My heart ached immediately from just seeing his handwriting.

I fell down into the kitchen chair as my eyes started flying across the words, eating them up with an intensity like a starving man's first smell of food in years.

*Puppet,*

*My achingly beautiful Puppet. I've started and stopped this letter a hundred different times since finally locating you four days ago. I haven't been able to stop the spiral inside of my head every time I realized you were finally within reach for the first time in months.*

*I can't describe the burning need building inside of me every single second of every day since you ran away from me.*

*I'm crazed by your absence.*

*I'm feral for your touch.*

*I'm desperate for your love, again.*

*Puppet, I love you. And I can confidently say I've never loved another human being on this planet before. Not once.*

*Not until I met you. It wasn't by choice; it wasn't a decision I had any control over. It was necessary.*

*You. Are. Necessary. Peyton.*

*I love you.*

*And I know I shouldn't have lied to you about who I really was. I simply didn't know how to convince you to love both sides of me.*

*The sane, and the not.*

*The good man, and the wicked one.*

*But fuck, Puppet, loving you is easy. God, it's the most natural thing I've ever felt before. It gives my deepest troubles peace for the first time in my life. I'm so sorry I broke you before I told you that.*

*I'm so sorry you know what happened to you that night, because the only thing I ever wanted was to shield you from that memory returning. I never wanted that pain in your soul. I wanted to burden that for you. Damnit Peyton, I wanted your soul free of that darkness.*

*I should have given you that choice, and I should have been there to hold you when you saw it. I should have done better.*

*I'm sorry.*

*You came into my life because I needed you. My need manipulated every single piece of our story past you applying for a random job. My desires and needs were the driving force for everything.*

*But no more.*

*I'm giving you the choice to let me back in or not. I'm begging you to give me the chance.*

*The cell phone and the tablet were programmed specifically for you by a friend of mine. They're completely impenetrable to me, I can't access them no matter how hard I try.*

*And I'll fucking try, because I'm that obsessed with you.*

*But you're safe, and you're in control. Because they're not only impenetrable to me, but they're also linked to me.*

*To my phone.*

*To my cameras.*

*To my life. You have full access to every single second of my life.*

*Watch me. Study me.*

*Stalk me, Puppet.*

*You're in control of this, from this moment on. Learn as little or as much about me, both sides of me, as you want. But I beg of you, baby, give me the chance.*

*Give me the chance to show you every part of me before you decide if you can let me in again.*

*I love you.*

*I'll always love you.*

*I'll always want you.*

*Come home to me, Puppet.*

*Come home to your monster and let me feed your needs the way only I can.*

*-Yours, Dane.*

My tears blurred the ink at the bottom of the page and I tipped my head back to staunch the flow as I waved the paper back and forth through the air, trying desperately to dry it.

I wanted to reread his words every single day because they were the truest things I'd ever been given from someone before. I believed every one of them.

But I didn't know how to go back to him after everything, so much time had passed.

Wiping away the tears and taking a deep breath, I eyed the electronics again like I was staring at Pandora's box.

All the secrets to Dane's world laid at my fingertips, but I knew if I gave in to taking even just a peek, I'd be even further from moving on than I'd got in the three months since leaving.

If I was being honest, though, I wasn't any closer to being over him. I didn't think I ever would be.

Before I could convince myself not to, I powered on the tablet and felt my heart do somersaults in my chest as it loaded. As soon as the menu popped up, I gasped as I saw all the available cameras to view.

Forty-two.

Forty-two different angles to use, to watch him. There was nowhere to hide from me.

The camera's with movement on them were highlighted in red to signal which ones were active and before I could stop myself, I clicked on the one that was labeled office.

And then there he was.

In vivid color was Lincoln. But he didn't look like anything I'd ever seen the mysterious businessman look like before.

He sat in the chair at his desk, working on something, but I couldn't see the screens because the camera seemed to be tucked between two of the screens, facing him.

"My god." I whispered as I let my eyes rove over the man sitting there.

Man didn't quite describe him, though. Because the figure sitting in the chair looked *wild*.

His hair was longer, mussed up like he constantly ran his fingers through it instead of the effortless style he normally wore it in. He also had a full beard covering his jaw, adding to that animalistic look he had.

He was shirtless, showing my hungry eyes all of his delicious tattoos I only saw in the picture he first sent me.

My mouth fucking watered as I stared at him, and my pulse picked up, thrumming through my entire body.

Specifically, low in my stomach. God, I missed the monster in front of me more than I could bear to admit. In the bottom corner of my screen, other camera views were available, and I flicked through them, looking down on my monster from every angle in his office.

He didn't have the cameras before everything happened; I was sure of it.

He did it for me.

So I could stalk him.

I stood up from the table, staring at the screen uninterested in anything else around me as I crawled into my bed, covering my body up with the thick blankets and propped the tablet up so I could keep watching him.

He was coding something on his computer screen and I simply stared at him, memorizing every inch of his face and body now that

I knew he wasn't just my boss that I lusted after, but really the man that had touched my body deeper than any other man ever had.

Every night shared with Dane played on repeat in my head as I watched him on the screen. But as the memories played out, I finally had a face to put on my monster's body as he fucked me wildly in my biggest fantasies.

He stopped typing suddenly and clicked something as I switched views to see his screens.

My breath caught when I saw that every single screen on the wall had changed to—me.

Pictures of me, from so many different times covered the screens. Dane sat back in his chair and ran his hand over his face and sighed as he stared, and I leaned closer to the screen to watch him. Part of me wanted to get in my car and drive straight back to Massachusetts and back to Hartington.

Another part of me felt like I didn't know the man in front of me at all, though. He was a mystery. And that was why I stayed still, watching him as he stared at pictures of me for a while before going back to whatever he was doing before that.

And I just kept watching.

# CHAPTER 33 - LINCOLN

THE LINE WALKERS

Not knowing if she was watching was the hardest part.

Thanks to a one text update from Maddox reading 'Package was delivered', I knew she got the phone and tablet. I just didn't know if she turned them on, though.

Which was the point, after all. I wanted her to have full control over the situation, but it didn't mean I didn't *ache* to know if she at least was open to the idea.

I spent days hanging cameras through my estate, covering every single inch of space I used so she'd have full access to me. But being patient and letting someone else have control over me was turning out to be agonizing.

I got up from my desk and walked away from the work I desperately needed to finish, but no different from the last three months, I couldn't focus.

I couldn't think about anything but Peyton. Distraction wasn't working, so I gave into the need I had that was even greater than my hunger or thirst.

It was carnal.

It was Peyton.

Walking through my bedroom doors used to be so meaningless to me, but now it was the only place I allowed myself to give in to my desperate need for closeness to my pretty little Puppet.

My shower was barely ice cold when I stripped my pants off and walked into it, letting the sting of the icy water cut into me. I welcomed the burn before it warmed up and soothed something inside me.

And then I turned to face the camera I installed on the tile wall and stared at it.

Was she watching?

Who fucking knew.

But I stared at it, nonetheless, hoping the intensity of my gaze made her skin pebble to life and her pussy throb. The same way my body reacted viscerally every time I thought about her.

My cock already throbbed before I even pumped soap into my palm, and then firmly gripped it. "Peyton." I moaned as my eyes closed and my head tipped back as I fisted my cock and remembered the way she felt wrapped around it. "Mmh."

I could have exploded in no time at all, and I would have had the process been only for my sexual satisfaction. But I was hoping it was doing more than just releasing my pent-up need as I slowed my strokes and stared back at the camera.

I hoped she was watching me lose myself for her. It was always her in my brain, like my favorite drug I couldn't ever get enough of. I started seducing Peyton Everett, hoping I would become her special kind of high, but instead, I became the junkie constantly seeking his next fix, not the other way around.

And I prayed I'd get her back so I could feel like I could breathe again.

"Fuck, I miss you, Puppet." I groaned, twisted my palm over the hypersensitive head of my cock. "Sometimes I can still smell you. But it's fading." I swallowed while that burning in my chest returned as I voiced out loud just how fucked I was over her. "The day I wake up and your presence no longer lingers around me is the day I'm past the chance of redemption. There will be no sanity left inside of me if I can't feel you here, even if it's in my head."

The base of my cock burned with pleasure, tempting me to give into it and explode for her, causing me to growl.

"I miss the way you smile to yourself when you paint your fingernails." With a hiss, I disclosed the parts of her she didn't know I knew. Proving to her, I was within every part of her. "I miss the way you sway your hips back and forth when you listen to those girly songs in the shower." Licking my lips, I pressed on, knowing I wasn't going to be able to hold back anymore. "I miss the way you sigh almost silently right after I make you come, like you've never felt more fulfilled than in that moment. As if I've met your needs so completely, you ache for nothing else."

I tightened my palm around my cock and bit my lip, fighting the roar that built in my chest.

"Come back to me, P." I sighed as I started coming for her, covering the shower floor and growling. "Come back."

There was no response through the camera, and even though I knew there wouldn't be, it didn't stop me from hoping.

I stared at the unmoving eye of the camera and closed mine so I could pretend for even just a moment that I wasn't alone.

I spent my entire life alone, yet it had never felt as suffocating as it did right now.

# CHAPTER 34 – PEYTON

**M**y hand itched to pull the phone out of my purse as I walked up the steps to my apartment so I could look in on Dane.

Lincoln.

*Fuck*, whatever his name was.

But I refrained, because who knew what I'd see when I opened the cameras to stalk him. It seemed like his favorite activity was jacking off for me.

Me.

For me. To me. About me.

All of it.

He did it multiple times a day. And I was *obsessed*. My mouth literally salivated when he'd strip down and wrap his big hand around his cock to stroke it for me. But my favorite part of all was what he said when he did it.

Damn, his mouth was filthy.

And endearing.

Who knew a man could be both at the same time?

But Dane could.

Or Lincoln.

*Fuck!*

So instead of spying on him again for the millionth time this week, I refrained while I walked through my front door and even longer as I stripped out of my clothes and crawled into bed. I didn't even bother with a shower.

Because I'd work up a sweat playing with myself while he jacked off at some point in the next few hours, I just knew it.

I was a sucker for that man.

My monster.

He didn't need a name; I knew him inside and out. When I first opened the package, the idea of stalking him and spying on his every move had unnerved me. I didn't understand why he'd want me to do that for him.

But it took only 2 days of watching him to understand his motive.

I finally *knew* him.

The real him. From watching him in his unguarded movements around the house and through his day without him putting on his mask or pretending to be anything else. Every now and then, he'd look at a camera I was watching him through, like he was trying to tell if I was there or not, but from what I could tell, he was clueless.

Which added to the appeal of it.

I was a ghost, afforded privileges that no one else in the world had. I had free access to my monster, and it almost felt as good as being there with him in person. Almost.

Not sure how much longer I'd be able to hold back from driving back to Hartington and begging him to let me back in, I promised myself that I'd lurk for tonight.

Hidden behind the screen of technology for just a little while longer. I thought he'd groveled for me long enough.

Even though it was late, thanks to yet again, another long shift at the hotel, I wasn't surprised to find my monster still awake. I was, however, surprised to find him standing at the back door to the main house, looking out over the pool deck in silent thought.

"What are you doing, Monster?" I whispered to myself as I watched him. He stood there for a few minutes longer before silently opening the door and walking across the illuminated pool deck. At first, I cringed as he walked across the stone patio with his bare feet. The surface must have been heated because, despite there being a foot or more of snow on the grass, not a single flake was on the stone.

Brr. It was December in Boston, I'm sure it was still fucking cold.

He walked past the hot tub, eyeing it briefly like he was remembering the first night we met when he caught me coming on the jet, because that was the only thing I could think of every time I saw it.

But what had me sitting up in bed clinging to the screen like a lifeline was when he walked into the guest house and shut the door behind him.

I quickly changed views to the cameras he hid in the residence when I stayed there and found him walking through the dark space, straight into the bedroom. He pulled his shirt off over the back of his head and then crawled into the bed between the blankets. Grabbing the pillows that I had slept on, he brought one to his chest and buried his face into it, taking a deep breath as he burrowed deeper into the bedding.

"Come back to me, baby." He sighed, laying on his side and staring at the wall. The night vision feature on the camera made his eyes glow, giving them an unhuman like hue. "Please, baby."

He was sleeping in my bed because he missed me.

Before I could even think twice, I clicked the grayed-out icon on the bottom of the screen, turning it red as the microphone feature came to life.

"Dane." I whispered, suddenly shy and second guessing my actions. I was revealing myself to him for the first time in months. But as he shot up in bed and stared directly at the camera in the corner with a look of pure shock on his face, I knew it had to be done. "I'm here."

"Puppet." He growled, kicking the blankets off and standing on the bed to get closer to the camera, and I'm guessing the speaker playing my voice. "Puppet!" He yelled when I hesitated.

"I'm here." I repeated, as I sank back down into my own bed fighting the urge to pass out in anticipation of what he'd do now that I had crossed that divide between us.

"My god," He whispered and sank to his knees in the center of my bed. His mouth opened and closed as he blinked at the camera like he suddenly was at a loss for words, before blurting out, "I love you."

I smiled to myself and sighed at his declaration. Out of everything he could have said in that moment, his proclamation of love was most important to him. "Why are you in my bed?"

His lips turned up briefly in a devastating grin, and he scrubbed a hand over his face. "Because it's the only place left that smells like you. It's the only place I feel sane.""I know the feeling." I admitted.

"Have you been stalking me, Puppet?" He asked, still staring up at the camera.

I could hear the smile in my voice, "Nearly every second I can."

"Let me see you." He demanded, pulling his phone out of his pocket in a hurry, "Link to my phone."

I hesitated, knowing once I did it, I'd be his again. Forever.

There would be no walking away for me after making that move. But it was what I wanted more than anything. So I changed cameras to his phone, overwhelmed by just how devastatingly sexy he was up close, and then clicked the camera icon to open my camera.

The relief in his body language took my breath away as his shoulders sagged and his eyes roved over the entire screen like he was trying to take in every last one of my features.

I was lying on my side with my phone held tight in my hands so he could see only my face as he laid back down on the bed and turned onto his side, mirroring me. It almost felt like we were laying in bed like two normal people, side by side instead of in the weird technological limbo we were always in.

"There she is." He whispered with the ghost of a smile on his face. He looked so tired compared to what he looked like as my boss before everything fell to pieces. "Hi."

"Hi." I whispered back, fighting back the tears that always burned in the back of my eyes as I stared at his perfect face on my secret phone.

"Don't cry, Puppet." He sighed, "I'm sorry Peyton, you'll never understand how fucking sorry I am."

I shook my head and closed my eyes as the tears escaped, rolling down my temple into my pillow. "I know you are. It makes sense to me why you lied and chose to keep your true identity a secret." I took a shuddering breath and opened my eyes again, "I don't blame you for that anymore."

Confusion furrowed his dark eyebrows together as he asked, "Then why are you crying?"

"Because I miss you." I admitted, as fresh tears fell. "I miss both sides of you."

He swallowed, staring back at me so intently. "Come home to me, baby. Just come back and we can start fresh."

"How?" I wondered, "I have a job and responsibilities here," I shook my head. "I can't just quit."

"Why?"

"Because there are no alternative options for a hotel manager near Hartington Estate, that's why. And I have bills and—"

He growled and clenched his teeth together, silencing me with effortless power. "I'm a fucking billionaire, Puppet. Do you think I can't take care of you?" He scowled deeper, "Or that I'd let you out of my sight again to go work for someone else?"

"I don't understand."

"I'm going to take care of you, every second moving forward, Peyton. You don't need to work. You don't need to worry about anything ever again." I started to protest simply because no one had ever taken care of me before since I was a child, but he shook his head and silenced me. "I told you the very first time I slid inside of your body that I perfected myself for your wants and needs. Let me be your everything, because you're mine."

I mulled his words over in my head and couldn't voice a single reason I shouldn't give in and take everything he was offering me. Until the one reason reared its ugly head in the back of my conscience.

"Tell me about Tyson." I said in response. "I need to know the truth."

He watched me silently for a moment and then nodded. "He raped you, Peyton." His words were so steady and strong it was like they held my frantically beating heart in place as I processed them. "He deserved far worse than I gave him."

"You blinded him, didn't you?" I questioned.

"He shared that video with his friends. He also watched it almost daily. So I took what was most precious to him." As my heart stopped beating completely, he let out a sigh. "He'll never see you again. He'll never get to watch your pain and get pleasure from it, ever again."

"Thank you." I whispered, meaning it fully. "Thank you."

He didn't respond immediately, as if he wasn't prepared for the gratitude I expressed for such a heinous act. "You're welcome."

I swallowed and took a deep breath, feeling lighter with the truth coming out between us, so there were no more secrets. "I hate Florida." Admitting it made me sad, because it made me long for him again that much more.

"Come home to me then." He demanded passionately. "Come back."

"I don't even know what to call you." I reminded him. "I don't know how to just pick up my life and trust in someone else to carry it for me."

He held my stare and took a deep breath, "Then I guess we keep doing this." He nodded at the phone. "I guess we get to know each other the right way. Once you feel comfortable enough to trust me again, I'll diligently gather every shattered fragment of your heart. The ones that are sharp, fragmented, and disintegrating, I'll pick them all up every single day that you're struggling to keep them all together. And only then will you know you're safe. And loved. And mine."

Tears fell again, but not in sadness this time, instead they fell for hope. Hope was more terrifying than anything else. But I still wanted to trust in it.

"Okay." I smiled through the tears and nodded to him. "My name is Peyton Everett." I wiped at my cheeks and braved on. "I'm a little dark and twisted on the inside, but I don't know how to embrace it on the outside."

He grinned wolfishly at me and then perfected his face like he was all business, "Peyton. My name is Lincoln Dane Bryce. And I'm a whole lot of dark and twisted on the inside and out. And I'll teach you how to love all of that darkness inside of you."

# CHAPTER 35 - LINCOLN

I growled as I took another drink and cracked my neck angrily.

She was ignoring me.

My pretty fucking Puppet was tempting the monster in me with every minute she stayed dark on me. The urge to fly my private jet down to Miami to kidnap her and make her come back to Hartington was quickly becoming one I couldn't keep restrained. I was going to do something stupid if she kept it up.

She was at work today, a place that couldn't keep staff and constantly forced her to work doubles. And going sixteen hours straight with limited interactions from her after just getting her back in my life, even digitally, a few days ago, was making my darkness grow. She didn't need to work; I could easily take care of her for the rest of her life. But she was stubborn simply because she believed she should be.

I needed to hear her voice and see her face to calm my demons. She was the only salve for the noises and constant chaos that tried to rip apart my psyche.

"Fuck!" I roared, throwing the bottle at the wall of my office as I lost the hold of my darkness. Before I could lift the chair and add it to the pile of broken glass, an alarm sounded through the system, drawing my attention.

*Perimeter Breech Alarm – Guest House – Ten seconds ago.*

I grinned as I moved over to my computer, knowing somebody had chosen the wrong fucking day to mess with me. I pulled up the security footage for the guest house and the backyard, but both had gone black.

Cut connection.

Someone had gotten through my other alarms and disabled the ones near my home.

"Game on, fucker." I growled, sliding my gun into my waistband. My fingertips itched to feel the recoil of my pistol as I pumped iron into some piece of shit.

I didn't recognize any bit of Lincoln in my body as I tore through the house to the backyard. Dane completely overpowered me.

And instead of fighting it, I let that power take control of me.

*Fucking have at it,* I grinned sadistically as I left the main house onto the patio deck. As soon as my feet touched the cold stone, though, I froze. Fucking solid.

"Puppet." I whispered in disbelief as her head turned to me and a glassy eyed, sweet smile transformed her face. Her head tipped back, and a moan fell from her lips as she gripped the edge of the hot tub.

My pretty fucking Puppet was right in front of me, but I shook my head and blinked. Afraid she'd vanish like a mirage if I looked away too quickly. But she was still there when my vision cleared again. Peyton was recreating the first time we met, and she was naked in my hot tub, pleasuring herself on the jets.

I set my gun down on a sun chair in a pile of snow, uncaring as I slowly walked across the wet patio to her. The intense rush of adrenaline and primal hunger surged through my body as I continued to approach her, all while moving at a relaxed and unhurried pace.

I was stalking my prey.

Her eyes opened as she bit her lip and looked up at me as I came to a stop right above her. "Mr. Bryce," she moaned in a breathy voice, rocking forward on the jet that I figured was aimed directly at her clit as I came to a stop right above her. "What are you doing home, Sir?"

"Apparently catching my dirty little housekeeper masturbating." I growled, "Again."

She purred with that same lazy smile on her face and leaned up on her knees so her lush tits came above the water and my mouth watered as her dusty rose nipples were revealed to me for the first time in months. "I wouldn't have to masturbate if my grumpy old boss would lend a helping hand." She parted her lips and moaned, sinking back down into the water, "Or cock."

"Is that what you want, Puppet?" I fell to my knees on the ledge right above her and wrapped my hand around her throat, pulling her up out of the water again so her needy little clit would be free of the delicious pleasure she was searching for. "Do you want your monster's cock?""Mmh," she hummed before reaching between my thighs and fisting my rock-hard erection and licking her lips. "I want to taste you first." Her boldness made me raise my eyebrow, and I had to fight every urge rushing through my body to jump into the hot tub and slam deep inside her after being apart for so long. "I want to suck your cock with no blindfold on so I can see you lose yourself to me." She tightened her hold, dragging her nails down the length of me, still trapped in my sweatpants. "I want to watch you shatter for little old me."

"I've never been able to tell you no, P." I growled, standing up and pushing my pants down, freeing my aching cock for her hungry eyes.

"Come here, Mr. Bryce," She patted the edge of the hot tub and shimmied her tits for me as I sat down, legs spread wide on each side of her. She hummed again and licked her lips as she slid her wet hands up my thighs. "I've fantasized about seeing you naked a million times." She admitted and I could tell she wasn't role playing anymore as she spoke her truths.

"I'm all yours, Puppet." I ran my hand over her cheek and she leaned into my palm, staring into my eyes as her hands wrapped around my cock for the first time like this.

It was intimate.

It was meaningful.

It was new.

"I've missed you so much, Dane." She purred, leaning forward to twirl her tongue around the head of my cock and moaned when she tasted me.

"Not nearly as much as I've missed you." I hissed when she bared her teeth and then pulled back right before using them with a wicked grin. "You at least got to watch me." I groaned when she sucked the head into her mouth and hollowed out her cheeks. "You know my favorite pastime is stalking you, Puppet."

She hummed and then spit on my cock, using her hands to stroke me as she leaned up so her face was close to mine. "Do you have any idea how many times I played with my pussy watching you jack off for me?"Growling, I buried my hand in the back of her hair that was tied up in a messy bun, exactly like that first time. "Tell me."

"The shower ones were my favorite." She licked her lips, twirling her hands around the head of my cock just like I did each time she apparently watched me. "The way you called out for me." She pulled out of my hold and lowered her mouth back onto my cock, sucking me deep and then looking back up, "The way you *begged* me to come back." Her eyelids fluttered as I fought like hell to keep mine open. "Every time you came for me, I shot off in sync."

"Puppet." I warned.

"Every. Single. Time." She purred, diving back down onto my cock and deep throating it.

"Fuck, baby. Just like that. You know just how I like it."

"I studied you." She stared up at me with such depth in her mystical green eyes. "I perfected myself for you." Reaching down, she ran her nails over my tight balls and I tipped my head back, roaring with release as she leaned forward, aiming my cock at her big sexy tits, coating them with my come. "I love you, Dane."

I sank down into the water and pulled her face to mine, crushing her against me as I kissed her with everything I had, as hope bloomed in my chest for the first time in my life. "No one has ever loved me as Dane before. No one has ever loved me before, period." Her eyes widened as sadness filled her bright eyes. So I gave her something to take it all away. "I love you, Peyton. So fucking much."

"I know you do." She smiled up at me as she wrapped her arms around my neck and leaned into me. "You're the monster of my dreams."

I chuckled and turned her around so she straddled the jet again, holding her hands in mine on the ledge as I pressed myself against her back. She was pinned, directly over the jet and she dropped her head to my shoulder as her hips started rocking against it.

"And you, my pretty little Puppet, are never leaving me again." I bit her neck, and she moaned, rocking back against my still hard cock. "From this moment on, I'm always watching you. Stalking you is my entire purpose on this earth. Nothing else."

"Promise?" She gasped as she started orgasming in my arms.

I pulled her hips back and lined up with pussy and slammed in deep. "I fucking promise, Puppet. You have nowhere to hide from me anymore."

# Epilogue – Peyton

"I fucking hate this shit." I gritted my teeth and peeked around the corner, half expecting Dane to jump scare me at any second.

Yeah, well, he'd be the jumpy one when I was done with him. Two years later and his crazy ass still talked me into stupid situations. Just like this one.

It was nearly midnight, and my dumbass was back in the corn maze, trying to beat him to the exit.

I never beat him anywhere.

Well, except to ecstasy, I was usually one or two ahead of him before he reached it himself most days.

I grinned to myself, knowing how fucking good he thought he was going to give it to me when he won his little challenge. It was two years after our first night in the maze, and I stupidly came back for a little rendezvous.

Turns out I hated dark spooky mazes just as much as I did that first night. That hadn't changed even though so much in our life had.

I did, however, like being chased by my monster in his sexy Ghost-face mask, so I showed up. With a little treat for Dane to find when he caught me. Because he *always* caught me.

The snap of a stalk behind me had me jumping into the rows between paths, hoping to hide from my monster long enough to surprise him, but who was I kidding, the man was a stalker for fuck's sake.

I backed up further, content to cheat and push my way through the rows instead of sticking to the path like he thought I would.

It was what he would do, after all.

I cleared one path and pushed my way into the corn to the next one when I heard him enter the corn behind me.

"Fuck!" I screeched and took off running as his evil chuckle weaved through the corn stalks after me.

"You can run, but you can't hide, Puppet." He teased, catching up to me as I made it into a clearing that was so similar to the one that reminded me of that first night. Two benches stood in the clearing, and my eyes fixated on the cuffs hanging off one of them, causing my feet to freeze as I realized I had already been caught. He had herded me right where he wanted me.

"Fuck." I hissed, turning and running square into his chest as he silently appeared behind me.

"It's my intent to, P." He cocked his mask covered head and my body shivered as I looked down at his bare chest to his jeans just barely hanging on his hips.

God, my monster was delicious.

"You cheated." I squinted my eyes up at him and put my hands on my hips.

"Duh." He chided, pressing his chest into mine and pushing me back toward the benches. "I figured it was only appropriate to bring the past back to life completely."

My ass bumped into the back of the bench with the cuffs and my pussy throbbed as my heart raced in my chest. I was out of time if my plan was going to work.

He leaned down to bend me backward over the bench, dominating me, "Tell me Puppet, are you going to beg for my cock tonight, or are you going to fight me kicking and screaming?"

My fingers brushed against the trusty tool strapped in a garter on my thigh under the hem of my white summer dress and I felt like I was going to pass out as I worked it free while he was distracted.

"What do you think?" I hummed, dragging the nails of my free hand down his exposed abs, covered in ink dedicated to us and our love story.

"Hmm. I hope you fight." He replied and I could hear his smile beneath his mask as he wrapped his hand around my wrist and pulled it away from his jeans where I was trying to distract him and moved it toward the cuff. "You know I love it when you kick and scream for me."

"Same." I gritted out and brought my stun gun up from my leg and jabbed it into his side as he tried to jump back. "Too slow." I chided as he grunted and locked up tight from ears to toes, and then fell in a heap on the ground. "Holy fuck." I whispered in awe as my big terrible monster, once again, laid defeated because of me. Shit, now I had to hurry. "Oh, yeah." I jumped over his body, tucking the taser far enough away that I knew he couldn't reach it. Not that he would ever use such a tool of torture on me, but still.

I pushed my big man onto his back and then pulled his arms up over his head, fastening him into the cuffs on the bench working my ass off under pressure knowing he'd wake back up in a minute or two, based on the other time I outsmarted him with it.

With both his arms cuffed, I hefted him as best I could up onto his ass so his back was leaned against the back of the bench. Then I stood at his feet, huffing air like I hadn't just manhandled my two-hundred-pound boyfriend into captivity in the middle of a dark corn maze in the ass crack of nowhere.

My guess was, we were somewhere near the middle of the maze, so I didn't have time to run to the truck to get anything else to secure him to the bench. I had to trust that his favorite leather cuffs would keep him restrained.

Or I was in trouble.

Big, *big* trouble.

He groaned from the ground where he sat with his chin against his chest in his mask and jeans and I stepped back further, watching him slowly come to.

"Puppet." He hissed, lifting his head to look at me through the creepy hot mask and then pulled at his bindings. "Naughty, naughty Puppet."

I stood taller, feeling brave and high on his special kind of high as I stared down at my very unwilling victim. I rarely ever saw the upside of control where Dane was considered, and normally I didn't mind. But I craved the power tonight.

Oh, the things I was going to do to him—.

"This is your own fault." I walked toward him and crouched down in front of him and cocked my head to the side, just like he did in that creepy way. "You were way too excited to string me up and use me tonight, I couldn't just be a willing plaything for you. And you wanted me to fight back."

"So now what, Puppet." He shook his hands out, rattling the cuffs. "You've got me at your mercy, what are you going to do to me?"

"Now," I crawled forward onto my hands and knees and made sure to shake my hair behind my shoulders so he could see my tits down the front of my low cut dress. As predicted, my actions distracted him as he tilted his face down, watching my show. "I torture you in the best way possible."

I quickly undid his jeans and pulled them down, already knowing I'd find him commando underneath. Instead of just pulling his jeans down enough to free his thick cock, I removed both his jeans and shoes completely, leaving him absolutely naked for me except for the mask.

I had no intention of removing that as I rode his cock tonight.

Tonight, my monster was going to play in my fantasies instead of the other way around.

I leaned down and left my ass arched up in the air as I dropped my wet lips to the crown of his leaking cock and sucked on it. As predicted, he arched his hips forward, trying to meet my lips to chase his pleasure.

But I was in control.

So I let my lips play with the head of his cock only, teasing him with a combination of suction and wet licks of my tongue until he was cursing and fighting the bindings, trying to free himself.

"Puppet." He growled, as his muscles bulged in his arms as he fought to get out. "I need you."

"Aww, come on big guy," I pretend pouted as I leaned up so my face was only a few inches from his. "I thought you had more fight in you than that. Begging me already?"

He cursed and lunged forward as if he could bite me through the mask, but I backed up onto my heels just in the nick of time. His restraint was slipping and his darkness was showing more and more as I teased him.

"There he is." I moaned, standing up and lifting my dress to pull my panties down, dropping them onto his cock before I lifted one foot onto the back of the bench. "There's my dark monster." I lifted his mask off his face until it sat on the top of his head and he tilted it back to look up at me and my bare pussy right above his face. "Show me how good my big, bad monster can beg for me."

He lunged forward, burying his mouth against my pussy and sucking on my clit without any further persuasion. He growled, leaning forward as much as he could as he ate me like a man possessed.

"Yes, baby." I tipped my head back as I rode his face. "God, you're so good with your tongue."

He growled, nipping my inner thigh with his teeth and then diving back in. He rocked against my pussy, using every inch of his mouth and jaw to stimulate and pleasure me and before long, I was coming, crying out for more like I wasn't the one in charge at all.

When I dropped my foot to the ground, I bent at the waist and kissed him, tasting my orgasm on his lips as he pushed his tongue into my mouth, eager for relief. "Good monster." I sank to my knees, straddling him, and pulled my dress off over my head, adding it to the growing pile and fisted his cock.

He leaned forward and bit my nipple before sucking it into his mouth and making me hiss from the intensity.

"Bad monster." I chided, pulling his mask back down and covering his sharp teeth as I rubbed the head of his cock through my soaking lips, coating him. "I wanted to reward you for being a good boy, but now I'm not sure you deserve it."

"Ride my cock, Puppet. Or the moment I'm free, I'm going to make you regret every single thing you've done tonight."

"Mmh," I moaned, sinking down onto him. I was taking his cock, regardless if he deserved it or not, we both knew that. "What will you do? Spank me?"

He growled as I took him deep inside of me. "Oh, the way I could turn your skin red for me, baby. You'd never be the same."

"I think I like the sounds of that." I moaned, riding him, grinding my hips back and forth to rub my clit on his pubic bone. "God, you feel so good, Dane."

"That's it, Puppet." He grabbed the top of the bench and used it for leverage to lift his hips, slamming his cock up into me with each thrust. "Take my cock like a good girl."

"Yes." I moaned, reaching up and playing with my nipples with one hand while rubbing my clit with the other. "Your thick cock feels so good, I'm going to come again."

He growled as I reached ecstasy, watching me come on his cock. My gasps filled the air as I held onto his shoulders, slowing down my thrusts to prolong his torture. "Puppet." He hissed, and I grinned, biting my lip as he caught on.

"What baby?" I moaned, leaning down to bite his neck as I stopped lifting my hips completely.

"Shh." He snapped, and I froze as his body went stiff under mine.

I turned my head around to look around us, not sure what it was that set of his internal alarms, and then I heard it.

*Voices!*

"Welcome to our haunted Halloween corn maze!" A loud voice boomed across a megaphone. "Enter if you dare! But be prepared to be scared along the way!"

"Oh, fuck." I scurried off Dane's lap and grabbed my dress as the voices got closer at an alarming rate of speed.

"Peyton!" He hissed, fighting the cuffs on his wrists. "Undo these!"

I fought with my dress, getting my head stuck in the armhole as I started panicking. "I can't!" As a flashlight shone down the path, I whipped my head to the side.

"I'm naked, Peyton!" He growled, getting his feet under him so he was in a crouch. The man didn't even have shoes on, just a mask.

"So am I!" I cried back and then started laughing, because I had no choice. But I was going to pay dearly for it. "I'm sorry!"

"Don't you dare." He warned, freezing his attempts to break free like he couldn't believe what I was about to do.

As the people drew closer to us, I snatched the pile of clothes and shoes off the ground and made my way towards the back of the maze. "I love you!"

"I'm going to make you pay for this Puppet!" He yelled as I started running. "I swear to God!"

Naked as a jaybird, I ran for my life, holding our belongings tightly. I ducked through the rows of corn, using them to stay as hidden as possible, as I got my dress on over my head the right way and ran out of the exit.

Screams of terror and delight rang out around me, mixed with the haunted noises of chainsaws and creepy Halloween music.

How the fuck did we not know there was a midnight event being held?

I ran through the darkness to where we parked Dane's truck, jumping inside and locking the doors as my chest rose and fell wildly from the excitement and horror of the whole thing.

But I couldn't stop laughing.

I jumped over into the driver's seat, ready to abandon Dane completely, when movement caught my eye at the side of the maze. "No. He. Didn't." I cackled as my big, terrible, masked monster came running through the middle of the corn maze, naked, with the bench hefted onto his shoulders.

His cock swung like a weapon as he ran toward the truck. When he was about halfway to the safety of the truck, a shadowed figure followed his path through the darkness at an alarming speed, like someone was actually chasing him.

Dane. My monster was being chased. The thought made me giggle.

I leaned over the steering wheel, squinting, as I stared past my naked man running for his life and covered my mouth when I finally made out what was chasing him.

Or who.

The naughty little old lady from the post office gave chase, swinging her arms back and forth over her head as she cackled merrily, dressed like a little spooky porcelain doll.

"Go, P!" Dane barked as he threw the bench and himself into the bed of the truck in a heap. "Now!"

I started the truck, and the headlights illuminated the old woman as she stopped running now that her target was out of reach and I spun the tires to get us both the fuck out of dodge.

As we tore past her, she tipped her head back and yelled, "Come back, Sunny! Don't you want to play with Dolly?"

And we never stepped foot in that fucking maze again.

Or the post office.

# SNEAK PEEK TIME

## THE LINE WALKERS

Want more of the Line Walker boys?

Here's a snippet of Olivia and Maddox's story in Book 2, Psycho.

## Chapter 1 – Olivia

My blood ran cold when I took the first punch. By the fourth, that coldness turned into agonizing pins and needles as each punch or kick landed against my body.

I curled into a ball, forcing myself to protect my vital organs and precious bits from the attack. I didn't know if it would work, but I had to try.

I had to fucking try.

"Stupid cunt!" Damon's demonic sneer made my skin crawl as he screamed at me from above. "You just couldn't do as you were told, could you!"

"I'm sorry!" With my face down and covered, I cried and hiccupped through the pain. I wasn't dumb enough to think he was done beating me for fucking up.

He never quit that fast.

"No, you're not!" He barked, grabbing me by my hair and picking me up until I dangled with my toes barely touching the floor. "But you will be when I'm done with you."

I finally opened my eyes, staring at the man I thought I loved through my blurry vision. He was unrecognizable to me anymore.

I guess that happened when drugs took hold of your soul like they had his. A few months ago, I'd been smitten with his bad boy vibes and dark lifestyle.

But as I stared it all in the eyes, I realized it was probably going to be what killed me. He was going to be what killed me.

If it wasn't from his physical violence, it'd be from dehydration or starvation. Because two days ago he locked me in the windowless room in the basement of his club, and I hadn't had a drop of water or a bit of food since. The only way I knew how many days I had been alone in the darkness was because of the bouts of vomiting that hit me each morning without fail.

Those had been reliable like clockwork for almost two weeks now, knocking the wind out of my every morning at six am.

Which meant I was running out of time. And I had to make a move, or I was going to disappear into nothingness like all the others before me. I couldn't do that. I couldn't just give up.

So as he slammed my back into the wall to scream at me some more about what a useless piece of shit I was, I fought back. Not because I thought I could actually win again his massive self, but because with each hit he returned, he didn't pay attention to me picking his pockets for his cell phone.

When I finally got it free, I pushed it behind the shelf on the wall stocked with toilet paper and then cowered away from him. I had absolutely no strength left in my body and he tired of me quickly.

I fell to a heap on the ground at his feet as he delivered one final kick to my side and spit on me. "Next time, maybe you'll fucking listen to me." He cursed.

And then he walked out of the room and locked the door behind him, trapping me in the darkness once again.

I weakly reached over to the shelf from my curled-up ball on the floor, feeling around for the brick of technology, and cried out silently when I found it. There wasn't much time before he realized he was missing his phone, and even less time before he traced it back to me.

If he came back in the room and found me with it, I was dead.

But if I didn't manage to pull off my escape. I was dead anyway.

So through the blood dripping down my face, I painstakingly typed in the only phone number I had memorized and prayed to God she answered.

I felt dizziness start making my world spin on the side as I listened to the line ring, and ring on.

And when her angelic voice finally answered, I sobbed in relief. It was the first time I cried since Damon first hit me two months ago. I wasn't sure I'd ever be able to get them to stop once the tears started, either.

"Peyton." I cried, slurring my words through the pain and fatigue. "Help."

Her voice echoed through the phone in panic. "Olivia? Livy!" She screamed when I didn't reply. I suddenly felt like I was lying under a blanket of water as my eyelids drooped closed. "Livy!"

"He's going to kill me." I whispered, hoping she could understand me through the gurgles of spit and blood pooling around my lips. "Help."

"Who? Who's going to kill you? Where are you?" She cried as air blew through the phone line before she screamed in the background, "Dane! Olivia's hurt. Help her!" There was a shuffling on the line and then my sister's boyfriend came on in her place.

"Olivia. Tell me what you can."

He was so calm and in charge, my split lip curled up in a faint smile. Dane would find me. If anyone could, he would. "Hell Eater's Lounge." I whispered, curling my arm over my stomach as each breath hurt more than the last. "Basement storeroom."

"Who hurt you?" He demanded with that same calmness, but I knew there was darkness deep inside of Dane that would show its ugly head for this.

"Dam—" I coughed as more blood filled my mouth from my split lips. "Damon Kirst."

"Stay with me, Liv." Dane commanded, and then I heard him talking to someone else in the background. "Maddox. I need your help, it's Peyton's sister."

I tried to focus as Dane literally assembled the troops for me, but I was so tired, sleep weighed down on me like a warm blanket. Dane's voice sounded so far away as he came back to me. "Liv. Talk to me. You have to stay with me, pretty girl. I've got someone coming to you. He's the best of the best and he's close. But you have to stay with me. C'mon, Olivia."

Peyton's fearful sobs echoed behind his voice and I felt bad that she was so sad. I never wanted to add to her burden like this. Our whole lives she took care of me, and now it seemed she'd do the same at my end.

"Tell P I love her." I slurred, "And I'm sorry."

"No!" My sister cried and Dane barked out loudly over her, finally raising his voice as he lost control of himself.

"Olivia, focus! Stay with us!"

The phone slipped from my fingers and I couldn't gather the strength to pick it up again as I hugged my stomach. "I'm so sorry, little baby. I tried."

# Acknowledgements

Three words...

**Thank you, Amanda.**

I'm not sure this book, or the next ones, would have turned out the way they have without your constant reassurance and insight when I hit walls and felt like deleting chapters at a time. I literally couldn't have crafted this story so perfectly without you, and I hope you understand how fricken awesome you are. I'd be lost if I couldn't bother you at all hours of the day and night with my randomness.

So thank you.

Again.

# Other Books

## THE LINE WALKERS

Did you know Ally writes across so many other types of tropes and themes?

Check out some of her other books here.

### Looking for Series and Duets?

**Beauty In the Ink Series:**
https://a.co/d/6tc8M7M
**Bailey Dunn & Co Duet:**
https://a.co/d/i9gwqL2
**Shadeport Crew Series:**
https://a.co/d/dVzGcyo
**Kings of Hawthorn Series:**

https://a.co/d/h1AITKM

## How about some spicy standalones?

**Sinister Vows:**
https://a.co/d/gbe35fF
**Guilty For You:**
**https://a.co/d/1ef3UPU**
**Secrets Within Us:**
https://a.co/d/cTZ04XQ

## Stalk Me!

### THE LINE WALKERS

Want to stay up to date with all of my shenanigans and upcoming news? Pretty Please?

Check out my website: www.ammccoybooks.com

How about TikTok, are you there? https://www.tiktok.com/@amm ccoy_author?is_from_webapp=1&sender_device=pc

Facebook? I've got a readers group there! Twisted After Dark: A.M. McCoy's Reader Group is mostly unhinged and full of exclusive news! https://www.facebook.com/share/g/b41rkBMkSurWz43i/

IG? https://www.instagram.com/ammccoy_author/

Amazon?
https://www.amazon.com/stores/A.-M.-McCoy/author/B07QNRJ

MLB?ref=ap_rdr&isDramIntegrated=true&shoppingPortalEnabled
=true

I think that's all for now!